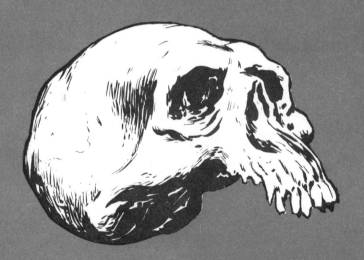

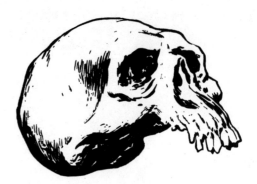

Great tales

illustrated by
Norman Nodel
Harry Borgman

# of horror and suspense

WEIRD TALES OF EDGAR ALLAN POE

THE GHOST SHIP AND OTHER GHOSTLY STORIES

DRACULA

GALAHAD BOOKS • NEW YORK CITY

TABLE OF CONTENTS

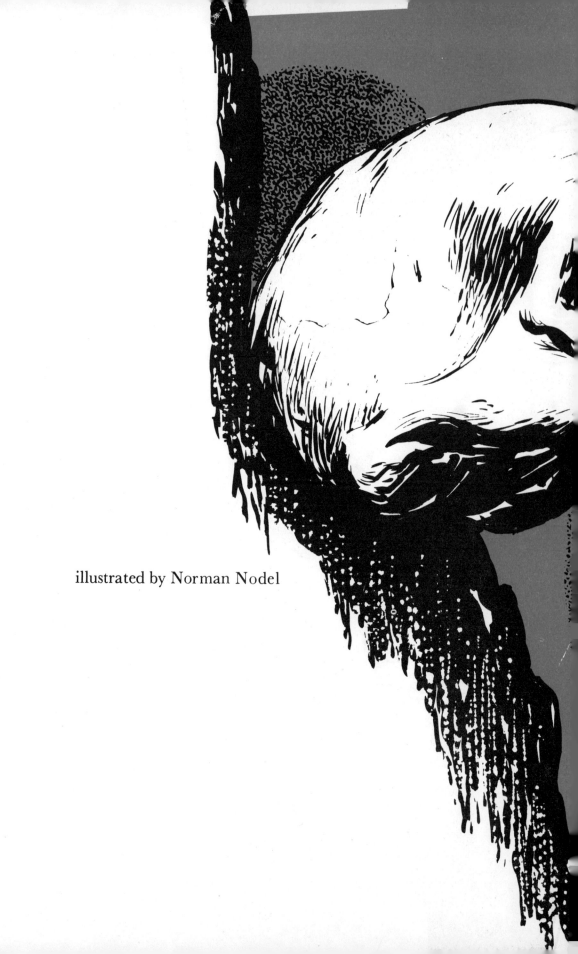

illustrated by Norman Nodel

ONE — THE CASK OF AMONTILLADO

The thousand injuries of Fortunato I had borne as I best could; but when he ventured upon insult, I vowed revenge. You, who so well know the nature of my soul, will not suppose, however, that I gave utterance to a threat. *At length* I would be avenged; this was a point definitely settled—but the very definitiveness with which it was resolved, precluded the idea of risk. I must not only punish, but punish with impunity. A wrong is unredressed when retribution overtakes its redresser. It is equally unredressed when the avenger fails to make himself felt as such to him who has done the wrong.

It must be understood, that neither by word nor deed had I given Fortunato cause to doubt my good-will. I continued, as was my wont, to smile in his face, and he did not perceive that my smile *now* was at the thought of his immolation.

He had a weak point—this Fortunato—although in other regards he was a man to be respected and even feared. He prided himself on his connoisseurship in wine. Few Italians have the true virtuoso spirit. For the most part their enthusiasm is adopted to suit the time and opportunity—to practice imposture upon the British and Austrian millionaires. In painting and gemmary Fortunato, like his countrymen, was a quack—but in the matter of old wines he was sincere. In this respect I did not differ from him materially: I was skillful in the Italian vintages myself, and bought largely whenever I could.

It was about dusk, one evening during the supreme madness of the carnival season, that I encountered my friend. He accosted me with excessive warmth, for he had been drinking much. The man wore motley. He had on a tight-fitting parti-striped dress, and his head was surmounted by the conical cap and bells. I was so pleased to see him, that I thought I should never have done wringing his hand.

I said to him, "My dear Fortunato, you are luckily met. How remarkably well you are looking to-day! But I have received a pipe of what passes for Amontillado, and I have my doubts."

"How?" said he. "Amontillado? A pipe? Impossible! And in the middle of the carnival!"

"I have my doubts," I replied; "and I was silly enough to pay the full Amontillado price without consulting you in the matter. You were not to be found, and I was fearful of losing a bargain."

"Amontillado!"

"I have my doubts."

"Amontillado!"

"And I must satisfy them."

"Amontillado!"

"As you are engaged, I am on my way to Luchesi. If anyone has a critical turn, it is he. He will tell me —"

"Luchesi cannot tell Amontillado from Sherry."

"And yet some fools will have it that his taste is a match for your own."

"Come, let us go."

"Whither?"

"To your vaults."

"My friend, no; I will not impose upon your good nature. I perceive you have an engagement. Luchesi —"

"I have no engagement; come."

"My friend, no. It is not the engagement, but the severe cold with which I perceive you are afflicted. The vaults are insufferably damp. They are encrusted with niter."

"Let us go, nevertheless. The cold is merely nothing. Amontillado! You have been imposed upon. And as for Luchesi, he cannot distinguish sherry from Amontillado."

Thus speaking, Fortunato possessed himself of my arm. Putting on a mask of black silk, and drawing a *roquelaire* closely about my person, I suffered him to hurry me to my palazzo.

There were no attendants at home; they had absconded to make merry in honor of the time. I had told them that I should not return until the morning, and had given them explicit orders not to stir from the house. These orders were sufficient, I well knew, to insure their immediate disappearance, one and all, as soon as my back was turned.

I took from their sconces two flambeaux, and giving one to Fortunato, bowed him through several suites of rooms to the archway that led into the vaults. I passed down a long and winding staircase, re-

questing him to be cautious as he followed. We came at length to the foot of the descent, and stood together on the damp ground of the catacombs of the Montresors.

The gait of my friend was unsteady, and the bells upon his cap jingled as he strode.

"The pipe?" said he.

"It is farther on," said I, "but observe the white webwork which gleams from these cavern walls."

He turned toward me, and looked into my eyes with two filmy orbs that distilled the rheum of intoxication.

"Niter?" he asked, at length.

"Niter," I replied. "How long have you had that cough?"

"Ugh! ugh! ugh! — ugh! ugh! ugh! — ugh! ugh! ugh! — ugh! ugh! ugh! — ugh! ugh! ugh!"

My poor friend found it impossible to reply for many minutes.

"It is nothing," he said, at last.

"Come," I said, with decision, "we will go back; your health is precious. You are rich, respected, admired, beloved; you are happy, as once I was. You are a man to be missed. For me it is no matter. We will go back; you will be ill, and I cannot be responsible. Besides, there is Luchesi—"

"Enough," he said. "The cough is a mere nothing; it will not kill me. I shall not die of a cough."

"True—true," I replied, "and,

indeed, I had no intention of alarming you unnecessarily; but you should use all proper caution. A draught of this Medoc will defend us from the damps."

Here I knocked off the neck of a bottle which I drew from a long row of its fellows that lay upon the mold.

"Drink," I said, presenting him the wine.

He raised it to his lips with a leer. He paused and nodded to me familiarly, while his bells jingled.

"I drink," he said, "to the buried that repose around us."

"And I to your long life."

He again took my arm, and we proceeded.

"These vaults," he said, "are extensive."

"The Montresors," I replied, "were a great and numerous family."

"I forget your arms."

"A huge human foot d'or, in a field azure; the foot crushes a serpent rampant whose fangs are imbedded in the heel."

"And the motto?"

"Nemo me impune lacessit."

"Good!" he said.

The wine sparkled in his eyes and the bells jingled. My own fancy grew warm with the Medoc. We had passed through walls of piled bones, with casks and puncheons intermingling, into the inmost recesses of the catacombs. I paused again, and this time I made bold to seize Fortunato by an arm above the elbow.

"The niter!" I said. "See, it increases. It hangs like moss upon the vaults. We are below the river's bed. The drops of moisture trickle among the bones. Come, we will go back ere it is too late. Your cough —"

"It is nothing," he said. "Let us go on. But first, another draught of the Medoc."

I broke and reached him a flagon of De Grâve. He emptied it at a breath. His eyes flashed with a fierce light. He laughed and threw the bottle upward with a gesticulation I did not understand.

I looked at him in surprise. He repeated the movement — a grotesque one.

"You do not comprehend?" he said.

"Not I," I replied.

"Then you are not of the brotherhood."

"How?"

"You are not of the masons."

"Yes, yes," I said, "yes, yes."

"You? Impossible! A mason?"

"A mason," I replied.

"A sign," he said.

"It is this," I answered, producing a trowel from beneath the folds of my *roquelaire*.

"You jest," he exclaimed, recoiling a few paces. "But let us proceed to the Amontillado."

"Be it so," I said, replacing the tool beneath the cloak, and again offering him my arm. He leaned upon it heavily. We continued our route in search of the Amontillado. We passed through a range of low arches, descended, passed on, and descending again, arrived at a deep crypt, in which the foulness of the air caused our flambeaux rather to glow than flame.

At the most remote end of the crypt there appeared another less spacious. Its walls had been lined with human remains, piled to the vault overhead, in the fashion of the great catacombs of Paris. Three sides of this interior crypt were still ornamented in this manner. From the fourth the bones had been thrown down, and lay promiscuously upon the earth, forming at one point a mound of some size. Within the wall thus exposed by the displacing of the bones, we perceived a still interior recess, in depth about four feet, in width three, in height six or seven. It seemed to have been constructed for no especial use within itself, but formed merely the interval between two of the colossal supports of the roof of the catacombs, and was backed by one of their circumscribing walls of solid granite.

It was in vain that Fortunato, uplifting his dull torch, endeavored to pry into the depth of the recess. Its termination the feeble light did not enable us to see.

"Proceed," I said. "Herein is the Amontillado. As for Luchesi —"

"He is an ignoramus," interrupted my friend, as he stepped unsteadily forward, while I followed immediately at his heels. In an instant he had reached the extremity of the niche, and finding his progress arrested by the rock, stood stupidly bewildered. A moment more and I had fettered him to the granite. In its surface were two iron staples, distant from each other about two feet, horizontally. From one of these depended a short chain, from the other a padlock. Throwing the links about his waist, it was but the work of a few seconds to secure it. He was too much astounded to resist. Withdrawing the key I stepped back from the

recess.

"Pass your hand," I said, "over the wall; you cannot help feeling the niter. Indeed it is *very* damp. Once more let me *implore* you to return. No? Then I must positively leave you. But I must first render you all the little attentions in my power."

"The Amontillado!" ejaculated my friend, not yet recovered from his astonishment.

"True," I replied; "the Amontillado."

As I said these words I busied myself among the pile of bones of which I have before spoken. Throwing them aside, I soon uncovered a quantity of building stone and mortar. With these materials and with the aid of my trowel, I began vigorously to wall up the entrance of the niche.

I had scarcely laid the first tier of the masonry when I discovered that the intoxication of Fortunato had in a great measure worn off. The earliest indication I had of this was a low moaning cry from the depth of the recess. It was *not* the cry of a drunken man. There was then a long and obstinate silence. I laid the second tier, and the third, and the fourth; and then I heard the furious vibrations of the chain. The noise lasted for several minutes, during which, that I might hearken to it with the more satisfaction, I ceased my labors and sat down upon the bones. When at last the clanking subsided, I resumed the trowel, and finished without interruption the fifth, the sixth, and the seventh tier. The wall was now nearly upon a level with my breast. I again paused, and holding the flambeaux over the mason work, threw a few feeble rays upon the figure within.

A succession of loud and shrill screams, bursting suddenly from the throat of the chained form, seemed to thrust me violently back. For a brief moment I hesitated—I trembled. Unsheathing my rapier, I began to grope with it about the recess; but the thought of an instant reassured me. I placed my hand upon the solid fabric of the catacombs, and felt satisfied. I reapproached the wall. I replied to the yells of him who clamored. I re-echoed—I aided—I surpassed them in volume and in strength. I did this, and the clamorer grew still.

It was now midnight, and my task was drawing to a close. I had completed the eighth, the ninth, and the tenth tier. I had finished a portion of the last and the eleventh; there remained but a single stone to be fitted and plastered in. I struggled with its weight; I placed it partially in its destined position. But now there came from out of the niche a low laugh that erected the hairs upon my head. It was succeeded by a sad voice, which I had difficulty in recognizing as that of the noble Fortunato. The voice said:

"Ha! ha! ha! — he! he! — a very good joke indeed—an excellent jest. We will have many a rich laugh about it at the palazzo—he! he! he! —over our wine—he! he! he!"

"The Amontillado!" I said.

"He! he! he! — he! he! he! — yes, the Amontillado. But is it not getting late? Will not they be awaiting us at the palazzo, the Lady Fortunato and the rest? Let us be gone."

"Yes," I said, "let us be gone."

"For the love of God, Montresor!"

"Yes," I said, "for the love of God!"

But to these words I harkened in vain for a reply. I grew impatient. I called aloud:

"Fortunato!"

No answer. I called again:

"Fortunato!"

No answer still. I thrust a torch through the remaining aperture and let it fall within. There came forth in return only a jingling of the bells. My heart grew sick—on account of the dampness of the catacombs. I hastened to make an end of my labor. I forced the last stone into its position; I plastered it up. Against the new masonry I re-erected the old rampart of bones. For the half of a century no mortal has disturbed them. *In pace requiescat!*

TWO THE PURLOINED LETTER

At Paris, just after dark one gusty evening in the autumn of 18—, I was enjoying the twofold luxury of meditation and a meerschaum, in company with my friend, C. Auguste Dupin, in his little back library, or book closet, *au troisième*, No. 33 *Rue Dunôt, Faubourg St. Germain*. For one hour at least we had maintained a profound silence; while each, to any casual observer, might have seemed intently and exclusively occupied with the curling eddies of smoke that oppressed the atmosphere of the chamber. For myself, however, I was mentally discussing certain topics which had formed matter for conversation between us at an earlier period of the evening; I mean the affair of the Rue Morgue, and the mystery attending the murder of Marie Rogêt. I looked upon it, therefore, as something of a coincidence, when the door of our apartment was thrown open and admitted our old acquaintance, Monsieur G——, the Prefect of the Parisian police.

We gave him a hearty welcome; for there was nearly half as much of the entertaining as of the contemptible about the man, and we had not seen him for several years. We had been sitting in the dark, and Dupin now arose for the purpose of lighting a lamp, but sat down again, without doing so, upon G.'s saying that he had called to consult us, or rather to ask the opinion of my friend, about some official business which had occasioned a great deal of trouble.

"If it is any point requiring reflection," observed Dupin, as he forbore to enkindle the wick, "we shall examine it to better purpose in the dark."

"That is another of your odd notions," said the Prefect, who had the fashion of calling everything "odd" that was beyond his comprehension, and thus lived amid an absolute legion of "oddities."

"Very true," said Dupin, as he supplied his visitor with a pipe, and rolled toward him a comfortable chair.

"And what is the difficulty now?"

I asked. "Nothing more in the assassination way I hope?"

"Oh, no; nothing of that nature. The fact is, the business is *very* simple indeed, and I make no doubt that we can manage it sufficiently well ourselves; but then I thought Dupin would like to hear the details of it because it is so excessively *odd.*"

"Simple and odd," said Dupin.

"Why, yes; and not exactly that either. The fact is, we have all been a good deal puzzled because the affair *is* so simple, and yet baffles us altogether."

"Perhaps it is the very simplicity of the thing which puts you at fault," said my friend.

"What nonsense you *do* talk!" replied the Prefect, laughing heartily.

"Perhaps the mystery is a little *too* plain," said Dupin.

"Oh, good heavens! who ever heard of such an idea?"

"A little *too* self-evident."

"Ha! ha! ha! — ha! ha! ha! — ho! ho! ho!" roared our visitor, profoundly amused, "oh, Dupin, you will be the death of me yet!"

"And what, after all, *is* the matter on hand?" I asked.

"Why, I will tell you," replied the Prefect, as he gave a long, steady, and contemplative puff, and settled himself in his chair. "I will tell you in a few words; but, before I begin, let me caution you that this is an affair demanding the greatest secrecy, and that I should most probably lose the position I now hold, were it known that I confided it to any one."

"Proceed," said I.

"Or not," said Dupin.

"Well, then; I have received personal information, from a very high quarter, that a certain document of the last importance has been purloined from the royal apartments. The individual who purloined it is known; this beyond a doubt; he was seen to take it. It is known, also, that it still remains in his possession."

"How is this known?" asked Dupin.

"It is clearly inferred," replied the Prefect, "from the nature of the document, and from the non-appearance of certain results which would at once arise from its passing *out* of the robber's possession—that is to say, from his employing it as he must design in the end to employ it."

"Be a little more explicit," I said.

"Well, I may venture so far as to say that the paper gives its holder a certain power in a certain quarter where such power is immensely valuable." The Prefect was fond of the cant of diplomacy.

"Still I do not quite understand," said Dupin.

"No? Well, the disclosure of the document to a third person, who shall be nameless, would bring in question the honor of a personage of most exalted station; and this fact gives the holder of the document an ascendancy over the illustrious personage whose honor and peace are so jeopardized."

"But this ascendancy," I interposed, "would depend upon the robber's knowledge of the loser's knowledge of the robber. Who would dare—"

"The thief," said G., "is the Minister D——, who dares all things, those unbecoming as well as those becoming a man. The method of the theft was not less ingenious than bold. The document in question—a letter, to be frank—had been received by the personage robbed while alone in the royal *boudoir*. During its perusal she was suddenly interrupted by the entrance of the other exalted personage from whom especially it was her wish to conceal it. After a hurried and vain endeavor to thrust it in a drawer, she was forced to place it, open as it was, upon a table. The address, however, was uppermost, and, the contents thus unexposed, the letter escaped notice. At this juncture enters the Minister D——. His lynx eye immediately perceives the paper, recognizes the handwriting of the address, observes the confusion of the personage addressed, and fathoms her secret. After some business transactions, hurried through in his ordinary manner, he produces a letter somewhat similar to the one in question, opens it, pretends to read it, and then places it in close juxtaposition to the other. Again he converses, for some fifteen minutes, upon the public affairs. At length, in taking leave, he takes also from the table the letter to which he had no claim. Its rightful owner saw, but, of course, dared not call attention to the act, in the presence of the third personage who stood at her elbow. The minister decamped, leaving his own letter—one of no importance — upon the table."

"Here, then," said Dupin to me, "you have precisely what you demand to make the ascendancy complete—the loser's knowledge of the robber."

"Yes," replied the Prefect, "and   23

the power thus attained has, for some months past, been wielded, for political purposes, to a very dangerous extent. The personage robbed is more thoroughly convinced, every day, of the necessity of reclaiming her letter. But this, of course, cannot be done openly. In fine, driven to despair, she has committed the matter to me."

"Than whom," said Dupin, amid a perfect whirlwind of smoke, "no more sagacious agent could, I suppose, be desired, or even imagined."

"You flatter me," replied the Prefect; "but it is possible that some such opinion may have been entertained."

"It is clear," said I, "as you observe, that the letter is still in the possession of the minister; since it is this possession, and not any employment of the letter, which bestows the power. With the employment the power departs."

"True," said G., "and upon this conviction I proceeded. My first care was to make thorough search of the minister's hotel; and here my chief embarrassment lay in the necessity of searching without his knowledge. Beyond all things, I have been warned of the danger which would result from giving him reason to suspect our design."

"But," said I, "you are quite *au fait* in these investigations. The Parisian police have done this thing often before."

"Oh, yes; and for this reason I did not despair. The habits of the minister gave me, too, a great advantage. He is frequently absent from home all night. His servants are by no means numerous. They sleep at a distance from their master's apartment, and, being chiefly Neapolitans, are readily made drunk. I have keys, as you know, with which I can open any chamber or cabinet in Paris. For three months a night has not passed, during the greater part of which I have not been engaged, personally, in ransacking the D—— Hotel. My honor is interested, and, to mention a great secret, the reward is enormous. So I did not abandon the search until I had become fully satisfied that the thief is a more astute man than myself. I fancy that I have investigated every nook and corner of the premises in which it is possible that the paper can be concealed."

"But is it not possible," I suggested, "that although the letter may be in possession of the minister, as it unquestionably is, he may have concealed it elsewhere than

25

upon his own premises?"

"This is barely possible," said Dupin. "The present peculiar condition of affairs at court, and especially of those intrigues in which D——is known to be involved, would render the instant availability of the document—its susceptibility of being produced at a moment's notice—a point of nearly equal importance with its possession."

"Its susceptibility of being produced?" said I.

"That is to say, of being *destroyed*," said Dupin.

"True," I observed. "The paper is clearly then upon the premises. As for its being upon the person of the minister, we may consider that as out of the question."

"Entirely," said the Prefect. "He has been twice waylaid, as if by footpads, and his person rigidly searched under my own inspection."

"You might have spared yourself this trouble," said Dupin. "D——, I presume, is not altogether a fool, and, if not, must have anticipated these waylayings, as a matter of course."

"Not *altogether* a fool," said G., "but then he is a poet, which I take to be only one remove from a fool."

"True," said Dupin, after a long

and thoughtful whiff from his meer-schaum, "although I have been guilty of certain doggerel myself."

"Suppose you detail," said I, "the particulars of your search."

"Why, the fact is, we took our time, and we searched *everywhere*. I have had long experience in these affairs. I took the entire building, room by room; devoting the nights of a whole week to each. We examined, first, the furniture of each apartment. We opened every possible drawer; and I presume you know that, to a properly trained police agent, such a thing as a *secret* drawer is impossible. Any man is a dolt who permits a 'secret' drawer to escape him in a search of this kind. The thing is *so* plain. There is a certain amount of bulk —of space—to be accounted for in every cabinet. Then we have accurate rules. The fiftieth part of a line could not escape us. After the cabinets we took the chairs. The cushions we probed with the fine long needles you have seen me employ. From the tables we removed the tops."

"Why so?"

"Sometimes the top of a table, or other similarly arranged piece of furniture, is removed by the person wishing to conceal an article; then the leg is excavated, the article deposited within the cavity, and the top replaced. The bottoms and tops of bedposts are employed in the same way."

"But could not the cavity be detected by sounding?" I asked.

"By no means, if, when the article is deposited, a sufficient wadding of cotton be placed around it. Besides, in our case, we were obliged to proceed without noise."

"But you could not have removed —you could not have taken to pieces *all* articles of furniture in which it would have been possible to make a deposit in the manner you mention. A letter may be compressed into a thin spiral roll, not differing much in shape or bulk from a large knitting needle, and in this form it might be inserted into the rung of a chair, for example. You did not take to pieces all the chairs?"

"Certainly not; but we did better—we examined the rungs of every chair in the hotel, and, indeed, the jointings of every description of furniture, by the aid of a most powerful microscope. Had there been any traces of recent disturbance we should not have failed to detect it instantly. A single grain of gimlet dust, for example, would have been as obvious as an apple. Any dis-

order in the gluing—any unusual gaping in the joints — would have sufficed to insure detection."

"I presume you looked to the mirrors, between the boards and the plates, and you probed the beds and the bedclothes, as well as the curtains and carpets."

"That of course; and when we had absolutely completed every particle of the furniture in this way, then we examined the house itself. We divided its entire surface into compartments, which we numbered, so that none might be missed; then we scrutinized each individual square inch throughout the premises, including the two houses immediately adjoining, with the microscope, as before."

"The two houses adjoining!" I exclaimed. "You must have had a great deal of trouble."

"We had; but the reward offered is prodigious."

"You include the *grounds* about the houses?"

"All the grounds are paved with brick. They gave us comparatively little trouble. We examined the moss between the bricks, and found it undisturbed."

"You looked among D——'s papers, of course, and into the books of the library?"

"Certainly; we opened every package and parcel; we not only opened every book, but we turned over every leaf in each volume, not contenting ourselves with a mere shake, according to the fashion of some of our police officers. We also measured the thickness of every book *cover,* with the most accurate admeasurement, and applied to each the most jealous scrutiny of the microscope. Had any of the bindings been recently meddled with, it would have been utterly impossible that the fact should have escaped observation. Some five or six volumes, just from the hands of the binder, we carefully probed, longitudinally, with the needles."

"You explored the floors beneath the carpets?"

"Beyond doubt. We removed every carpet, and examined the boards with the microscope."

"And the paper on the walls?"

"Yes."

"You looked into the cellars?"

"We did."

"Then," I said, "you have been making a miscalculation and the letter is *not* upon the premises, as you suppose."

"I fear you are right there," said the Prefect. "And now, Dupin,

what would you advise me to do?"

"To make a thorough research of the premises."

"That is absolutely needless," replied G——. "I am not more sure that I breathe than I am that the letter is not at the hotel."

"I have no better advice to give you," said Dupin. "You have, of course, an accurate description of the letter?"

"Oh, yes!" — And here the Prefect, producing a memorandum book, proceeded to read aloud a minute account of the internal, and especially of the external, appearance of the missing document. Soon after finishing the perusal of this description, he took his departure, more entirely depressed in spirits than I had ever known the good gentleman before.

In about a month afterward he paid us another visit, and found us occupied very nearly as before. He took a pipe and a chair and entered into some ordinary conversation. At length I said:

"Well, but G., what of the purloined letter? I presume you have at last made up your mind that there is no such thing as overreaching the Minister?"

"Confound him, say I—yes; I made the re-examination, however, 29

as Dupin suggested—but it was all labor lost, as I knew it would be."

"How much was the reward offered, did you say?" asked Dupin.

"Why, a very great deal—a *very* liberal reward—I don't like to say how much, precisely; but one thing I *will* say, that I wouldn't mind giving my individual check for fifty thousand francs to any one who could obtain me that letter. The fact is, it is becoming of more and more importance every day; and the reward has been lately doubled. If it were trebled, however, I could do no more than I have done."

"The Prefect, producing a memorandum-book, proceeded to read aloud a minute account of the internal, and especially of the external, appearance of the missing document."

"Why, yes," said Dupin, drawlingly, between the whiffs of his meerschaum, "I really—think, G., you have not exerted yourself—to the utmost in this matter. You might — do a little more, I think, eh?"

"How?—in what way?"

"Why—puff, puff—you might—

puff, puff—employ counsel in the matter, eh?—puff, puff, puff. Do you remember the story they tell of Abernethy?"

"No; hang Abernethy!"

"To be sure! hang him and welcome. But, once upon a time, a certain rich miser conceived the design of sponging upon this Abernethy for a medical opinion. Getting up, for this purpose, an ordinary conversation in a private company, he insinuated his case to the physician, as that of an imaginary individual."

" 'We will suppose,' said the miser, 'that his symptoms are such and such; now, doctor, what would *you* have directed him to take?'

" 'Take!' said Abernethy, 'why, take *advice,* to be sure.' "

"But," said the Prefect, a little discomposed, "*I* am *perfectly* willing to take advice, and to pay for it. I would *really* give fifty thousand francs to any one who would aid me in the matter."

"In that case," replied Dupin, opening a drawer, and producing a checkbook, "you may as well fill me up a check for the amount mentioned. When you have signed it, I will hand you the letter."

I was astounded. The Prefect appeared absolutely thunderstricken.

For some minutes he remained speechless and motionless, looking incredulously at my friend with open mouth, and eyes that seemed starting from their sockets; then apparently recovering himself in some measure, he seized a pen, and after several pauses and vacant stares, finally filled up and signed a check for fifty thousand francs, and handed it across the table to Dupin. The latter examined it carefully and deposited it in his pocketbook; then, unlocking an *escritoire,* took thence a letter and gave it to the Prefect. This functionary grasped it in a perfect agony of joy, opened it with a trembling hand, cast a rapid glance at its contents, and then, scrambling and struggling to the door, rushed at length unceremoniously from the room and from the house, without having uttered a syllable since Dupin had requested him to fill up the check.

When he had gone, my friend entered into some explanations.

"The Parisian police," he said, "are exceedingly able in their way. They are persevering, ingenious, cunning, and thoroughly versed in the knowledge which their duties seem chiefly to demand. Thus, when G—— detailed to us his mode of searching the premises at the

31

Hotel D——, I felt entire confidence in his having made a satisfactory investigation—so far as his labors extended."

"So far as his labors extended?" said I.

"Yes," said Dupin. "The measures adopted were not only the best of their kind, but carried out to absolute perfection. Had the letter been deposited within the range of their search, these fellows would, beyond a question, have found it."

I merely laughed—but he seemed quite serious in all that he said.

"The measures, then," he continued, "were good in their kind, and well executed; their defect lay in their being inapplicable to the case and to the man. A certain set of highly ingenious resources are, with the Prefect, a sort of Procrustean bed, to which he forcibly adapts his designs. But he perpetually errs by being too deep or too shallow for the matter in hand; and many a schoolboy is a better reasoner than he. I knew one about eight years of age, whose success at guessing in the game of 'even and odd' attracted universal admiration. This game is simple, and is played with marbles. One player holds in his hand a number of these toys, and demands of another whether that number is even or odd. If the guess is right, the guesser wins one; if wrong, he loses one. The boy to whom I allude won all the marbles of the school. Of course he had some principle of guessing; and this lay in mere observation and admeasurement of the astuteness of his opponents. For example, an arrant simpleton is his opponent, and, holding up his closed hand, asks, 'Are they even or odd?' Our schoolboy replies, 'Odd,' and loses; but upon the second trial he wins, for he then says to himself: 'The simpleton had them even upon the first trial, and his amount of cunning is just sufficient to make him have them odd upon the second; I will therefore guess odd'; — he guesses odd, and wins. Now, with a simpleton a degree above the first, he would have reasoned thus: 'This fellow finds that in the first instance I guessed odd, and, in the second, he will propose to himself, upon the first impulse, a simple variation from even to odd, as did the first simpleton; but then a second thought will suggest that this is too simple a variation, and finally he will decide upon putting it even as before. I will therefore guess even'; —he guesses even, and wins. Now this mode of reasoning in the schoolboy, whom his fellows termed 'lucky,'—what, in its last analysis, is it?"

"It is merely," I said, "an identification of the reasoner's intellect with that of his opponent."

"It is," said Dupin, "and, upon inquiring of the boy by what means he effected the *thorough* identification in which his success consisted, I received answer as follows: 'When I wish to find out how wise, or how stupid, or how good, or how wicked is any one, or what are his thoughts at the moment, I fashion the expression of my face, as accurately as possible, in accordance with the expression of his, and then wait to see what thoughts or sentiments arise in my mind or heart, as if to match or correspond with the expression.' This response of the schoolboy lies at the bottom of all the spurious profundity which has been attributed to La Rochefoucauld, to La Bougive, to Machiavelli, and to Campanella."

"And the identification," I said, "of the reasoner's intellect with that of his opponent, depends, if I understand you aright, upon the accuracy with which the opponent's intellect is admeasured."

"For its practical value it depends upon this," replied Dupin, "and the Prefect and his cohort fail so frequently, first, by default of this identification, and, secondly, by ill-admeasurement, or rather through non-admeasurement, of the intellect with which they are engaged. They consider only their *own* ideas of ingenuity; and, in searching for anything hidden, advert only to the modes in which *they* would have hidden it. They are right in this much—that their own ingenuity is a faithful representative of that of *the mass;* but when the cunning of the individual felon is diverse in character from their own, the felon foils them, of course. This always happens when it is above their own, and very usually when it is below. They have no variation of principle in their investigations; at best, when urged by some unusual emergency — by some extraordinary reward — they extend or exaggerate their old modes of *practice,* without touching their principles. What, for example, in this case of D——, has been done to vary the principle of action? What is all this boring, and probing, and sounding and scrutinizing with the microscope, and dividing the surface of the building into registered square inches—what is it all but an exaggeration *of the application* of the one principle or 33 set of principles of search, which are based upon the one set of notions regarding human ingenuity, to which the Prefect, in the long routine of his duty, has been accustomed? Do you not see he has taken it for granted that *all* men proceed to conceal a letter, not exactly in a gimlet hole bored in a chair leg, but, at least, in *some* out-of-the-way hole or corner suggested by the same tenor of thought which would urge a man to secrete a letter in a gimlet hole bored in a chair leg? And do you not see also, that such *recherché* nooks for concealment are adapted only for ordinary occasions, and would be adopted only by ordinary intellects; for, in all cases of concealment, a disposal of the article concealed—a disposal of it in this *recherché* manner —is, in the very first instance, presumable and presumed; and thus its discovery depends, not at all upon the acumen, but altogether upon the mere care, patience, and determination of the seekers; and where the case is of importance — or, what amounts to the same thing in the political eyes, when the reward is of magnitude —the qualities in question have *never* been known to fail. You will now understand what I meant in suggesting that, had the

purloined letter been hidden anywhere within the limits of the Prefect's examination—in other words, had the principle of its concealment been comprehended within the principles of the Prefect—its discovery would have been a matter altogether beyond question. This functionary, however, has been thoroughly mystified; and the remote source of his defeat lies in the supposition that the Minister is a fool, because he has acquired renown as a poet. All fools are poets; this the Prefect *feels;* and he is merely guilty of a *non distributio medii* in thence inferring that all poets are fools."

"But is this really the poet?" I asked. "There are two brothers, I know, and both have attained reputation in letters. The Minister I believe has written learnedly on the Differential Calculus. He is a mathematician, and no poet."

"You are mistaken; I know him well; he is both. As poet *and* mathematician, he would reason well; as mere mathematician, he could not have reasoned at all, and thus would have been at the mercy of the Prefect."

"I mean to say," continued Dupin, while I merely laughed at his last observations, "that if the Minister had been no more than a mathematician, the Prefect would have been under no necessity of giving me this check. I knew him, however, as both mathematician and poet, and my measures were adapted to his capacity, with reference to the circumstances by which he was surrounded. I knew him as a courtier, too, and as a bold *intriguant*. Such a man, I considered, could not fail to be aware of the ordinary political modes of action. He could not have failed to anticipate—and events have proved that he did not fail to anticipate — the waylayings to which he was subjected. He must have foreseen, I reflected, the secret investigations of his premises. His frequent absences from home at night, which were hailed by the Prefect as certain aids to his success, I regarded only as *ruses,* to afford opportunity for thorough search to the police, and thus the sooner to impress them with the conviction to which G——, in fact, did finally arrive — the conviction that the letter was not upon the premises. I felt, also, that the whole train of thought, which I was at some pains in detailing to you just now, concerning the invariable principle of political action in searches for articles concealed — I felt that this whole train of thought

would necessarily pass through the mind of the Minister. It would imperatively lead him to despise all the ordinary *nooks* of concealment. *He* could not, I reflected, be so weak as not to see that the most intricate and remote recess of his hotel would be as open as his commonest closets to the eyes, to the probes, to the gimlets, and to the microscopes of the Prefect. I saw, in fine, that he would be driven, as a matter of course, to *simplicity,* if not deliberately induced to it as a matter of choice. You will remember, perhaps, how desperately the Prefect laughed when I suggested, upon our first interview, that it was just possible this mystery troubled him so much on account of its being *so very* self-evident."

"Yes," said I, "I remember his merriment well. I really thought he would have fallen into convulsions."

"The material world," continued Dupin, "abounds with very strict analogies to the immaterial; and thus some color of truth has been given to the rhetorical dogma, that metaphor, or simile, may be made to strengthen an argument as well as to embellish a description. The principle of the *vis inertioe,* for example, seems to be identical in 35 physics and metaphysics. It is not more true in the former, that a large body is with more difficulty set in motion than a smaller one, and that its subsequent *momentum* is commensurate with this difficulty, than it is, in the latter, that intellects of the vaster capacity, while more forcible, more constant, and more eventful in their movements than those of inferior grade, are yet the less readily moved, and more embarrassed, and full of hesitation in the first few steps of their progress. Again: have you ever noticed which of the street signs, over the shop doors, are the most attractive of attention?"

"I have never given the matter a thought," I said.

"There is a game of puzzles," he resumed, "which is played upon a map. One party playing requires another to find a given word — the name of town, river, state, or empire—any word, in short, upon the motley and perplexed surface of the chart. A novice in the game generally seeks to embarrass his opponents by giving them the most minutely lettered names; but the adept selects such words as stretch, in large characters, from one end of the chart to the other. These, like the over-largely lettered signs and placards of the street, escape observation by dint of being excessively obvious; and here the physical oversight is precisely analogous with the moral inapprehension by which the intellect suffers to pass unnoticed those considerations which are too obtrusively and too palpably self-evident. But this is a point, it appears, somewhat above or beneath the understanding of the Prefect. He never once thought it probable, or possible, that the Minister had deposited the letter immediately beneath the nose of the whole world, by way of best preventing any portion of that world from perceiving it.

"But the more I reflected upon the daring, dashing, and discriminating ingenuity of D——; upon the fact that the document must always have been *at hand,* if he intended to use it to good purpose; and upon the decisive evidence, obtained by the Prefect, that it was not hidden within the limits of that dignitary's ordinary search—the more satisfied I became that, to conceal this letter, the Minister had resorted to the comprehensive and sagacious expedient of not attempting to conceal it at all.

"Full of these ideas, I prepared myself with a pair of green spectacles, and called one fine morning, quite by accident, at the Ministerial hotel. I found D—— at home, yawning, lounging, and dawdling, as usual, and pretending to be in the last extremity of *ennui*. He is, perhaps, the most really energetic human being now alive—but that is only when nobody sees him.

"To be even with him, I complained of my weak eyes, and lamented the necessity of the spectacles, under cover of which I cautiously and thoroughly surveyed the whole apartment, while seemingly intent only upon the conversation of my host.

"I paid especial attention to a large writing table near which he sat, and upon which lay confusedly, some miscellaneous letters and other papers, with one or two musical instruments and a few books. Here, however, after a long and very deliberate scrutiny, I saw nothing to excite particular suspicion.

"At length my eyes, in going the circuit of the room, fell upon a trumpery filigree card rack of pasteboard, that hung dangling by a dirty blue ribbon, from a little brass knob just beneath the middle of the mantelpiece. In this rack, which had three or four compartments, were five or six visiting cards and a solitary letter. This last was much soiled and crumpled. It was torn nearly in two, across the middle—as if a design, in the first instance, to tear it entirely up as worthless, had been altered, or stayed, in the second. It had a large black seal, bearing the D—— cipher *very* conspicuously, and was addressed, in a diminutive female hand, to D——, the Minister, himself. It was thrust carelessly, and even, as it seemed, contemptuously, into one of the uppermost divisions of the rack.

"No sooner had I glanced at this letter than I concluded it to be that of which I was in search. To be sure, it was, to all appearance, radically different from the one of which the Prefect had read us so minute a description. Here the seal was large and black, with the D—— cipher; there it was small and red with the ducal arms of the S—— family. Here, the address, to the Minister, was diminutive and feminine; there the superscription, to a certain royal personage, was markedly bold and decided; the size alone formed a point of correspondence. But, then the *radicalness* of these differences, which was excessive; the dirt; the soiled and torn condition of the paper, so inconsistent with the *true* methodical habits of D——, and so suggestive of a design to delude the beholder into an idea of the worthlessness of the document — these things, together with the hyperobtrusive situation of this document, full in the view of every visitor, and thus exactly in accordance with the conclusions to which I had previously arrived; these things, I say, were strongly corroborative of suspicion, in one who came with the intention to suspect.

"I protracted my visit as long as possible, and, while I maintained a most animated discussion with the Minister, upon a topic which I knew well had never failed to interest and excite him, I kept my attention really riveted upon the letter. In this examination, I committed to memory its external appearance and arrangement in the rack; and also fell, at length, upon a discovery which set at rest whatever trivial doubt I might have entertained. In scrutinizing the edges of the paper, I observed them to be more *chafed* than seemed necessary. They presented the *broken* appearance which is manifested when a stiff paper, having been once folded and pressed with a folder, is refolded in a reversed direction, in the same

creases or edges which had formed the original fold. This discovery was sufficient. It was clear to me that the letter had been turned, as a glove, inside out, redirected and re-sealed. I bade the Minister good morning, and took my departure at once, leaving a gold snuffbox upon the table.

"The next morning I called for the snuffbox, when we resumed, quite eagerly, the conversation of the preceding day. While thus engaged, however, a loud report, as if of a pistol, was heard immediately beneath the windows of the hotel, and was succeeded by a series of fearful screams, and the shoutings of a terrified mob. D—— rushed to a casement, threw it open, and looked out. In the meantime I stepped to the card rack, took the letter, put it in my pocket, and replaced it by a facsimile, (so far as regards externals) which I had carefully prepared at my lodgings—imitating the D— cipher very readily, by means of a seal formed of bread.

"The disturbance in the street had been occasioned by the frantic behavior of a man with a musket. He had fired it among a crowd of women and children. It proved, however, to have been without ball, and the fellow was suffered to go his way as a lunatic or a drunkard. When he had gone, D—— came from the window, whither I had followed him immediately upon securing the object in view. Soon afterward I bade him farewell. The pretended lunatic was a man in my own pay."

"But what purpose had you," I asked, "in replacing the letter by a facsimile? Would it not have been better, at the first visit, to have seized it openly, and departed?"

"D——," replied Dupin, "is a desperate man, and a man of nerve. His hotel, too, is not without attendants devoted to his interests. Had I made the wild attempt you suggest, I might never have left the Ministerial presence alive. The good people of Paris might have heard of me no more. But I had an object apart from these considerations. You know my political prepossessions. In this matter, I act as a partisan of the lady concerned. For eighteen months the Minister has had her in his power. She has now him in hers—since, being unaware that the letter is not in his possession, he will proceed with his exactions as if it was. Thus will he inevitably commit himself, at once, to his political destruction. His downfall, too, will not be more pre-

cipitate than awkward. It is all very well to talk about the *facilis descensus Averni;* but in all kinds of climbing, as Catalani said of singing, it is far more easy to get up than to come down. In the present instance I have no sympathy—at least no pity—for him who descends. He is that *monstrum horrendum,* an unprincipled man of genius. I confess, however, that I should like very well to know the precise character of his thoughts, when, being defied by her whom the Prefect terms 'a certain personage,' he is reduced to opening the letter which I left for him in the card rack."

"How? Did you put anything particular in it?"

"Why—it did not seem altogether right to leave the interior blank— that would have been insulting. D——, at Vienna once, did me an evil turn, which I told him, quite good-humoredly, that I should remember. So, as I knew he would feel some curiosity in regard to the identity of the person who had outwitted him, I thought it a pity not to give him a clue. He is well acquainted with my MS., and I just copied into the middle of the blank sheet the words—

"—— —— Un dessein si funeste,
S'il n'est digne d'Atrée, est
digne de Thyeste."

They are to be found in Crébillon's *Atrée.*"

THREE

THE TELL-TALE HEART

True! — nervous — very, very dreadfully nervous I had been and am; but why *will* you say that I am mad? The disease had sharpened my senses — not destroyed — not dulled them. Above all was the sense of hearing acute. I heard all things in the heaven and in the earth. I heard many things in hell. How, then, am I mad? Harken! and observe how healthily—how calmly I can tell you the whole story.

It is impossible to say how first the idea entered my brain; but once conceived, it haunted me day and night. Object there was none. Passion there was none. I loved the old man. He had never wronged me. He had never given me insult. For his gold I had no desire. I think it was his eye! Yes, it was this! One of his eyes resembled that of a vulture —a pale blue eye, with a film over it. Whenever it fell upon me, my blood ran cold; and so by degrees—very gradually—I made up my mind to take the life of the old man, and thus rid myself of the eye forever.

Now this is the point. You fancy me mad. Madmen know nothing. But you should have seen *me*. You should have seen how wisely I proceeded — with what caution — with what foresight—with what dissimulation I went to work! I was never kinder to the old man than during the whole week before I killed him. And every night, about midnight, I turned the latch of his door and opened it—oh, so gently! And then, when I had made an opening sufficient for my head, I put in a dark lantern, all closed, closed, so that no light shone out, and then I thrust in my head. Oh, you would have laughed to see how cunningly I thrust it in! I moved it slowly — very, very slowly, so that I might not disturb the old man's sleep. It took me an hour to place my whole head within the opening so far that I could see him as he lay upon his bed. Ha!—would a madman have been so wise as this? And then, when my head was well in the room, I undid the lantern cautiously—oh, so cautiously — cautiously (for the

41

hinges creaked)—I undid it just so much that a single thin ray fell upon the vulture eye. And this I did for seven long nights—every night just at midnight—but I found the eye always closed; and so it was impossible to do the work; for it was not the old man who vexed me, but his Evil Eye. And every morning, when the day broke, I went boldly into the chamber, and spoke courageously to him, calling him by name in a hearty tone, and inquiring how he had passed the night. So you see he would have been a very profound old man, indeed, to suspect that every night, just at twelve, I looked in upon him while he slept.

Upon the eighth night I was more than usually cautious in opening the door. A watch's minute hand moves more quickly than did mine. Never before that night had I *felt* the extent of my own powers— of my sagacity. I could scarcely contain my feelings of triumph. To think that there I was, opening the door, little by little, and he not even to dream of my secret deeds or thoughts. I fairly chuckled at the idea; and perhaps he heard me; for he moved on the bed suddenly, as if startled. Now you may think that I drew back—but no. His room was as black as pitch with the thick dark-

ness (for the shutters were close fastened, through fear of robbers), and so I knew that he could not see the opening of the door, and I kept pushing it on steadily, steadily.

"And then, when my head was well in the room, I undid the lantern cautiously—oh, so cautiously—cautiously (for the hinges creaked) —I undid it just so much that a single thin ray fell upon the vulture eye."

I had my head in, and was about to open the lantern, when my thumb slipped upon the tin fastening, and the old man sprang up in the bed, crying out—"Who's there?"

I kept quite still and said nothing. For a whole hour I did not move a muscle, and in the meantime I did not hear him lie down. He was still sitting up in the bed listening — just as I have done, night after night, harkening to the death watches in the wall.

Presently I heard a slight groan, and I knew it was the groan of mortal terror. It was not a groan of pain or of grief—oh, no!—it was the low stifled sound that arises from the bottom of the soul when overcharged with awe. I knew the sound well. Many a night, just at midnight, when all the world slept, it has welled up from my own bosom, deepening, with its dreadful echo, the terrors that distracted me. I say I knew it well. I knew what the old man felt, and pitied him, although I chuckled at heart. I knew that he had been lying awake ever since the first slight noise, when he had turned in the bed. His fears had been ever since growing upon him. He had been trying to fancy them causeless, but could not. He had been saying to himself, "It is nothing but the wind in the chimney— it is only a mouse crossing the floor," or "It is merely a cricket which has made a single chirp." Yes, he has been trying to comfort himself with these suppositions; but he had found all in vain. *All in vain;* because Death in approaching him, had stalked with his black shadow before him, and enveloped the victim. And it was the mournful influence of the unperceived shadow that caused him to feel — although he neither saw nor heard — to *feel* the presence of my head within the room.

When I had waited a long time, very patiently, without hearing him lie down, I resolved to open a little —a very, very little crevice in the lantern. So I opened it—you can-

not imagine how stealthily, stealthily—until, at length, a single dim ray, like the thread of the spider, shot from out the crevice and full upon the vulture eye.

It was open—wide, wide open—and I grew furious as I gazed upon it. I saw it with perfect distinctness—all a dull blue, with a hideous veil over it that chilled the very marrow in my bones; but I could see nothing else of the old man's face or person: for I had directed the ray as if by instinct, precisely upon the damned spot.

And now have I not told you that what you mistake for madness is but over-acuteness of the senses? Now, I say, there came to my ears a low, dull, quick sound, such as a watch makes when enveloped in cotton. I knew *that* sound well too. It was the beating of the old man's heart. It increased my fury, as the beating of a drum stimulates the soldier into courage.

But even yet I refrained and kept still. I scarcely breathed. I held the lantern motionless. I tried how steadily I could maintain the ray upon the eye. Meantime the hellish tattoo of the heart increased. It grew quicker and quicker, and louder and louder every instant. The old man's terror *must* have

been extreme! It grew louder, I say, louder every moment! — do you mark me well? I have told you that I am nervous; so I am. And now at the dead hour of the night, amid the dreadful silence of that old house, so strange a noise as this excited me to uncontrollable terror. Yet, for some minutes longer I refrained and stood still. But the beating grew louder, louder! I thought the heart must burst. And now a new anxiety seized me—the sound would be heard by a neighbor! The old man's hour had come! With a loud yell, I threw open the lantern and leaped into the room. He shrieked once—once only. In an instant I dragged him to the floor, and pulled the heavy bed over him. I then smiled gaily, to find the deed so far done. But, for many minutes, the heart beat on with a muffled sound. This, however, did not vex me; it would not be heard through the wall. At length it ceased. The old man was dead. I removed the bed and examined the corpse. Yes, he was stone, stone dead. I placed my hand upon the heart and held it there many minutes. There was no pulsation. He was stone dead. His eye would trouble me no more.

If still you think me mad, you

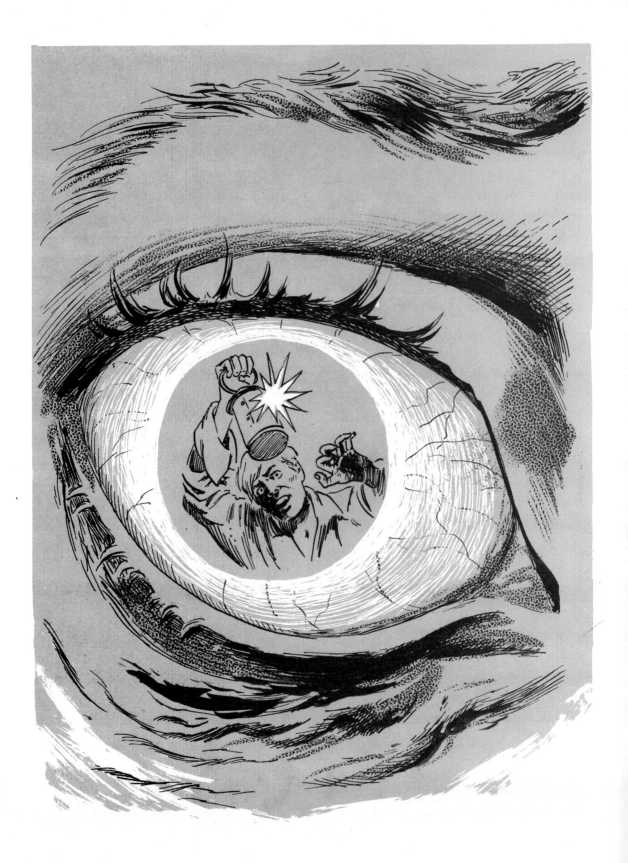

will think so no longer when I describe the wise precautions I took for the concealment of the body. The night waned, and I worked hastily, but in silence. First of all I dismembered the corpse. I cut off the head and the arms and the legs.

I then took up three planks from the flooring of the chamber, and deposited all between the scantlings. I then replaced the boards so cleverly, so cunningly, that no human eye —not even *his*—could have detected anything wrong. There was nothing to wash out — no stain of any kind—no blood-spot whatever. I had been too wary for that. A tub had caught all—ha! ha!

When I had made an end of these labors, it was four o'clock—still dark as midnight. As the bell sounded the hour, there came a knocking at the street door. I went down to open it with a light heart —for what had I *now* to fear? There entered three men, who introduced themselves, with perfect suavity, as officers of the police. A shriek had been heard by a neighbor during the night; suspicion of foul play had been aroused; information had been lodged at the police office, and they (the officers) had been deputed to search the premises.

I smiled — for *what* had I to fear? I bade the gentlemen welcome. The

shriek, I said, was my own in a dream. The old man, I mentioned, was absent in the country. I took my visitors all over the house. I bade them search — search *well*. I led them, at length, to *his* chamber. I showed them his treasures, secure, undisturbed. In the enthusiasm of my confidence, I brought chairs into the room, and desired them *here* to rest from their fatigues, while I myself, in the wild audacity of my perfect triumph, placed my own seat upon the very spot beneath which reposed the corpse of the victim.

The officers were satisfied. My *manner* had convinced them. I was singularly at ease. They sat, and while I answered cheerily, they chatted familiar things. But, ere long, I felt myself getting pale and wished them gone. My head ached, and I fancied a ringing in my ears; but still they sat and still chatted. The ringing became more distinct —it continued and became more distinct. I talked more freely to get rid of the feeling, but it continued and gained definitiveness—until, at length, I found that the noise was *not* within my ears.

No doubt I now grew *very* pale; —but I talked more fluently, and with a heightened voice. Yet the

sound increased—and what could I do? It was a *low, dull, quick sound* —*much such a sound as a watch makes when enveloped in cotton.* I gasped for breath—and yet the officers heard it not. I talked more quickly—more vehemently; but the noise steadily increased. I arose and argued about trifles, in a high key and with violent gesticulations, but the noise steadily increased. Why *would* they not be gone? I paced the floor to and fro with heavy strides, as if excited to fury by the observation of the men — but the noise steadily increased. Oh God! what

could I do? I foamed—I raved—I swore! I swung the chair upon which I had been sitting, and grated it upon the boards, but the noise arose over all and continually increased. It grew louder—louder—*louder!* And still the men chatted pleasantly, and smiled. Was it possible they heard not? Almighty God!—no, no! They heard!—they suspected!—they *knew!*—they were making a mockery of my horror!— this I thought, and this I think. But anything was better than this agony! Anything was more tolerable than this derision! I could bear those 49

hypocritical smiles no longer! I felt that I must scream or die!—and now — again! — hark! louder! louder! louder! *louder!*—

"Villains!" I shrieked, "dissemble no more! I admit the deed!—tear up the planks!—here, here!—it is the beating of his hideous heart!"

FOUR · THE PIT AND THE PENDULUM

I was sick—sick unto death with that long agony; and when they at length unbound me, and I was permitted to sit, I felt that my senses were leaving me. The sentence—the dread sentence of death — was the last of distinct accentuation which reached my ears. After that, the sound of the Inquisitorial voices seemed merged in one dreamy indeterminate hum. It conveyed to my soul the idea of revolution—perhaps from its association in fancy with the burr of a mill wheel. This only for a brief period, for presently I heard no more. Yet, for a while, I saw—but with how terrible an exaggeration! I saw the lips of the black-robed judges. They appeared to me white—whiter than the sheet upon which I trace these words—and thin even to grotesqueness; thin with the intensity of their expression of firmness—of immovable resolution—of stern contempt of human torture. I saw that the decrees of what to me was Fate were still issuing from those lips. I saw them writhe with a deadly locution. I saw them fash-

ion the syllables of my name; and I shuddered because no sound succeeded. I saw, too, for a few moments of delirious horror, the soft and nearly imperceptible waving of the sable draperies which enwrapped the walls of the apartment. And then my vision fell upon the seven tall candles upon the table. At first they wore the aspect of charity, and seemed white slender angels who would save me; but then, all at once, there came a most deadly nausea over my spirit, and I felt every fibre in my frame thrill as if I had touched the wire of a galvanic battery, while the angel forms became meaningless specters, with heads of flame, and I saw that from them there would be no help. And then there stole into my fancy, like a rich musical note, the thought of what sweet rest there must be in the grave. The thought came gently and stealthily, and it seemed long before it attained full appreciation; but just as my spirit came at length properly to feel and entertain it, the figures of the judges vanished, as if

51

magically, from before me; the tall candles sank into nothingness; their flames went out utterly; the blackness of darkness supervened; all sensations appeared swallowed up in a mad rushing descent as of the soul into Hades. Then silence, and stillness, and night were the universe.

I had swooned; but still will not say that all of consciousness was lost. What of it there remained I will not attempt to define, or even to describe; yet all was not lost. In the deepest slumber—no! In delirium—no! In a swoon—no! In death—no! Even in the grave all *is not* lost. Else there is no immortality for man. Arousing from the most profound of slumbers, we break the gossamer web of *some* dream. Yet in a second afterward (so frail may that web have been) we remember not that we have dreamed. In the return to life from the swoon there are two stages: first, that of the sense of mental or spiritual; secondly, that of the sense of physical, existence. It seems probable that if, upon reaching the second stage, we could recall the impressions of the first, we should find these impressions eloquent in memories of the gulf beyond. And that gulf is — what? How at least shall we distinguish its shadows from those of the tomb?

But if the impressions of what I have termed the first stage are not, at will, recalled, yet, after long interval, do they not come unbidden, while we marvel whence they come? He who has never swooned, is not he who finds strange palaces and wildly familiar faces in coals that glow; is not he who beholds floating in midair the sad visions that the many may not view; is not he who ponders over the perfume of some novel flower; is not he whose brain grows bewildered with the meaning of some musical cadence which has never before arrested his attention.

Amid frequent and thoughtful endeavors to remember, amid earnest struggles to regather some token of the state of seeming nothingness into which my soul had lapsed, there have been moments when I have dreamed of success; there have been brief, very brief periods when I have conjured up remembrances which the lucid reason of a later epoch assures me could have had reference only to that condition of seeming unconsciousness. These shadows of memory tell, indistinctly, of tall figures that lifted and bore me in silence down — down — still down—till a hideous dizziness oppressed me at the mere idea of the interminableness of the descent. They tell also of a vague horror at my heart, on account of that heart's unnatural stillness. Then comes a sense of sudden motionlessness throughout all things; as if those who bore me (a ghastly train!) had outrun, in their descent, the limits of the limitless, and paused from the wearisomeness of their toil. After this I call to mind flatness and dampness; and then all is *madness*—the madness of a memory which busies itself among forbidden things.

Very suddenly there came back to my soul motion and sound—the tumultuous motion of the heart, and, in my ears, the sound of its beating. Then a pause in which all is blank. Then again sound, and motion, and touch—a tingling sensation pervading my frame. Then the mere consciousness of existence, without thought—a condition which lasted long. Then, very suddenly, *thought,* and shuddering terror, and earnest endeavor to comprehend my true state. Then a strong desire to lapse into insensibility. Then a rushing revival of soul and a successful effort to move. And now a full memory of the trial, of the judges, of the sable draperies, of the sentence, of the sickness, of the swoon. Then entire forgetfulness of all that followed; of all that a later day and much earnestness of endeavor have enabled me vaguely to recall.

So far, I had not opened my eyes. I felt that I lay upon my back, unbound. I reached out my hand, and it fell heavily upon something damp and hard. There I suffered it to remain for many minutes, while I strove to imagine where and *what* I could be. I longed, yet dared not, to employ my vision. I dreaded the first glance at objects around me. It was not that I feared to look upon things horrible, but that I grew aghast lest there should be *nothing* to see. At length, with a wild desperation at heart, I quickly unclosed my eyes. My worst thoughts, then, were confirmed. The blackness of eternal night encompassed me. I struggled for breath. The intensity of the darkness seemed to oppress and stifle me. The atmosphere was intolerably close. I still lay quietly, and made effort to exercise my reason. I brought to mind the Inquisitorial proceedings, and attempted from that point to deduce my real condition. The sentence had passed; and it appeared to me that a very long interval of time had since elapsed. Yet not for a moment did I suppose myself actually dead. Such a supposition, notwithstanding what we read in fiction, is altogether inconsistent with real existence — but where and in what state was I? The condemned to death, I knew, perished usually at the *auto-da-fés*, and one of these had been held on the very night of the day of my trial. Had I been remanded to my dungeon, to await the next sacrifice, which would not take place for many months? This I at once saw could not be. Victims had been in immediate demand. Moreover, my dungeon, as well as all the condemned cells at Toledo, had stone floors, and light was not altogether excluded.

A fearful idea now suddenly drove the blood in torrents upon my heart, and for a brief period I once more relapsed into insensibility. Upon recovering, I at once started to my feet, trembling convulsively in every fibre. I thrust my arms wildly above and around me in all directions. I felt nothing; yet dreaded to move a step, lest I should be impeded by the walls of a *tomb*. Perspiration burst from every pore, and stood in cold big beads upon my forehead. The agony of suspense grew at length intolerable, and I cautiously moved forward, with my arms extended, and my eyes straining from their sockets in the hope of catching some faint ray of light. I proceeded for many paces; but still all was blackness and vacancy. I breathed more freely. It seemed evident that mine was not, at least, the most hideous of fates.

And now, as I still continued to step cautiously onward, there came thronging upon my recollection a thousand vague rumors of the horrors of Toledo. Of the dungeons there had been strange things narrated—fables I had always deemed them,—but yet strange, and too ghastly to repeat, save in a whisper. Was I left to perish of starvation in this subterranean world of darkness; or what fate, perhaps even more fearful, awaited me? That the result would be death, and a death of more than customary bitterness, I knew too well the character of my judges to doubt. The mode and the hour were all that occupied or distracted me.

My outstretched hands at length encountered some solid obstruction. It was a wall, seemingly of stone masonry — very smooth, slimy, and cold. I followed it up, stepping with all the careful distrust with which certain antique narratives had inspired me. This process,

55

however, afforded me no means of ascertaining the dimensions of my dungeon, as I might make its circuit and return to the point whence I set out without being aware of the fact, so perfectly uniform seemed the wall. I therefore sought the knife which had been in my pocket when led into the inquisitorial chamber; but it was gone; my clothes had been exchanged for a wrapper of coarse serge. I had thought of forcing the blade in some minute crevice of the masonry, so as to identify my point of departure. The difficulty, nevertheless, was but trivial; although, in the disorder of my fancy, it seemed at first insuperable. I tore a part of the hem from the robe and placed the fragment at full length, and at right angles to the wall. In groping my way around the prison, I could not fail to encounter this rag upon completing the circuit. So, at least, I thought; but I had not counted upon the extent of the dungeon, or upon my own weakness. The ground was moist and slippery. I staggered onward for some time, when I stumbled and fell. My excessive fatigue induced me to remain prostrate; and sleep soon overtook me as I lay.

Upon awaking, and stretching forth an arm, I found beside me a

loaf and a pitcher with water. I was
too much exhausted to reflect upon
this circumstance, but ate and drank
with avidity. Shortly afterward, I
resumed my tour around the prison,
and with much toil, came at last
upon the fragment of the serge. Up
to the period when I fell, I had
counted fifty-two paces, and, upon
resuming my walk, I had counted
forty-eight more—when I arrived at
the rag. There were in all, then, a
hundred paces; and, admitting two
paces to the yard, I presumed the
dungeon to be fifty yards in circuit.
I had met, however, with many
angles in the wall, and thus I could
form no guess at the shape of the
vault, for vault I could not help
supposing it to be.

I had little object—certainly no
hope—in these researches; but a
vague curiosity prompted me to
continue them. Quitting the wall,
I resolved to cross the area of the
enclosure. At first, I proceeded with
extreme caution, for the floor, although seemingly of solid material,
was treacherous with slime. At
length, however, I took courage,
and did not hesitate to step firmly—
endeavoring to cross in as direct a
line as possible. I had advanced
some ten or twelve paces in this
manner, when the remnant of the

torn hem of my robe became entangled between my legs. I stepped on it, and fell violently on my face.

In the confusion attending my fall, I did not immediately apprehend a somewhat startling circumstance, which yet, in a few seconds afterward, and while I still lay prostrate, arrested my attention. It was this: my chin rested upon the floor of the prison, but my lips, and the upper portion of my head, although seemingly at a less elevation than the chin, touched nothing. At the same time, my forehead seemed bathed in a clammy vapor, and the peculiar smell of decayed fungus arose to my nostrils. I put forward my arm, and shuddered to find that I had fallen at the very brink of a circular pit, whose extent, of course, I had no means of ascertaining at the moment. Groping about the masonry just below the margin, I succeeded in dislodging a small fragment, and let it fall into the abyss. For many seconds I harkened to its reverberations as it dashed against the sides of the chasm in its descent; at length, there was a sullen plunge into water, succeeded by loud echoes. At the same moment, there came a sound resembling the quick opening and as rapid closing of a door overhead, while a faint gleam of light flashed suddenly through the gloom, and as suddenly faded away.

I saw clearly the doom which had been prepared for me, and congratulated myself upon the timely accident by which I had escaped. Another step before my fall, and the world had seen me no more. And the death just avoided was of that very character which I had regarded as fabulous and frivolous in the tales respecting the Inquisition. To the victims of its tyranny, there was the choice of death with its direst physical agonies, or death with its most hideous moral horrors. I had been reserved for the latter. By long suffering my nerves had been unstrung, until I trembled at the sound of my own voice, and had become in every respect a fitting subject for the species of torture which awaited me.

Shaking in every limb, I groped my way back to the wall—resolving there to perish rather than risk the terrors of the wells, of which my imagination now pictured many in various positions about the dungeon. In other conditions of mind, I might have had courage to end my misery at once, by a plunge into one of these abysses; but now I was the veriest of cowards. Neither could I forget what I had read of these pits —that the *sudden* extinction of life formed no part of their most horrible plan.

Agitation of spirit kept me awake for many long hours, but at length I again slumbered. Upon arousing, I found by my side, as before, a loaf and a pitcher of water. A burning thirst consumed me, and I emptied the vessel at a draught. It must have been drugged — for scarcely had I drunk, before I became irresistibly drowsy. A deep sleep fell upon me —a sleep like that of death. How long it lasted, of course I know not; but when, once again, I unclosed my eyes, the objects around me were visible. By a wild, sulphurous luster, the origin of which I could not at first determine, I was enabled to see the extent and aspect of the prison.

In its size I had been greatly mistaken. The whole circuit of its walls did not exceed twenty-five yards. For some minutes this fact occasioned me a world of vain trouble; vain indeed—for what could be of less importance, under the terrible circumstances which environed me, than the mere dimensions of my dungeon? But my soul took a wild interest in trifles, and I busied myself in endeavors to account for the error I had committed in my measurement. The truth at length flashed upon me. In my first attempt at exploration I had counted fifty-two paces, up to the period when I fell: I must then have been within a pace or two of the fragment of serge; in fact, I had nearly performed the circuit of the vault. I then slept—and, upon awaking, I must have returned upon my steps —thus supposing the circuit nearly double what it actually was. My confusion of mind prevented me from observing that I began my tour with the wall to the left, and ended it with the wall to the right.

I had been deceived, too, in respect to the shape of the enclosure. In feeling my way I had found many angles, and thus deduced an idea of great irregularity; so potent is the effect of total darkness upon one arousing from lethargy or sleep! The angles were simply those of a few slight depressions, or niches, at odd intervals. The general shape of the prison was square. What I had taken for masonry seemed now to be iron, or some other metal, in huge plates, whose sutures or joints occasioned the depression. The entire surface of this metallic enclosure was rudely daubed in all the hideous and repulsive devices to which the charnel superstition of the monks has given rise. The figures of fiends in aspects of menace, with skeleton forms, and other more really fearful images, overspread and disfigured the walls. I observed that the outlines of these monstrosities were sufficiently distinct, but that the colors seemed faded and blurred, as if from the effects of a damp atmosphere. I now noticed the floor, too, which was of stone. In the center yawned the circular pit from whose jaws I had escaped; but it was the only one in the dungeon.

All this I saw indistinctly and by much effort—for my personal condition had been greatly changed during slumber. I now lay upon my back, and at full length, on a species of low framework of wood. To this I was securely bound by a long strap resembling a surcingle. It passed in many convolutions about my limbs and body, leaving at liberty only my head, and my left arm to such extent, that I could, by dint of much exertion, supply myself with food from an earthen dish which lay by my side on the floor. I saw, to my horror, that the pitcher had been removed. I say to my horror—for I was consumed with intolerable thirst. This thirst it appeared to be

the design of my persecutors to stimulate—for the food in the dish was meat pungently seasoned.

Looking upward, I surveyed the ceiling of my prison. It was some thirty or forty feet overhead, and constructed much as the side walls. In one of its panels a very singular figure riveted my whole attention. It was the painted figure of Time as he is commonly represented, save that, in lieu of a scythe, he held what, at a casual glance, I supposed to be the pictured image of a huge pendulum, such as we see on antique clocks. There was something, however, in the appearance of this machine which caused me to regard it more attentively. While I gazed directly upward at it (for its position was immediately over my own) I fancied that I saw it in motion. In an instant afterward the fancy was confirmed. Its sweep was brief, and of course slow. I watched it for some minutes somewhat in fear, but more in wonder. Wearied at length with observing its dull movement, I turned my eyes upon the other objects in the cell.

A slight noise attracted my notice, and, looking to the floor, I saw several enormous rats traversing it. They had issued from the well which lay just within view to my right. Even then, while I gazed, they came up in troops, hurriedly, with ravenous eyes, allured by the scent of the meat. From this it required much effort and attention to scare them away.

It might have been half an hour, perhaps even an hour (for I could take but imperfect note of time), before I again cast my eyes upward. What I then saw confounded and amazed me. The sweep of the pendulum had increased in extent by nearly a yard. As a natural consequence its velocity was also much greater. But what mainly disturbed me was the idea that it had perceptibly *descended*. I now observed —with what horror it is needless to say—that its nether extremity was formed of a crescent of glittering steel, about a foot in length from horn to horn; the horns upward, and the under edge evidently as keen as that of a razor. Like a razor also, it seemed massy and heavy, tapering from the edge into a solid and broad structure above. It was appended to a weighty rod of brass, and the whole *hissed* as it swung through the air.

I could no longer doubt the doom prepared for me by monkish ingenuity in torture. My cognizance of the pit had become known to the Inquisitorial agents—*the pit*, whose horrors had been destined for so bold a recusant as myself—*the pit* typical of hell and regarded by rumor as the Ultima Thule of all their punishments. The plunge into this pit I had avoided by the merest of accidents, and I knew that surprise, or entrapment into torment, formed an important portion of all the grotesquerie of these dungeon deaths. Having failed to fall, it was no part of the demon plan to hurl me into the abyss, and thus (there being no alternative) a different and a milder destruction awaited me. Milder! I half smiled in my agony as I thought of such application of such a term.

What boots it to tell of the long, long hours of horror more than mortal, during which I counted the rushing oscillations of the steel! Inch by inch—line by line—with a descent only appreciable at intervals that seemed ages — down and still down it came! Days passed — it might have been that many days passed—ere it swept so closely over me as to fan me with its acrid breath. The odor of the sharp steel forced itself into my nostrils. I prayed—I wearied heaven with my prayer for its more speedy descent. I grew frantically mad, and strug-

gled to force myself upward against the sweep of the fearful scimitar. And then I fell suddenly calm, and lay smiling at the glittering death, as a child at some rare bauble.

There was another interval of utter insensibility; it was brief; for, upon again lapsing into life, there had been no perceptible descent in the pendulum. But it might have been long—for I knew there were demons who took note of my swoon, and who could have arrested the vibration at pleasure. Upon my recovery, too, I felt very—oh! inexpressibly—sick and weak, as if through long inanition. Even amid the agonies of that period, the human nature craved food. With painful effort I outstretched my left arm as far as my bonds permitted, and took possession of the small remnant which had been spared me by the rats. As I put a portion of it. within my lips, there rushed to my mind a half-formed thought of joy —of hope. Yet what business had *I* with hope? It was, as I say, a half-formed thought — man has many such, which are never completed. I felt that it was of joy—of hope; but I felt also that it had perished in its formation. In vain I struggled to perfect—to regain it. Long suffering had nearly annihilated all my

ordinary powers of mind. I was an imbecile—an idiot.

The vibration of the pendulum was at right angles to my length. I saw that the crescent was designed to cross the region of the heart. It would fray the serge of my robe—it would return and repeat its operations—again—and again. Notwithstanding its terrifically wide sweep (some thirty feet or more), and the hissing vigor of its descent, sufficient to sunder these very walls of iron, still the fraying of my robe would be all that, for several minutes, it would accomplish. And at this thought I paused. I dared not go further than this reflection. I dwelt upon it with a pertinacity of attention—as if, in so dwelling, I could arrest *here* the descent of the steel. I forced myself to ponder upon the sound of the crescent as it should pass across the garment— upon the peculiar thrilling sensation which the friction of cloth produces on the nerves. I pondered upon all this frivolity until my teeth were on edge.

Down—steadily down it crept. I took a frenzied pleasure in contrasting its downward with its lateral velocity. To the right—to the left— far and wide—with the shriek of a damned spirit! to my heart, with the stealthy pace of the tiger! I alternately laughed and howled, as the one or the other idea grew predominant.

Down — certainly, relentlessly down! It vibrated within three inches of my bosom! I struggled violently—furiously—to free my left arm. This was free only from the elbow to the hand. I could reach the latter, from the platter beside me, to my mouth, with great effort, but no farther. Could I have broken the fastenings above the elbow, I would have seized and attempted to arrest the pendulum. I might as well have attempted to arrest an avalanche!

Down—still unceasingly—still inevitably down! I gasped and struggled at each vibration. I shrunk convulsively at its every sweep. My eyes followed its outward or upward whirls with the eagerness of the most unmeaning despair; they closed themselves spasmodically at the descent, although death would have been a relief, oh, how unspeakable! Still I quivered in every nerve to think how slight a sinking of the machinery would precipitate that keen, glistening axe upon my bosom. It was *hope* that prompted the nerve to quiver—the frame to shrink. It was *hope*—the hope that

triumphs on the rack—that whispers to the death-condemned even in the dungeons of the Inquisition.

I saw that some ten or twelve vibrations would bring the steel in actual contact with my robe—and with this observation there suddenly came over my spirit all the keen, collected calmness of despair. For the first time during many hours—or perhaps days—I *thought*. It now occurred to me, that the bandage, or surcingle, which enveloped me, was *unique*. I was tied by no separate cord. The first stroke of the razor-like crescent athwart any portion of the band would so detach it that it might be unwound from my person by means of my left hand. But how fearful, in that case, the proximity of the steel! The result of the slightest struggle, how deadly! Was it likely, moreover, that the minions of the torturer had not foreseen and provided for this possibility? Was it probable that the bandage crossed my bosom in the track of the pendulum? Dreading to find my faint and, as it seemed, my last hope frustrated, I so far elevated my head as to obtain a distinct view of my breast. The surcingle enveloped my limbs and body close in all directions—*save in the path of the destroying crescent.*

Scarcely had I dropped my head back into its original position, when there flashed upon my mind what I cannot better describe than as the unformed half of that idea of deliverance to which I have previously alluded, and of which a moiety only floated indeterminately through my brain when I raised food to my burning lips. The whole thought was now present — feeble, scarcely sane, scarcely definite—but still entire. I proceeded at once, with the nervous energy of despair, to attempt its execution.

For many hours the immediate vicinity of the low framework upon which I lay had been literally swarming with rats. They were wild, bold, ravenous—their red eyes glaring upon me as if they waited but for motionlessness on my part to make me their prey. "To what food," I thought, "have they been accustomed in the well?"

They had devoured, in spite of all my efforts to prevent them, all but a small remnant of the contents of the dish. I had fallen into an habitual see-saw or wave of the hand about the platter; and, at length, the unconscious uniformity of the movement deprived it of effect. In their voracity, the vermin frequently fastened their sharp fangs in my fingers. With the particles of the oily and spicy viand which now remained, I thoroughly rubbed the bandage wherever I could reach it; then, raising my hand from the floor, I lay breathlessly still.

At first, the ravenous animals were startled and terrified at the change—at the cessation of movement. They shrank alarmedly back; many sought the well. But this was only for a moment. I had not counted in vain upon their voracity. Observing that I remained without motion, one or two of the boldest leaped upon the framework, and smelt at the surcingle. They seemed the signal for a general rush. Forth from the well they hurried in fresh troops. They clung to the wood—they overran it, and leaped in hundreds upon my person. The measured movement of the pendulum disturbed them not at all. Avoiding its strokes, they busied themselves with the anointed bandage. They pressed—they swarmed upon me in ever accumulating heaps. They writhed upon my throat; their cold lips sought my own; I was half stifled by their thronging pressure; disgust, for which the world has no name, swelled my bosom, and chilled, with a heavy clamminess, my heart. Yet one minute, and I felt that the struggle would be over. Plainly I perceived the loosening of the bandage. I knew that in more than one place it must be already severed. With a more than human resolution I lay *still*.

Nor had I erred in my calculations—nor had I endured in vain. I at length felt that I was *free*. The surcingle hung in ribands from my body. But the stroke of the pendulum already pressed upon my bosom. It had divided the serge of the robe. It had cut through the linen beneath. Twice again it swung, and a sharp sense of pain shot through every nerve. But the moment of escape had arrived. At a wave of my hand my deliverers hurried tumultuously away. With a steady movement—cautious, sidelong, shrinking, and slow — I slid from the embrace of the bandage and beyond the reach of the scimitar. For the moment, at least, *I was free*.

Free!—and in the grasp of the Inquisition! I had scarcely stepped from my wooden bed of horror upon the stone floor of the prison, when the motion of the hellish machine ceased, and I beheld it drawn up, by some invisible force, through the ceiling. This was a les-son which I took desperately to heart. My every motion was undoubtedly watched. Free! — I had but escaped death in one form of agony, to be delivered unto worse than death in some other. With that thought I rolled my eyes nervously around on the barriers of iron that hemmed me in. Something unusual—some change which, at first, I could not appreciate distinctly—it was obvious, had taken place in the apartment. For many minutes of a dreamy and trembling abstraction, I busied myself in vain, unconnected conjecture. During this period, I became aware, for the first time, of the origin of the sulphurous light which illumined the cell. It proceeded from a fissure, about half an inch in width, extending entirely around the prison at the base of the walls, which thus appeared, and were completely separated from the floor. I endeavored, but of course in vain, to look through the aperture.

As I arose from the attempt, the mystery of the alteration in the chamber broke at once upon my understanding. I have observed that, although the outlines of the figures upon the walls were sufficiently distinct, yet the colors seemed blurred and indefinite. These colors had now assumed, and were momentarily assuming, a startling and most intense brilliancy, that gave to the spectral and fiendish portraitures an aspect that might have thrilled even firmer nerves than my own. Demon eyes, of a wild and ghastly vivacity, glared upon me in a thousand directions, where none had been visible before, and gleamed with the lurid luster of a fire that I could not force my imagination to regard as unreal.

Unreal!—Even while I breathed there came to my nostrils the breath of the vapor of heated iron! A suffocating odor pervaded the prison! A deeper glow settled each moment in the eyes that glared at my agonies! A richer tint of crimson diffused itself over the pictured horrors of blood. I panted! I gasped for breath! There could be no doubt of the design of my tormentors—oh! most unrelenting! oh! most demoniac of men! I shrank from the glowing metal to the center of the cell. Amid the thought of the fiery destruction that impended, the idea of the coolness of the well came over my soul like balm. I rushed to its deadly brink. I threw my straining vision below. The glare from the enkindled roof illumined its inmost recesses. Yet, for a wild moment, did my spirit refuse to comprehend the meaning of what I saw. At length it forced—it wrestled its way into my soul — it burned itself in upon my shuddering reason. Oh! for a voice to speak! —oh! horror!—oh! any horror but this! With a shriek, I rushed from the margin, and buried my face in my hands—weeping bitterly.

The heat rapidly increased, and once again I looked up, shuddering as with a fit of the ague. There had been a second change in the cell— and now the change was obviously in the *form*. As before, it was in vain that I at first endeavored to appreciate or understand what was taking place. But not long was I left in doubt. The Inquisitorial vengeance had been hurried by my two-fold escape, and there was to be no more dallying with the King of Terrors. The room had been square. I saw that two of its iron angles were now acute—two, consequently, obtuse. The fearful difference quickly increased with a low rumbling or moaning sound. In an instant the apartment had shifted its form into that of a lozenge. But the alteration stopped not here — I neither hoped nor desired it to stop. I could have clasped the red walls to my bosom as a garment of eter-

nal peace. "Death," I said, "any death but that of the pit!" Fool! Might I not have known that *into the pit* it was the object of the burning iron to urge me? Could I resist its glow? or if even that, could I withstand its pressure? And now, flatter and flatter grew the lozenge, with a rapidity that left me no time for contemplation. Its center, and of course its greatest width, came just over the yawning gulf. I shrank back—but the closing walls pressed me resistlessly onward. At length for my seared and writhing body there was no longer an inch of foothold on the firm floor of the prison.

I struggled no more, but the agony of my soul found vent in one loud, long, and final scream of despair. I felt that I tottered upon the brink—I averted my eyes—

There was a discordant hum of human voices! There was a loud blast as of many trumpets! There was a harsh grating as of a thousand thunders! The fiery walls rushed back! An outstretched arm caught my own as I fell, fainting, into the abyss. It was that of General Lasalle. The French army had entered Toledo. The Inquisition was in the hands of its enemies.

FIVE

THE FALL OF THE HOUSE OF USHER

During the whole of a dull, dark, and soundless day in the autumn of the year, when the clouds hung oppressively low in the heavens, I had been passing alone, on horseback, through a singularly dreary tract of country, and at length found myself, as the shades of the evening drew on, within view of the melancholy House of Usher. I know not how it was — but, with the first glimpse of the building, a sense of insufferable gloom pervaded my spirit. I say insufferable; for the feeling was unrelieved by any of that half-pleasurable, because poetic, sentiment with which the mind usually receives even the sternest natural images of the desolate or terrible. I looked upon the scene before me—upon the mere house, and the simple landscape features of the domain—upon the bleak walls—upon the vacant eye-like windows—upon a few rank sedges—and upon a few white trunks of decayed trees—with an utter depression of soul which I can compare to no earthly sensation more properly than to the after-dream of the reveler upon opium—the bitter lapse into everyday life—the hideous dropping off of the veil. There was an iciness, a sinking, a sickening of the heart—an unredeemed dreariness of thought which no goading of the imagination could torture into aught of the sublime. What was it —I paused to think—what was it that so unnerved me in the contemplation of the House of Usher? It was a mystery all insoluble; nor could I grapple with the shadowy fancies that crowded upon me as I pondered. I was forced to fall back upon the unsatisfactory conclusion, that while, beyond doubt, there *are* combinations of very simple natural objects which have the power of thus affecting us, still the analysis of this power lies among considerations beyond our depth. It was possible, I reflected, that a mere different arrangement of the particulars of the scene, of the details of the picture, would be sufficient to modify, or perhaps to annihilate its capacity for sorrowful impression;

and, acting upon this idea, I reined my horse to the precipitous brink of a black and lurid tarn that lay in unruffled luster by the dwelling, and gazed down—but with a shudder even more thrilling than before —upon the remodeled and inverted images of the gray sedge, and the ghastly tree stems, and the vacant and eye-like windows.

Nevertheless, in this mansion of gloom I now proposed to myself a sojourn of some weeks. Its proprietor, Roderick Usher, had been one of my boon companions in boyhood; but many years had elapsed since our last meeting. A letter, however, had lately reached me in a distant part of the country—a letter from him—which, in its wildly importunate nature, had admitted of no other than a personal reply. The MS. gave evidence of nervous agitation. The writer spoke of acute bodily illness—of a mental disorder which oppressed him—and of an earnest desire to see me, as his best and indeed his only personal friend, with a view of attempting, by the cheerfulness of my society, some alleviation of his malady. It was the manner in which all this, and much more, was said—it was the apparent *heart* that went with his

71

request—which allowed me no room for hesitation; and I accordingly obeyed forthwith what I still considered a very singular summons.

Although, as boys, we had been even intimate associates, yet I really knew little of my friend. His reserve had been always excessive and habitual. I was aware, however, that his very ancient family had been noted, time out of mind, for a peculiar sensibility of temperament, displaying itself, through long ages, in many works of exalted art, and manifested, of late, in repeated deeds of munificent yet unobtrusive charity, as well as in a passionate devotion to the intricacies, perhaps even more than to the orthodox and easily recognizable beauties, of musical science. I had learned, too, the very remarkable fact, that the stem of the Usher race, all time-honored as it was, had put forth, at no period, any enduring branch; in other words, that the entire family lay in the direct line of descent, and had always, with very trifling and very temporary variation, so lain. It was this deficiency, I considered, while running over in thought the perfect keeping of the character of the premises with the accredited character of the people, and while speculating upon the possible in-fluence which the one, in the long lapse of centuries, might have exercised upon the other—it was this deficiency, perhaps, of collateral issue, and the consequent undeviating transmission, from sire to son, of the patrimony with the name, which had, at length, so identified the two as to merge the original title of the estate in the quaint and equivocal appellation of the "House of Usher" — an appellation which seemed to include, in the minds of the peasantry who used it, both the family and the family mansion.

I have said that the sole effect of my somewhat childish experiment—that of looking down within the tarn—had been to deepen the first singular impression. There can be no doubt that the consciousness of the rapid increase of my superstition—for why should I not so term it?—served mainly to accelerate the increase itself. Such, I have long known, is the paradoxical law of all sentiments having terror as a basis. And it might have been for this reason only, that, when I again uplifted my eyes to the house itself, from its image in the pool, there grew in my mind a strange fancy—a fancy so ridiculous, indeed, that I but mention it to show the vivid force of the sensations which oppressed me. I had so worked upon my imagination as really to believe that about the whole mansion and domain there hung an atmosphere peculiar to themselves and their immediate vicinity — an atmosphere which had no affinity with the air of heaven, but which had reeked up from the decayed trees, and the gray wall, and the silent tarn—a pestilent and mystic vapor, dull, sluggish, faintly discernible, and leaden-hued.

Shaking off from my spirit what *must* have been a dream, I scanned more narrowly the real aspect of the building. Its principal feature seemed to be that of an excessive antiquity. The discoloration of ages had been great. Minute fungi overspread the whole exterior, hanging in a fine tangled webwork from the eaves. Yet all this was apart from any extraordinary dilapidation. No portion of the masonry had fallen; and there appeared to be a wild inconsistency between its still perfect adaptation of parts, and the crumbling condition of the individual stones. In this there was much that reminded me of the specious totality of old woodwork which has rotted for long years in some neglected vault, with no disturbance from the breath of the external air. Beyond this indication of extensive decay, however, the fabric gave little token of instability. Perhaps the eye of a scrutinizing observer might have discovered a barely perceptible fissure, which, extending from the roof of the building in front, made its way down the wall in a zigzag direction, until it became lost in the sullen wastes of the tarn.

Noticing these things, I rode over a short causeway to the house. A servant in waiting took my horse, and I entered the Gothic archway of the hall. A valet, of stealthy step, thence conducted me, in silence, through many dark and intricate passages in my progress to the studio of his master. Much that I encountered on the way contributed, I know not how, to heighten the vague sentiments of which I have already spoken. While the objects around me—while the carvings of the ceilings, the sombre tapestries of the walls, the ebon blackness of the floors, and the phantasmagoric armorial trophies which rattled as I strode, were but matters to which, or to such as which, I had been accustomed from my infancy—while I hesitated not to acknowledge how familiar was all this—I still wondered to find how unfamiliar were

73

from a sofa on which he had been lying at full length, and greeted me with a vivacious warmth which had much in it, I at first thought, of an overdone cordiality — of the constrained effort of the *ennuyé* man of the world. A glance, however, at his countenance convinced me of his perfect sincerity. We sat down; and for some moments, while he spoke not, I gazed upon him with a feeling half of pity, half of awe. Surely, man had never before so terribly altered, in so brief a period, as had Roderick Usher! It was with difficulty that I could bring myself to admit the identity of the wan being before me with the companion of my early boyhood. Yet the character of his face had been at all times remarkable. A cadaverousness of complexion; an eye large, liquid, and luminous beyond comparison; lips somewhat thin and very pallid, but of a surpassingly beautiful curve; a nose of a delicate Hebrew model, but with a breadth of nostril unusual in similar formations; a finely molded chin, speaking, in its want of prominence, of a want of moral energy; hair of a more than weblike softness and tenuity— these features, with an inordinate expansion above the regions of the temple, made up altogether a coun-

tenance not easily to be forgotten. And now in the mere exaggeration of the prevailing character of these features, and of the expression they were wont to convey, lay so much of change that I doubted to whom I spoke. The now ghastly pallor of the skin, and the now miraculous luster of the eye, above all things startled and even awed me. The silken hair, too, had been suffered to grow all unheeded, and as, in its wild gossamer texture, it floated rather than fell about the face, I could not, even with effort, connect its Arabesque expression with any idea of simple humanity.

In the manner of my friend I was at once struck with an incoherence —an inconsistency; and I soon found this to arise from a series of feeble and futile struggles to overcome an habitual trepidancy — an excessive nervous agitation. For something of this nature I had indeed been prepared, no less by his letter, than by reminiscences of certain boyish traits, and by conclusions deduced from his peculiar physical confirmation and temperament. His action was alternately vivacious and sullen. His voice varied rapidly from a tremulous indecision (when the animal spirits seemed utterly in abeyance) to that

species of energetic concision—that abrupt, weighty, unhurried, and hollow-sounding enunciation—that leaden, self-balanced, and perfectly modulated guttural utterance, which may be observed in the lost drunkard, or the irreclaimable eater of opium, during the periods of his most intense excitement.

It was thus that he spoke of the object of my visit, of his earnest desire to see me, and of the solace he expected me to afford him. He entered, at some length, into what he conceived to be the nature of his malady. It was, he said, a constitutional and a family evil, and one for which he despaired to find a remedy —a mere nervous affection, he immediately added, which would undoubtedly soon pass off. It displayed itself in a host of unnatural sensations. Some of these, as he detailed them, interested and bewildered me; although, perhaps, the terms and the general manner of their narration had their weight. He suffered much from a morbid acuteness of the senses; the most insipid food was alone endurable; he could wear only garments of certain texture; the odors of all flowers were oppressive; his eyes were tortured by even a faint light; and there were but peculiar sounds, and these from stringed instruments, which did not inspire him with horror.

To an anomalous species of terror I found him a bounden slave. "I shall perish," said he, "I *must* perish in this deplorable folly. Thus, thus, and not otherwise, shall I be lost. I dread the events of the future, not in themselves, but in their results. I shudder at the thought of any, even the most trivial, incident, which may operate upon this intolerable agitation of soul. I have, indeed, no abhorrence of danger, except in its absolute effect—in terror. In this unnerved, in this pitiable, condition I feel that the period will sooner or later arrive when I must abandon life and reason together, in some struggle with the grim phantasm, FEAR."

I learned, moreover, at intervals, and through broken and equivocal hints, another singular feature of his mental condition. He was enchained by certain superstitious impressions in regard to the dwelling which he tenanted, and whence, for many years, he had never ventured forth — in regard to an influence whose supposititious force was conveyed in terms too shadowy here to be restated — an influence which some peculiarities in the mere form and substance of his family mansion had, by dint of long sufferance, he said, obtained over his spirit — an effect which the physique of the gray walls and turrets, and of the dim tarn into which they all looked down, had, at length, brought about upon the morale of his existence.

He admitted, however, although with hesitation, that much of the peculiar gloom which thus afflicted him could be traced to a more natural and far more palpable origin —to the severe and long-continued illness—indeed to the evidently approaching dissolution—of a tenderly beloved sister, his sole companion for long years, his last and only relative on earth. "Her decease," he said, with a bitterness which I can never forget, "would leave him (him, the hopeless and the frail) the last of the ancient race of the Ushers." While he spoke, the lady Madeline (for so was she called) passed through a remote portion of the apartment, and, without having noticed my presence, disappeared. I regarded her with an utter astonishment not unmingled with dread; and yet I found it impossible to account for such feelings. A sensation of stupor oppressed me as my eyes followed her retreating steps. When a door, at length, closed upon her, my glance sought instinctively and

77

the fancies which ordinary images were stirring up. On one of the staircases, I met the physician of the family. His countenance, I thought, wore a mingled expression of low cunning and perplexity. He accosted me with trepidation and passed on. The valet now threw open a door and ushered me into the presence of his master.

The room in which I found myself was very large and lofty. The windows were long, narrow, and pointed, and at so vast a distance from the black oaken floor as to be altogether inaccessible from within. Feeble gleams of encrimsoned light made their way through the trellissed panes, and served to render sufficiently distinct the more prominent objects around; the eye, however, struggled in vain to reach the remoter angles of the chamber, or the recesses of the vaulted and fretted ceiling. Dark draperies hung upon the walls. The general furniture was profuse, comfortless, antique, and tattered. Many books and musical instruments lay scattered about, but failed to give any vitality to the scene. I felt that I breathed an atmosphere of sorrow. An air of stern, deep, and irredeemable gloom hung over and pervaded all.

Upon my entrance, Usher arose

eagerly the countenance of the brother; but he had buried his face in his hands, and I could only perceive that a far more than ordinary wanness had overspread the emaciated fingers through which trickled many passionate tears.

The disease of the lady Madeline had long baffled the skill of her physicians. A settled apathy, a gradual wasting away of the person, and frequent although transient afflictions of a partially cataleptical character were the unusual diagnosis. Hitherto she had steadily borne up against the pressure of her malady, and had not betaken herself finally to bed; but on the closing in of the evening of my arrival at the house, she succumbed (as her brother told me at night with inexpressible agitation) to the prostrating power of the destroyer; and I learned that the glimpse I had obtained of her person would thus probably be the last I should obtain—that the lady, at least while living, would be seen by me no more.

For several days ensuing, her name was unmentioned by either Usher or myself; and during this period I was busied in earnest endeavors to alleviate the melancholy of my friend. We painted and read together, or I listened, as if in a dream, to the wild improvisations of his speaking guitar. And thus, as a closer and still closer intimacy admitted me more unreservedly into the recesses of his spirit, the more bitterly did I perceive the futility of all attempt at cheering a mind from which darkness, as if an inherent positive quality, poured forth upon all objects of the moral and physical universe in one unceasing radiation of gloom.

I shall ever bear about me a memory of the many solemn hours I thus spent alone with the master of the House of Usher. Yet I should fail in any attempt to convey an idea of the exact character of the studies, or of the occupations, in which he involved me, or led me the way. An excited and highly distempered ideality threw a sulphurous luster over all. His long improvised dirges will ring forever in my ears. Among other things, I hold painfully in mind a certain singular perversion and amplification of the wild air of the last waltz of Von Weber. From the paintings over which his elaborate fancy brooded, and which grew, touch by touch, into vaguenesses at which I shuddered the more thrillingly, because I shuddered knowing not why — from these paintings (vivid as their

images now are before me) I would in vain endeavor to educe more than a small portion which should lie within the compass of merely written words. By the utter simplicity, by the nakedness of his designs, he arrested and overawed attention. If ever mortal painted an idea, that mortal was Roderick Usher. For me at least, in the circumstances then surrounding me, there arose out of the pure abstractions which the hypochondriac contrived to throw upon his canvas, an intensity of intolerable awe, no shadow of which felt I ever yet in the contemplation of the certainly glowing yet too concrete reveries of Fuseli.

One of the phantasmagoric conceptions of my friend, partaking not so rigidly of the spirit of abstraction, may be shadowed forth, although feebly, in words. A small picture presented the interior of an immensely long and rectangular vault or tunnel, with low walls, smooth, white, and without interruption or device. Certain accessory points of the design served well to convey the idea that this excavation lay at an exceeding depth below the surface of the earth. No outlet was observed in any portion of its vast extent, and no torch or other artificial source of light was discernible; yet a flood of intense rays rolled throughout, and bathed the whole in a ghastly and inappropriate splendor.

I have just spoken of that morbid condition of the auditory nerve which rendered all music intolerable to the sufferer, with the exception of certain effects of stringed instruments. It was, perhaps, the narrow limits to which he thus confined himself upon the guitar which gave birth, in great measure, to the fantastic character of his performances. But the fervid facility of his impromptus could not be so accounted for. They must have been, and were, in the notes, as well as in the words of his wild fantasias (for he not unfrequently accompanied himself with rhymed verbal improvisations), the result of that intense mental collectedness and concentration to which I have previously alluded as observable only in particular moments of the highest artificial excitement. The words of one of these rhapsodies I have easily remembered. I was, perhaps, the more forcibly impressed with it as he gave it, because, in the under or mystic current of its meaning, I fancied that I perceived, and for the first time, a full consciousness on the part of Usher of the tottering of his lofty reason upon her throne. The verses, which were entitled "The Haunted Palace," ran very nearly, if not accurately, thus—

I

In the greenest of our valleys,
    By good angels tenanted,
Once a fair and stately palace—
    Radiant palace—reared its head.
In the monarch Thought's dominion—
    It stood there!
Never seraph spread a pinion
    Over fabric half so fair.

II

Banners yellow, glorious, golden,
    On its roof did float and flow
(This—all this—was in the olden
    Time long ago);
And every gentle air that dallied,
    In that sweet day,
Along the ramparts plumed and pallid,
    A winged odor went away.

III

Wanderers in that happy valley
    Through two luminous windows saw
Spirits moving musically
    To a lute's well-tuned law;
Round about a throne, where sitting
    (Porphyrogene!)
In state his glory well befitting,
    The ruler of the realm was seen.

IV

And all with pearl and ruby glowing
    Was the fair palace door,

81

Through which came flowing, flowing,
    flowing
  And sparkling evermore,
A troop of Echoes whose sweet duty
  Was but to sing,
In voices of surpassing beauty,
  The wit and wisdom of their king.

v

But evil things, in robes of sorrow,
  Assailed the monarch's high estate;
(Ah, let us mourn, for never morrow
  Shall dawn upon him, desolate!)
And, round about his home, the glory
  That blushed and bloomed
Is but a dim-remembered story
  Of the old time entombed.

vi

And travellers now within that valley,
  Through the red-litten windows see
Vast forms that move fantastically
  To a discordant melody;
While, like a rapid ghastly river,
  Through the pale door;
A hideous throng rush out forever,
  And laugh—but smile no more.

I well remember that suggestions arising from this ballad led us into a train of thoughts wherein there became manifest an opinion of Usher's which I mention not so much on account of its novelty (for other men have thought thus), as on account of the pertinacity with

which he maintained it. This opinion, in its general form, was that of the sentience of all vegetable things. But, in his disordered fancy, the idea had assumed a more daring character, and trespassed, under certain conditions, upon the kingdom of inorganization. I lack words to express the full extent, or the earnest abandon of his persuasion. The belief, however, was connected (as I have previously hinted) with the gray stones of the home of his forefathers. The conditions of the sentience had been here, he imagined, fulfilled in the method of collocation of these stones—in the order of their arrangement, as well as in that of the many fungi which overspread them, and of the decayed trees which stood around — above all, in the long undisturbed endurance of this arrangement, and in its reduplication in the still waters of the tarn. Its evidence — the evidence of the sentience—was to be seen, he said (and I here started as he spoke), in the gradual yet certain condensation of an atmosphere of their own about the waters and the walls. The result was discoverable, he added, in that silent yet importunate and terrible influence which for centuries had molded the destinies of his family, and which made *him* what I now saw him—what he was. Such opinions need no comment, and I will make none.

Our books—the books which, for years, had formed no small portion of the mental existence of the invalid—were, as might be supposed, in strict keeping with this character of phantasm. We pored together over such works as the "Ververt et Chartreuse" of Gresset; the "Belphegor" of Machiavelli; the "Heaven and Hell" of Swedenborg; the "Subterranean Voyage of Nicholas Klimm" of Holberg; the "Chiromancy" of Robert Flud, of Jean D'Indaginé, and of Dela Chambre; the "Journey into the Blue Distance of Tieck"; and the "City of the Sun of Campanella." One favorite volume was a small octavo edition of the "Directorium Inquisitorium," by the Dominican Eymeric de Gironne; and there were passages in Pomponius Mela, about the old African Satyrs and Egipans, over which Usher would sit dreaming for hours. His chief delight, however, was found in the perusal of an exceedingly rare and curious book in quarto Gothic—the manual of a forgotten church—the *Vigilioe Mortuorum secundum Chorum Ecclesioe Maguntinoe.*

I could not help thinking of the wild ritual of this work, and of its probable influence upon the hypochondriac, when, one evening, having informed me abruptly that the lady Madeline was no more, he stated his intention of preserving her corpse for a fortnight (previously to its final interment), in one of the numerous vaults within the main walls of the building. The worldly reason, however, assigned for this singular proceeding, was one which I did not feel at liberty to dispute. The brother had been led to his resolution (so he told me) by consideration of the unusual character of the malady of the deceased, of certain obtrusive and eager inquiries on the part of her medical men, and of the remote and exposed situation of the burial ground of the family. I will not deny that when I called to mind the sinister countenance of the person whom I met upon the staircase, on the day of my arrival at the house, I had no desire to oppose what I regarded as at best but a harmless, and by no means an unnatural, precaution.

At the request of Usher, I personally aided him in the arrangements for the temporary entombment. The body having been encoffined, we two alone bore it to its rest. The vault in which we placed it (and

which had been so long unopened that our torches, half smothered in its oppressive atmosphere, gave us little opportunity for investigation) was small, damp, and entirely without means of admission for light; lying, at great depth, immediately beneath that portion of the building in which was my own sleeping apartment. It had been used, apparently, in remote feudal times, for the worst purposes of a donjon-keep, and, in later days, as a place of deposit for powder, or some other highly combustible substance, as a portion of its floor, and the whole interior of a long archway through which we reached it, were carefully sheathed with copper. The door, of massive iron, had been, also, similarly protected. Its immense weight caused an unusually sharp, grating sound, as it moved upon its hinges.

Having deposited our mournful burden upon tressels within this region of horror, we partially turned aside the yet unscrewed lid of the coffin, and looked upon the face of the tenant. A striking similitude between the brother and sister now first arrested my attention; and Usher, divining, perhaps, my thoughts, murmured out some few words from which I learned that the deceased and himself had been twins, and that sympathies of a scarcely intelligible nature had always existed between them. Our glances, however, rested not long upon the dead—for we could not regard her unawed. The disease which had thus entombed the lady in the maturity of youth, had left, as usual in all maladies of a strictly cataleptical character, the mockery of a faint blush upon the bosom and the face, and that suspiciously lingering smile upon the lip which is so terrible in death. We replaced and screwed down the lid, and, having secured the door of iron, made our way, with toil, into the scarcely less gloomy apartments of the upper portion of the house.

And now, some days of bitter grief having elapsed, an observable change came over the features of the mental disorder of my friend. His ordinary manner had vanished. His ordinary occupations were neglected or forgotten. He roamed from chamber to chamber with hurried, unequal, and objectless step. The pallor of his countenance had assumed, if possible, a more ghastly hue—but the luminousness of his eye had utterly gone out. The once occasional huskiness of his tone was heard no more; and a tremulous quaver, as if of extreme terror, habitually characterized his utterance. There were times, indeed, when I thought his unceasingly agitated mind was laboring with some oppressive secret, to divulge which he struggled for the necessary courage. At times, again, I was obliged to resolve all into the mere inexplicable vagaries of madness, for I beheld him gazing upon vacancy for long hours, in an attitude of the profoundest attention, as if listening to some imaginary sound. It was no wonder that his condition terrified—that it infected me. I felt creeping upon me, by slow yet certain degrees, the wild influences of his own fantastic yet impressive superstitions.

It was, especially, upon retiring to bed late in the night of the seventh or eighth day after the placing of the lady Madeline within the donjon, that I experienced the full power of such feelings. Sleep came not near my couch—while the hours waned and waned away. I struggled to reason off the nervousness which had dominion over me. I endeavored to believe that much, if not all of what I felt, was due to the bewildering influence of the gloomy furniture of the room—of the dark and tattered draperies, which, tortured into motion by the breath of a rising tempest, swayed fitfully to and fro upon the walls, and rustled uneasily about the decorations of the bed. But my efforts were fruitless. An irrepressible tremor gradually pervaded my frame; and, at length, there sat upon my very heart an incubus of utterly causeless alarm. Shaking this off with a gasp and a struggle, I uplifted myself upon the pillows, and, peering earnestly within the intense darkness of the chamber, harkened—I know not why, except that an instinctive spirit prompted me—to certain low and indefinite sounds which came, through the pauses of the storm, at long intervals, I knew not whence. Overpowered by an intense sentiment of horror, unaccountable yet unendurable, I threw on my clothes with haste (for I felt that I should sleep no more during the night), and endeavored to arouse myself from the pitiable condition into which I had fallen, by pacing rapidly to and fro through the apartment.

I had taken but few turns in this manner, when a light step on an adjoining staircase arrested my attention. I presently recognized it as that of Usher. In an instant afterward he rapped, with a gentle touch, at my door, and entered, bearing a lamp. His countenance was, as usual, cadaverously wan — but, moreover, there was a species of mad hilarity in his eyes—an evidently restrained hysteria in his whole demeanor. His air appalled me—but anything was preferable to the solitude which I had so long endured, and I even welcomed his presence as a relief.

"And you have not seen it?" he said abruptly, after having stared about him for some moments in silence—"you have not then seen it? —but, stay! you shall." Thus speaking, and having carefully shaded his lamp, he hurried to one of the casements, and threw it freely open to the storm.

The impetuous fury of the entering gust nearly lifted us from our feet. It was, indeed, a tempestuous yet sternly beautiful night, and one wildly singular in its terror and its beauty. A whirlwind had apparently collected its force in our vicinity; for there were frequent and violent alterations in the direction of the wind; and the exceeding density of the clouds (which hung so low as to press upon the turrets of the house) did not prevent our perceiving the lifelike velocity with which they flew careering from all points against each other, without passing away into the distance. I say that even their exceeding density did not prevent our perceiving this—yet we had no glimpse of the moon or stars, nor was there any flashing forth of the lightning. But the under surfaces of the huge masses of agitated vapor, as well as all terrestrial objects immediately around us, were glowing in the unnatural light of a faintly luminous and distinctly visible gaseous exhalation which hung about and enshrouded the mansion.

"You must not—you shall not behold this!" said I, shuddering, to Usher, as I led him, with a gentle violence, from the window to a seat. "These appearances, which bewilder you, are merely electrical phenomena not uncommon—or it may be that they have their ghastly origin in the rank miasma of the tarn. Let us close this casement—the air is chilling and dangerous to your frame. Here is one of your favorite romances. I will read, and you shall listen—and so we will pass away this terrible night together."

The antique volume which I had taken up was the "Mad Trist" of Sir Launcelot Canning; but I had called it a favorite of Usher's more in sad jest than in earnest; for, in truth, there is little in its uncouth and unimaginative prolixity which could have had interest for the lofty and spiritual ideality of my friend. It was, however, the only book immediately at hand; and I indulged a vague hope that the excitement which now agitated the hypochondriac, might find relief (for the history of mental disorder is full of similar anomalies) even in the extremeness of the folly which I should read. Could I have judged, indeed, by the wild overstrained air of vivacity with which he harkened, or apparently harkened, to the words of the tale, I might well have congratulated myself upon the success of my design.

I had arrived at that well-known portion of the story where Ethelred, the hero of the Trist, having sought in vain for peaceable admission into the dwelling of the hermit, proceeds to make good an entrance by force. Here, it will be remembered, the words of the narrative run thus:

"And Ethelred, who was by nature of a doughty heart, and who was now mighty withal, on account of the powerfulness of the wine which he had drunken, waited no longer to hold parley with the hermit, who, in sooth, was of an obstinate and maliceful turn, but, feeling the rain upon his shoulders, and fearing the rising of the tempest, uplifted his mace outright, and, with blows, made quickly room in the plankings of the door for his gauntleted hand; and now pulling therewith sturdily, he so cracked, and ripped, and tore all asunder. that the noise of the dry and hollow-sounding wood alarumed and reverberated throughout the forest.''

At the termination of this sentence I started and, for a moment, paused; for it appeared to me (although I at once concluded that my excited fancy had deceived me)—it appeared to me that, from some very remote portion of the mansion, there came, indistinctly to my ears, what might have been, in its exact similarity of character, the echo (but a stifled and dull one certainly) of the very cracking and ripping sound which Sir Launcelot had so particularly described. It was, beyond doubt, the coincidence alone which had arrested my attention; for, amid the rattling of the sashes of the casements, and the ordinary commingled noises of the still increasing storm, the sound, in itself, had nothing, surely, which should have interested or disturbed me. I continued the story:

"But the good champion Ethelred, now entering within the door, was sore enraged and amazed to per-
ceive no signal of the maliceful hermit; but, in the stead thereof, a dragon of a scaly and prodigious demeanor, and of a fiery tongue, which sate in guard before a palace of gold, with a floor of silver; and upon the wall there hung a shield of shining brass with this legend enwritten—

Who entereth herein, a conqueror hath bin;
Who slayeth the dragon, the shield he shall win.

And Ethelred uplifted his mace, and struck upon the head of the dragon, which fell before him, and gave up his pesty breath, with a shriek so horrid and harsh, and withal so piercing, that Ethelred had fain to close his ears with his hands against the dreadful noise of it, the like whereof was never before heard.''

Here again I paused abruptly, and now with a feeling of wild amazement—for there could be no doubt whatever that, in this instance, I did actually hear (although from what direction it proceeded I found it impossible to say) a low and apparently distant, but harsh, protracted, and most unusual screaming or grating sound—the exact counterpart of what my fancy had already conjured up for the dragon's unnatural shriek as described by the romancer.

Oppressed, as I certainly was, upon the occurrence of this second and most extraordinary coincidence, by a thousand conflicting sensations, in which wonder and extreme terror were predominant, I still retained sufficient presence of mind to avoid exciting, by any observation, the sensitive nervousness of my companion. I was by no means certain that he had noticed the sounds in question; although, assuredly, a strange alteration had, during the last few minutes, taken place in his demeanor. From a position fronting my own, he had gradually brought round his chair, so as to sit with his face to the door of the chamber; and thus I could but partially perceive his features, although I saw that his lips trembled as if he were murmuring inaudibly. His head had dropped upon his breast—yet I knew that he was not asleep, from the wide and rigid opening of the eye as I caught a glance of it in profile. The motion of his body, too, was at variance with this idea—for he rocked from side to side with a gentle yet constant and uniform sway. Having rapidly taken notice of all this, I resumed the narrative of Sir Launcelot, which thus proceeded:

"And now, the champion, having escaped from the terrible fury of the dragon, bethinking himself of the brazen shield, and of the breaking up of the enchantment which was upon it, removed the carcass from out of the way before him, and approached valorously over the silver pavement of the castle to where the shield was upon the wall; which in sooth tarried not for his full coming, but fell down at his feet upon the silver floor, with a mighty great and terrible ringing sound."

No sooner had these syllables passed my lips, than—as if a shield of brass had indeed, at the moment, fallen heavily upon a floor of silver—I became aware of a distinct, hollow, metallic, and clangorous, yet apparently muffled, reverberation. Completely unnerved, I leaped to my feet; but the measured rocking movement of Usher was undisturbed. I rushed to the chair in which he sat. His eyes were bent fixedly before him, and throughout his whole countenance there reigned a stony rigidity. But, as I placed my hand upon his shoulder, there came a strong shudder over his whole person; a sickly smile

89

quivered about his lips; and I saw that he spoke in a low, hurried, and gibbering murmur, as if unconscious of my presence. Bending closely over him, I at length drank in the hideous import of his words.

"Now hear it?—yes, I hear it, and *have* heard it. Long—long—long— many minutes, many hours, many days, have I heard it—yet I dared not—oh, pity me, miserable wretch that I am!—I dared not—I *dared* not speak! *We have put her living in the tomb!* Said I not that my senses were acute? I *now* tell you that I heard her first feeble movements in the hollow coffin. I heard them — many, many days ago—yet I dared not—*I dared not speak!* And now— tonight — Ethelred — ha! ha! — the breaking of the hermit's door, and the death cry of the dragon, and the clangor of the shield—say, rather, the rending of her coffin, and the grating of the iron hinges of her prison, and her struggles within the coppered archway of the vault! Oh! whither shall I fly? Will she not be here anon? Is she not hurrying to upbraid me for my haste? Have I not heard her footsteps on the stair? Do I not distinguish that heavy and horrible beating of her heart? Madman!"—here he sprang furiously to his feet, and shrieked out his sylla-

bles, as if in the effort he were giving up his soul—*"Madman! I tell you that she now stands without the door!"*

As if in the superhuman energy of his utterance there had been found the potency of a spell, the huge antique panels to which the speaker pointed threw slowly back, upon the instant, their ponderous and ebony jaws. It was the work of the rushing gust—but then without those doors there *did* stand the lofty and enshrouded figure of the lady Madeline of Usher. There was blood upon her white robes, and the evidence of some bitter struggle upon every portion of her emaciated frame. For a moment she remained trembling and reeling to and fro upon the threshold—then, with a low moaning cry, fell heavily inward upon the person of her brother, and in her violent and now final death agonies, bore him to the floor a corpse, and a victim to the terrors he had anticipated.

From that chamber, and from that mansion, I fled aghast. The storm was still abroad in all its wrath as I found myself crossing the old causeway. Suddenly there shot along the path a wild light, and I turned to see whence a gleam so unusual could have issued; for the vast

house and its shadows were alone behind me. The radiance was that of the full, setting, and blood-red moon; which now shone vividly through that once barely discernible fissure, of which I have before spoken as extending from the roof of the building, in a zigzag direction, to the base. While I gazed, this fissure rapidly widened—there came a fierce breath of the whirlwind—the entire orb of the satellite burst at once upon my sight—my brain reeled as I saw the mighty walls rushing asunder—there was a long tumultuous shouting sound like the voice of a thousand waters —and the deep and dank tarn at my feet closed sullenly and silently over the fragments of the House of Usher.

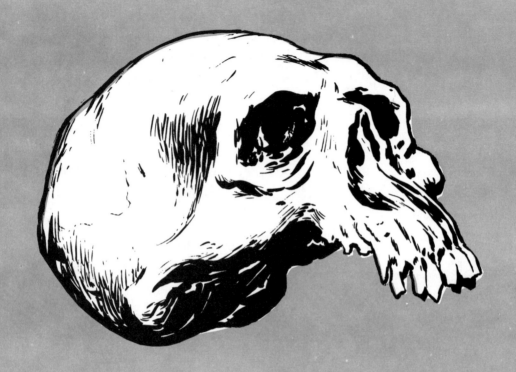

illustrated by Norman Nodel

The Ghost Ship

and other ghostly stories

1 The Ghost Ship

Fairfield is a little village lying near the Portsmouth Road about halfway between London and the sea. Strangers who find it by accident now and then, call it a pretty, old-fashioned place; we who live in it and call it home don't find anything very pretty about it, but we should be sorry to live anywhere else. Our minds have taken the shape of the inn and the church and the green, I suppose. At all events we never feel comfortable out of Fairfield.

Of course the Cockneys, with their vasty houses and noise-ridden streets, can call us rustics if they choose, but for all that Fairfield is a better place to live in than London. Doctor says that when he goes to London his mind is bruised with the weight of the houses, and he was a Cockney born. He had to live there himself when he was a little chap, but he knows better now. You gentlemen may laugh — perhaps some of you come from London way — but it seems to me that a witness like that is worth a gallon of arguments.

Dull? Well, you might find it dull, but I assure you that I've listened to all the London yarns you have spun tonight, and they're absolutely nothing to the things that happen at Fairfield. It's because of our way of thinking and minding our own business. If one of your Londoners were set down on the green of a Saturday night when the ghosts of the lads who died in the war keep tryst with the lasses who lie in the churchyard, he couldn't help being curious and interfering, and then the ghosts would go somewhere where it was quieter. But we just let them come and go and don't make any fuss, and in consequence Fairfield is the ghostiest place in all England. Why, I've seen a headless man sitting on the edge of the well in broad daylight, and the children playing about his feet as if he were their father. Take my word for it, spirits know when they are well off as much as human beings.

Still, I must admit that the thing I'm going to tell you about was queer even for our part of the world, where three packs of ghost-hounds hunt regularly during the season, and blacksmith's great-grandfather is busy all night shoeing the dead gentlemen's horses. Now that's a thing that wouldn't happen in London, because of their interfering way, but blacksmith he lies up aloft and sleeps as quiet as a lamb. Once when he had a bad head he shouted down to them not to make so much noise, and in the morning he found an old guinea left on the anvil as an apology. He wears it on his watch chain now. But I must get on with my story; if I start telling you about the queer happenings at Fairfield I'll never stop.

It all came of the great storm in the spring of '97, the year that we had two great storms. This was the first one, and I remember it very well, because I found in the morning that it had lifted the thatch of my pigsty into the widow's garden as clean as a boy's kite. When I looked over the hedge, widow — Tom Lamport's widow that was — was prodding for her nasturtiums with a daisy-grubber. After I had watched her for a little I went down to the Fox and Grapes to tell landlord what she had said to me. Landlord he laughed, being a married man and at ease with the sex. "Come to that," he said, "the tem-

pest had blowed something into my field. A kind of a ship I think it would be."

I was surprised at that until he explained that it was only a ghost ship and would do no hurt to the turnips. We argued that it had been blown up from the sea at Portsmouth, and then we talked of something else. There were two slates down at the parsonage and a big tree in Lumley's meadow. It was a rare storm.

I reckon the wind had blown our ghosts all over England. They were coming back for days afterward with foundered horses and as foot-sore as possible, and they were so glad to get back to Fairfield that some of them walked up the street crying like little children. Squire said that his great-grandfather's great-grandfather hadn't looked so dead beat since the battle of Nase-by, and he's an educated man.

What with one thing and anoth-er, I should think it was a week be-fore we got straight again, and then one afternoon I met the landlord on the green and he had a worried face. "I wish you'd come and have a look at that ship in my field," he said to me. "It seems to me it's leaning real hard on the turnips. I can't bear thinking what the missus will say when she sees it."

I walked down the lane with him, and sure enough there was a ship in the middle of his field, but such a ship as no man had seen on the water for three hundred years, let alone in the middle of a turnip field. It was all painted black and covered with carvings, and there was a great bay window in the stern for all the world like the squire's drawing-room. There was a crowd of little black cannon on deck and looking out of her portholes, and she was anchored at each end to the hard ground. I have seen the won-ders of the world on picture post-cards, but I have never seen any-thing to equal that.

"She seems very solid for a ghost ship," I said, seeing the landlord was bothered.

"I should say it's a betwixt and between," he answered, puzzling it over, "but it's going to spoil a mat-ter of fifty turnips, and missus she'll want it moved." We went up to her and touched the side, and it was as hard as a real ship. "Now there's folks in England would call that very curious," he said.

Now I don't know much about ships, but I should think that that ghost ship weighed a solid two hun-dred tons, and it seemed to me that she had come to stay, so that I felt sorry for landlord, who was a mar-

101

ried man. "All the horses in Fairfield won't move her out of my turnips," he said, frowning at her.

Just then we heard a noise on her deck, and we looked up and saw that a man had come out of her front cabin and was looking down at us very peaceably. He was dressed in a black uniform set out with rusty gold lace, and he had a great cutlass by his side in a brass sheath. "I'm Captain Bartholomew Roberts," he said, in a gentleman's voice, "put in for recruits. I seem to have brought her rather far up the harbor."

"Harbor!" cried landlord, "why, you're fifty miles from the sea."

Captain Roberts didn't turn a hair. "So much as that, is it?" he said coolly. "Well, it's of no consequence."

Landlord was a bit upset at this. "I don't want to be unneighborly," he said, "but I wish you hadn't brought your ship into my field. You see, my wife sets great store on these turnips."

The captain took a pinch of snuff out of a fine gold box that he pulled out of his pocket, and dusted his fingers with a silk handkerchief in a very genteel fashion. "I'm only here for a few months," he said, "but if a testimony of my esteem would pacify your good lady I should be content," and with the words he loosed a great gold brooch from the neck of his coat and tossed it down to landlord.

Landlord blushed as red as a strawberry. "I'm not denying she's fond of jewelry," he said, "but it's too much for half a sackful of turnips." And indeed it was a handsome brooch.

The captain laughed. "Tut, man," he said, "it's a forced sale, and you deserve a good price. Say no more about it," and nodding good day to us, he turned on his heel and went into the cabin. Landlord walked back up the lane like a man with a weight off his mind. "That tempest had blowed me a bit of luck," he said; "the missus will be main pleased with that brooch. It's better than blacksmith's guinea, any day."

Ninety-seven was Jubilee year, the year of the second Jubilee, you remember, and we had great doings at Fairfield, so that we hadn't much time to bother about the ghost ship, though anyhow it isn't our way to meddle in things that don't concern us. Landlord, he saw his tenant once or twice when he was hoeing his turnips and passed the time of day, and landlord's wife wore her new brooch to church every Sunday. But we didn't mix much with the ghosts at any time, all except an idiot lad there was in the village, and he didn't know the difference between a man and a ghost, poor innocent! On Jubilee Day, however, somebody told Captain Roberts why the church bells were ringing, and he hoisted a flag and fired off his guns like a loyal Englishman. 'Tis true the guns were shotted, and one of the round shot knocked a hole in Farmer Johnstone's barn, but nobody thought much of that in such a season of rejoicing.

It wasn't till our celebrations were over that we noticed that anything was wrong in Fairfield. 'Twas shoemaker who told me first about it one morning at the Fox and Grapes. "You know my great-uncle?" he said to me.

"You mean Joshua, the quiet lad," I answered, knowing him well.

"Quiet!" said shoemaker indignantly. "Quiet you call him, coming home at three o'clock every morning as drunk as a magistrate and waking up the whole house with his noise."

"Why, it can't be Joshua!" I said, for I knew him for one of the most respectable young ghosts in the village.

"Joshua it is," said shoemaker, "and one of these nights he'll find himself out in the street if he isn't careful."

This kind of talk shocked me, I can tell you, for I don't like to hear a man abusing his own family, and I could hardly believe that a steady youngster like Joshua had taken to drink. But just then in came butcher Aylwin in such a temper that he could hardly drink his beer. "The young puppy! the young puppy!" he kept on saying; and it was some time before shoemaker and I found out that he was talking about his ancestor that fell at Senlac.

"Drink?" said shoemaker hopefully, for we all like company in our misfortunes, and butcher nodded grimly.

"The young noodle," he said, emptying his tankard.

Well, after that I kept my ears open, and it was the same story all over the village. There was hardly a young man among all the ghosts of Fairfield who didn't roll home in the small hours of the morning the worse for liquor. I used to wake up in the night and hear them stumble past my house, singing outrageous songs. The worst of it was that we couldn't keep the scandal to ourselves, and the folk at Greenhill began to talk of "sodden Fairfield" and taught their children to sing a song about us:

"Sodden Fairfield, sodden Fairfield, has no use for bread-and-butter,
Rum for breakfast, rum for dinner, rum for tea, and rum for supper!"

We are easy-going in our village, but we didn't like that.

Of course we soon found out where the young fellows went to get the drink, and landlord was terribly cut up that his tenant should have turned out so badly, but his wife wouldn't hear of parting with the brooch, so that he couldn't give the Captain notice to quit. But as time went on, things grew from bad to worse, and at all hours of the day you would see those young reprobates sleeping it off on the village green. Nearly every afternoon a ghost wagon used to jolt down to the ship with a lading of rum, and though the older ghosts seemed inclined to give the Captain's hospitality the go-by, the youngsters were neither to hold nor to bind.

So one afternoon when I was taking my nap I heard a knock at the door, and there was Parson looking very serious, like a man with a job before him that he didn't altogether

relish. "I'm going down to talk to the Captain about all this drunkenness in the village, and I want you to come with me," he said straight out.

I can't say that I fancied the visit much myself, and I tried to hint to Parson that as, after all, they were only a lot of ghosts, it didn't very much matter.

"Dead or alive, I'm responsible for their good conduct," he said, "and I'm going to do my duty and put a stop to this continued disorder. And you are coming with me, John Simmons." So I went, Parson being a persuasive kind of man.

We went down to the ship, and as we approached her I could see the Captain tasting the air on deck. When he saw Parson he took off his hat very politely, and I can tell you that I was relieved to find that he had a proper respect for the cloth. Parson acknowledged his salute and spoke out stoutly enough. "Sir, I should be glad to have a word with you."

"Come on board, sir, come on board," said the Captain, and I could tell by his voice that he knew why we were there. Parson and I climbed up an uneasy kind of ladder, and the Captain took us into the great cabin at the back of the ship, where the bay window was. It was the most wonderful place you ever saw in your life, all full of gold and silver plate, swords with jeweled scabbards, carved oak chairs, and great chests that looked as though they were bursting with guineas. Even Parson was surprised, and he did not shake his head very hard when the Captain took down some silver cups and poured us out a drink of rum. I tasted mine, and I don't mind saying that it changed my view of things entirely. There was nothing betwixt and between about that rum, and I felt that it was ridiculous to blame the lads for drinking too much of stuff like that. It seemed to fill my veins with honey and fire.

Parson put the case squarely to the Captain, but I didn't listen much to what he said; I was busy sipping my drink and looking through the window at the fishes swimming to and fro over landlord's turnips. Just then it seemed the most natural thing in the world that they should be there, though afterwards, of course, I could see that that proved it was a ghost ship.

But even then I thought it was queer when I saw a drowned sailor float by in the thin air with his hair and beard all full of bubbles. It was the first time I had seen anything quite like that at Fairfield.

All the time I was regarding the wonders of the deep Parson was telling Captain Roberts how there was no peace or rest in the village owing to the curse of drunkenness, and what a bad example the youngsters were setting to the older ghosts. The Captain listened very attentively, and only put in a word now and then about boys being boys and young men sowing their wild oats. But when Parson had finished his speech he filled up our silver cups and said to Parson, with a flourish, "I should be sorry to cause trouble anywhere where I have been made welcome, and you will be glad to hear that I put to sea to-morrow night. And now you must drink me a prosperous voyage." So we all stood up and drank the toast with honor, and that noble rum was like hot oil in my veins.

After that Captain showed us some of the curiosities he had brought back from foreign parts, and we were greatly amazed, though afterwards I couldn't clearly remember what they were. And then I found myself walking across the turnips with Parson, and I was telling him of the glories of the deep that I had seen through the window of the ship. He turned on me severely. "If I were you, John Simmons," he said, "I should go straight home to bed." He has a way of putting things that wouldn't occur to an ordinary man, has Parson, and I did as he told me.

Well, next day it came on to blow, and it blew harder and harder, till about eight o'clock at night I heard a noise and looked out into the garden. I dare say you won't believe me, it seems a bit tall even to me, but the wind had lifted the thatch of my pigsty into the widow's garden a second time. I thought I wouldn't wait to hear what widow had to say about it, so I went across the green to the Fox and Grapes, and the wind was so strong that I danced along on tip-toe like a girl at the fair. When I got to the inn landlord had to help me shut the door; it seemed as though a dozen goats were pushing against it to come in out of the storm.

"It's a powerful tempest," he said, drawing the beer. "I hear there's a chimney down at Dickory End."

"It's a funny thing how these sailors know about the weather," I answered. "When Captain said he was going tonight, I was thinking it would take a capful of wind to carry the ship back to sea, but now here's more than a capful."

"Ah, yes," said landlord, "it's tonight he goes true enough and, mind you, though he treated me handsome over the rent, I'm not sure it's a loss to the village. I don't hold with gentry who fetch their drink from London instead of helping local traders to get their living."

"But you haven't got any rum like his," I said, to draw him out.

His neck grew red above his collar, and I was afraid I'd gone too far, but after a while he got his breath with a grunt.

"John Simmons," he said, "if you've come down here this windy night to talk a lot of fool's talk, you've wasted a journey."

Well, of course, then I had to smooth him down with praising his rum, and Heaven forgive me for swearing it was better than Captain's. For the like of that rum no living lips have tasted save mine and Parson's. But somehow or other I brought landlord round, and presently we must have a glass of his best to prove its quality.

"Beat that if you can!" he cried, and we both raised our glasses to our mouths, only to stop halfway and look at each other amazed.

106

For the wind that had been howling outside like an outrageous dog had all of a sudden turned as melodious as the carol boys of a Christmas Eve.

"Surely that's not my Martha," whispered landlord; Martha being his great-aunt that lived in the loft overhead.

We went to the door, and the wind burst it open so that the handle was driven clean into the plaster of the wall. But we didn't think about that at the time, for over our heads, sailing very comfortably through the windy stars, was the ship that had passed the summer in landlord's field. Her portholes and her bay window were blazing with lights, and there was a noise of singing and fiddling on her decks. "He's gone," shouted landlord above the storm, "and he's taken half the village with him!" I could only nod in answer, not having lungs like bellows of leather.

In the morning we were able to measure the strength of the storm, and over and above my pigsty there was damage enough wrought in the village to keep us busy. True it is that the children had to break down no branches for the firing that autumn, since the wind had strewn the woods with more than they could carry away. Many of our

ghosts were scattered abroad, but this time very few came back, all the young men having sailed with Captain; and not only ghosts, for a poor half-witted lad was missing, and we reckoned that he had stowed himself away or perhaps shipped as cabin boy, not knowing any better.

What with the lamentations of the ghost girls and the grumbling of families who had lost an ancestor, the village was upset for a while, and the funny thing was that it was the folk who had complained most of the carryings-on of the youngsters, who made most noise now that they were gone. I hadn't any sympathy with shoemaker or butcher, who ran about saying how much they missed their lads, but it made me grieve to hear the poor bereaved girls calling their lovers by name on the village green at nightfall. It didn't seem fair to me that they should have lost their men a second time, after giving up life in order to join them, as like as not. Still, not even a spirit can be sorry for ever, and after a few months we made up our minds that the folk who sailed in the ship were never coming back, and we didn't talk about it any more.

And then one day, I dare say it would be a couple of years after, when the whole business was quite forgotten, who should come traipsing along the road from Portsmouth but the daft lad who had gone away with the ship, without waiting till he was dead to become a ghost. You never saw such a boy as that in all your life. He had a great rusty cutlass hanging to a string at his waist, and he was tattooed all over in fine colors, so that even his face looked like a girl's sampler. He had a handkerchief in his hand full of foreign shells and old-fashioned pieces of small money, very curious, and he walked up to the well outside his mother's house and drew himself a drink as if he had been nowhere in particular.

The worst of it was that he had come back as soft-headed as he went, and try as we might we couldn't get anything reasonable out of him. He talked a lot of gibberish about keelhauling and walking the plank and crimson murders — things which a decent sailor should know nothing about, so that it seemed to me that for all his manners Captain had been more of a pirate than a gentleman mariner. But to draw sense out of that boy was as hard as picking cherries off a crab tree. One silly tale he had that he kept on drifting back to, and to hear him you would have thought that it was the only thing that happened to him in his life. "We was at anchor," he would say, "off an island called the Basket of Flowers, and the sailors had caught a lot of parrots and we were teaching them to swear. Up and down the decks, up and down the decks, and the language they used was dreadful. Then we looked up an saw the masts of the Spanish ship outside the harbor. Outside the harbor they were, so we threw the parrots into the sea and sailed out to fight. And all the parrots were drowned in the sea and the language they used was dreadful." That's the sort of boy he was, nothing but silly talk of parrots when we asked him about the fighting. And we never had a chance of teaching him better, for two days after he ran away again, and hasn't been seen since!

That's my story, and I assure you that things like that are happening at Fairfield all the time. The ship has never come back, but somehow as people grow older they seem to think that one of these windy nights she'll come sailing in over the hedges with all the lost ghosts on board. Well, when she comes, she'll be welcome. There's one ghost lass that has never grown tired of waiting for her lad to return. Every night you'll see her out on the green, straining her poor eyes with looking for the mast lights among the stars. A faithful lass you'd call her, and I'm thinking you'd be right.

Landlord's field wasn't a penny the worse for the visit, but they do say that since then the turnips that have been grown in it have tasted of rum.

2 Man-Size in Marble

Although every word of this story is as true as despair, I do not expect people to believe it. Nowadays a "rational explanation" is required before belief is possible. Let me then, at once, offer the "rational explanation" which finds most favor among those who have heard the tale of my life's tragedy. It is held that we were "under a delusion," Laura and I, on that thirty-first of October; and that this supposition places the whole matter on a satisfactory and believable basis. The reader can judge, when he, too, has heard my story, how far this is an "explanation," and in what sense it is "rational." There were three who took part in this: Laura and I and another man. The other man still lives, and can speak to the truth of the least credible part of my story.

I never in my life knew what it was to have as much money as I required to supply the most ordinary needs—good colors, books, and cab fares—and when we were married we knew quite well that we should only be able to live at all by "strict punctuality and attention to busi-

ness." I used to paint in those days, and Laura used to write, and we felt sure we could keep the pot at least simmering. Living in town was out of the question, so we went to look for a cottage in the country, which should be at once sanitary and picturesque. So rarely do these two qualities meet in one cottage that our search was for some time quite fruitless. We tried advertisements, but most of the desirable rural residences which we did look at proved to be lacking in both essentials, and when a cottage chanced to have drains it always had stucco as well and was shaped like a tea caddy. And if we found a vine or rose-covered porch, corruption invariably lurked within. Our minds got so befogged by the eloquence of house agents, and the rival disadvantages of the fever traps and outrages to beauty which we had seen and scorned, that I very much doubt whether either of us, on our wedding morning, knew the difference between a house and a haystack. But when we got away from friends and house agents, on our honeymoon, our wits grew clear again, and we knew a pretty cottage when at last we saw one. It was at Brenzett—a little village set on a hill over against the southern marshes. We had gone there, from the seaside village where we were staying, to see the church, and two fields from the church we found this cottage. It stood quite by itself, about two miles from the village. It was a long, low building, with rooms sticking out in unexpected places. There was a bit of stonework—ivy-covered and moss-grown, just two old rooms, all that was left of a big house that had once stood there—and round this stonework the house had grown up. Stripped of its roses and jasmine it would have been hideous. As it stood it was charming, and after a brief examination we took it. It was absurdly cheap. The rest of our honeymoon we spent in grubbing about in second-hand shops in the country town, picking up bits of old oak and Chippendale chairs for our furnishing. We wound up with a run up to town and a visit to Liberty's, and soon the low oak-beamed lattice-windowed rooms began to be home. There was a jolly old-fashioned garden with grass paths and no end of hollyhocks and sunflowers, and big lilies. From the window you could see the marsh pastures, and beyond them the blue, thin line of the sea. We were as happy as the summer was glorious, and settled down into work sooner than we ourselves expected. I was never tired of sketching the view and the wonderful cloud effects from the open lattice, and Laura would sit at the table and write verses about them, in which I mostly played the part of foreground.

We got a tall old peasant woman to do for us. Her face and figure were good, though her cooking was of the homeliest; but she understood all about gardening, and told us all the old names of the coppices and cornfields, and the stories of the smugglers and highwaymen, and, better still, of the "things that walked," and of the "sights" which met one in lonely glens of a starlight night. She was a great comfort to us, because Laura hated housekeeping as much as I loved folklore, and we soon came to leave all the domestic business to Mrs. Dorman, and to use her legends in little magazine stories which brought in the jingling guinea.

We had three months of married happiness, and did not have a single quarrel. One October evening I had been down to smoke a pipe with the doctor—our only neighbor

—a pleasant young Irishman. Laura had stayed at home to finish a comic sketch of a village episode for the *Monthly Marplot*. I left her laughing over her own jokes, and came in to find her a crumpled heap of pale muslin weeping on the window seat.

"Good heavens, my darling, what's the matter?' I cried, taking her in my arms. She leaned her little dark head against my shoulder and went on crying. I had never seen her cry before—we had always been so happy, you see—and I felt sure some frightful misfortune had happened.

"What *is* the matter? Do speak."

"It's Mrs. Dorman," she sobbed.

"What has she done?" I inquired, immensely relieved.

"She says she must go before the end of the month, and she says her niece is ill; she's gone down to see her now, but I don't believe that's the reason, because her niece is always ill. I believe someone has been setting her against us. Her manner was so queer—"

"Never mind, Pussy," I said, "whatever you do, don't cry, or I shall have to cry too, to keep you in countenance, and then you'll never respect your man again!"

She dried her eyes obediently on my handkerchief, and even smiled faintly.

"But you see," she went on, "it is really serious, because these village people are so sheepy, and if one won't do a thing you may be quite sure none of the others will. And I shall have to cook the dinners, and wash up the hateful greasy plates; and you'll have to carry cans of water about, and clean the boots and knives—and we shall never have any time for work, or earn any money, or anything. We shall have to work all day, and only be able to rest when we are waiting for the kettle to boil!"

I represented to her that even if we had to perform these duties, the day would still present some margin for other toils and recreations. But she refused to see the matter in any but the grayest light. She was very unseasonable, my Laura, but I could not have loved her any more if she had been as reasonable as Whately.

"I'll speak to Mrs. Dorman when she comes back, and see if I can't come to terms with her," I said. "Perhaps she wants a rise in her pay. It will be all right. Let's walk up to the church."

The church was a large and lonely one, and we loved to go there, es-

especially on bright nights. The path skirted a wood, cut through it once, and ran along the crest of the hill through two meadows, and round the churchyard wall, over which the old yews loomed in black masses of shadow. This path, which was partly paved, was called "the bierbalk," for it had long been the way by which the corpses had been carried to burial. The churchyard was richly treed, and was shaded by great elms which stood just outside and stretched their majestic arms in benediction over the happy dead. A large, low porch let one into the building by a Norman doorway and a heavy oak door studded with iron. Inside, the arches rose into darkness, and between them the reticulated windows, which stood out white in the moonlight. In the chancel, the windows were of rich glass, which showed in faint light their noble coloring, and made the black oak of the choir pews hardly more solid than the shadows. But on each side of the altar lay a gray marble figure of a knight in full plate armor lying upon a low slab, with hands held up in everlasting prayer, and these figures, oddly enough, were always to be seen if there was any glimmer of light in the church. Their names were lost, but the peasants told of them that they had been fierce and wicked men, marauders by land and sea, who had been the scourge of their time, and had been guilty of deeds so foul that the house they had lived in—the big house, by the way, that had stood on the site of our cottage—had been stricken by lightning and the vengeance of Heaven. But for all that, the gold of their heirs had bought them a place in the church. Looking at the bad hard faces reproduced in the marble, this story was easily believed.

The church looked at its best and weirdest on that night, for the shadows of the yew trees fell through the windows upon the floor of the nave and touched the pillars with tattered shade. We sat down together without speaking, and watched the solemn beauty of the old church, with some of that awe which inspired its early builders. We walked to the chancel and looked at the sleeping warriors. Then we rested some time on the stone seat in the porch, looking out over the stretch of quiet moonlit meadows, feeling in every fiber of our beings the peace of the night and of our happy love, and came away at last with a sense that even scrubbing and 113 black-leading were but small troubles at their worst.

Mrs. Dorman had come back from the village, and I at once invited her to a *tête-à-tête*.

"Now, Mrs. Dorman," I said, when I had got her into my painting room, "what's all this about your not staying with us?"

"I should be glad to get away, sir, before the end of the month," she answered, with her usual placid dignity.

"Have you any fault to find, Mrs. Dorman?"

"None at all, sir; you and your lady have always been most kind, I'm sure—"

"Well, what is it? Are your wages not high enough?"

"No, sir, I gets quite enough."

"Then why not stay?"

"I'd rather not"—with some hesitation—"my niece is ill."

"But your niece has been ill ever since we came."

No answer. There was a long and awkward silence. I broke it.

"Can't you stay for another month?" I asked.

"No, sir. I'm bound to go by Thursday."

And this was Monday!

"Well, I must say, I think you might have let us know before.

There's no time now to get any one else, and your mistress is not fit to do heavy housework. Can't you stay till next week?"

"I might be able to come back next week."

I was now convinced that all she wanted was a brief holiday, which we should have been willing enough to let her have, as soon as we could get a substitute.

"But why must you go this week?" I persisted. "Come, out with it."

Mrs. Dorman drew the little shawl, which she always wore, tightly across her bosom, as though she were cold. Then she said, with a sort of effort:

"They say, sir, as this was a big house in Catholic times, and there was a many deeds done here."

The nature of the "deeds" might be vaguely inferred from the inflection of Mrs. Dorman's voice—which was enough to make one's blood run cold. I was glad that Laura was not in the room. She was always nervous, as highly strung natures are, and I felt that these tales about our house, told by this old peasant woman, with her impressive manner and contagious credulity, might have made our home less dear to my wife.

"Tell me all about it, Mrs. Dorman," I said; "you needn't mind about telling me. I'm not like the young people who make fun of such things."

Which was partly true.

"Well, sir"—she sank her voice—"you may have seen in the church, beside the altar, two shapes."

"You mean the effigies of the knights in armor," I said cheerfully.

"I mean them two bodies, drawed out man-size in marble," she returned, and I had to admit that her description was a thousand times more graphic than mine, to say nothing of a certain weird force and uncanniness about the phrase "drawed out man-size in marble."

"They do say, as on All Saints' Eve them two bodies sits up on their slabs, and gets off of them, and then walks down the aisle, *in their marble*"—(another good phrase, Mrs. Dorman)—"and as the church clock strikes eleven they walks out of the church door, and over the graves, and along the bier balk, and if it's a wet night there's the marks of their feet in the morning."

"And where do they go?" I asked, rather fascinated.

"They comes back here to their home, sir, and if anyone meets them—"

"Well, what then?" I asked.

But no—not another word could I get from her, save that her niece was ill and she must go. After what I had heard I scorned to discuss the niece, and tried to get from Mrs. Dorman more details of the legend. I could get nothing but warnings.

"Whatever you do, sir, lock the door early on All Saints' Eve, and make the cross sign over the doorstep and on the windows."

"But has anyone ever seen these things?" I persisted.

"That's not for me to say. I know what I know, sir."

"Well, who was here last year?"

115

"No one, sir; the lady as owned the house only stayed here in summer, and she always went to London a full month afore *the* night. And I'm sorry to inconvenience you and your lady, but my niece is ill and I must go on Thursday."

I could have shaken her for her absurd reiteration of that obvious fiction, after she had told me her real reasons.

She was determined to go, nor could our united entreaties move her in the least.

I did not tell Laura the legend of the shapes that "walked in their marble," partly because a legend concerning our house might perhaps trouble my wife, and partly, I think, from some more occult reason. This was not quite the same to me as any other story, and I did not want to talk about it till the day was over. I had very soon ceased to think of the legend, however. I was painting a portrait of Laura, against the lattice window, and I could not think of much else. I had got a splendid background of yellow and gray sunset, and was working away with enthusiasm at her face. On Thursday Mrs. Dorman went. She relented, at parting, so far as to say:

"Don't you put yourself about too much, ma'am, and if there's any

little thing I can do next week, I'm sure I shan't mind."

From which I inferred that she wished to come back to us after Hallowe'en. Up to the last she adhered to the fiction of the niece with touching fidelity.

Thursday passed off pretty well. Laura showed marked ability in the matter of steak and potatoes, and I confess that my knives, and the plates, which I insisted upon washing, were better done than I had dared to expect.

Friday came. It is about what happened on that Friday that this is written. I wonder if I should have believed it, if anyone had told it to me. I will write the story of it as quickly and plainly as I can. Everything that happened on that day is burned into my brain. I shall not forget anything, nor leave anything out.

I got up early, I remember, and lighted the kitchen fire, and had just achieved a smoky success when my little wife came running down, as sunny and sweet as the clear October morning itself. We prepared breakfast together, and found it very good fun. The housework was soon done, and when brushes and brooms and pails were quiet again, the house was still indeed. It is wonderful what a difference one makes in a house. We really missed Mrs. Dorman, quite apart from considerations concerning pots and pans. We spent the day in dusting our books and putting them straight, and dined gaily on cold steak and coffee. Laura was, if possible, brighter and gayer and sweeter than usual, and I began to think that a little domestic toil was really good for her. We had never been so merry since we were married, and the walk we had that afternoon was, I think, the happiest time of all my life. When we had watched the deep scarlet clouds slowly pale into leaden gray against a pale green sky, and saw the white mists curl up along the hedgerows in the distant marsh, we came back to the house, silently, hand in hand.

"You are sad, my darling," I said, half jestingly, as we sat down together in our little parlor. I expected a disclaimer, for my own silence had been the silence of complete happiness. To my surprise she said:

"Yes. I think I am sad, or rather I am uneasy. I don't think I'm very well. I have shivered three or four times since we came in, and it is not cold, is it?"

"No," I said, and hoped it was not a chill caught from the treacherous mists that roll up from the marshes in the dying light. No—she said, she did not think so. Then, after a silence, she spoke suddenly:

"Do you ever have presentiments of evil?"

"No," I said, smiling, "and I shouldn't believe in them if I had."

"I do," she went on. "The night my father died I knew it, though he was right away in the North of Scotland." I did not answer in words.

She sat looking at the fire for some time in silence, gently stroking my hand. At last she sprang up, came behind me, and, drawing my head back, kissed me.

"There, it's over now," she said. "What a baby I am! Come, light the candles, and we'll have some of these new Rubinstein duets."

And we spent a happy hour or two at the piano.

At about half past ten I began to long for the good-night pipe, but Laura looked so white that I felt it would be brutal of me to fill our sitting room with the fumes of strong cavendish.

"I'll take my pipe outside," I said.

"Let me come, too."

"No, sweetheart, not tonight; you're much too tired. I shan't be   117 long. Get to bed, or I shall have an invalid to nurse tomorrow as well as the boots to clean.''

I kissed her and was turning to go, when she flung her arms round my neck and held me as if she would never let me go again. I stroked her hair.

"Come, Pussy, you're over tired. The housework has been too much for you."

She loosened her clasp a little and drew a deep breath.

"No. We've been very happy to-day, Jack, haven't we? Don't stay out too long."

"I won't, my dearie."

I strolled out of the front door, leaving it unlatched. What a night it was! The jagged masses of heavy dark clouds were rolling at intervals from horizon to horizon, and thin white wreaths covered the stars. Through all the rush of the cloud river, the moon swam, breasting the waves and disappearing again in the darkness. When now and again her light reached the woodlands they seemed to be slowly and noise-lessly waving in time to the swing of the clouds above them. There was a strange gray light over all the earth; the fields had that shadowy bloom over them which only comes from the marriage of dew and moonshine, or frost and starlight.

I walked up and down, drinking in the beauty of the quiet earth and the changing sky. The night was absolutely silent. Nothing seemed to be abroad. There was no scurry-ing of rabbits, or twitter of the half-asleep birds. And though the clouds went sailing across the sky, the wind that drove them never came low enough to rustle the dead leaves in the woodland paths. Across the meadows I could see the church tower standing out black and gray against the sky. I walked there thinking over our three months of happiness — and of my wife, her dear eyes, her loving ways. Oh, my little girl! My own little girl; what a vision came then of a long, glad life for you and me together!

I heard a bell-beat from the church. Eleven already! I turned to go in, but the night held me. I could not go back into our little warm rooms yet. I would go up to the church. I felt vaguely that it would be good to carry my love and thankfulness to the sanctuary whither so many loads of sorrow and gladness had been borne by the men and women of the dead years.

I looked in at the low window as I went by. Laura was half lying on her chair in front of the fire. I could not see her face, only her little head showed dark against the pale blue wall. She was quite still. Asleep, no doubt. My heart reached out to her as I went on. There must be a God, I thought, and a God Who was good. How otherwise could any-thing so sweet and dear as she have ever been imagined?

I walked slowly along the edge of the wood. A sound broke the still-ness of the night, it was a rustling in the wood. I stopped and listened.

The sound stopped too. I went on, and now distinctly heard another step than mine answer mine like an echo. It was a poacher or a wood stealer, most likely, for these were not unknown in our Arcadian neighborhood. But whoever it was, he was a fool not to step more light-ly. I turned into the wood, and now the footstep seemed to come from the path I had just left. It must be an echo, I thought. The wood looked perfect in the moonlight. The large dying ferns and the brushwood showed where through thinning foliage the pale light came down. The tree trunks stood up like Gothic columns all around me. They reminded me of the church, and I turned into the bier balk, and passed through the corpse gate be-tween the graves to the low porch. I paused for a moment on the stone seat where Laura and I had watched the fading landscape. Then I noticed that the door of the church was open, and I blamed myself for having left it unlatched the other night. We were the only people who ever cared to come to the church except on Sundays, and I was vexed to think that through our carelessness the damp autumn airs had had a chance of getting in and injuring the old fabric. I went in. It will seem strange, perhaps, that I

119

should have gone halfway up the aisle before I remembered—with a sudden chill, followed by as sudden a rush of self-contempt — that this was the very day and hour when, according to tradition, the "shapes drawed out man-size in marble" began to walk.

Having thus remembered the legend, and remembered it with a shiver, of which I was ashamed, I could not do otherwise than walk up toward the altar, just to look at the figures—as I said to myself; really what I wanted was to assure myself, first, that I did not believe the legend, and, secondly, that it was not true. I was rather glad that I had come. I thought now I could tell Mrs. Dorman how vain her fancies were, and how peacefully the marble figures slept on through the ghastly hour. With my hands in my pockets I passed up the aisle. In the gray dim light the eastern end of the church looked larger than usual, and the arches above the two tombs looked larger too. The moon came out and showed me the reason. I stopped short, my heart gave a leap that nearly choked me, and then sank sickeningly.

The "bodies drawed out man-size" *were gone,* and their marble slabs lay wide and bare in the vague moonlight that slanted through the east window.

Were they really gone or was I mad? Clenching my nerves, I stooped and passed my hand over the smooth slabs, and felt their flat unbroken surface. Had someone taken the things away? Was it some vile practical joke? I would make sure, anyway. In an instant I had made a torch of a newspaper, which happened to be in my pocket, and lighting it held it high above my head. Its yellow glare illumined the dark arches and those slabs. The figures *were* gone. And I was alone in the church; or was I alone?

And then a horror seized me, a horror indefinable and indescribable—an overwhelming certainty of supreme and accomplished calamity. I flung down the torch and tore along the aisle and out through the porch, biting my lips as I ran to keep myself from shrieking aloud. Oh, was I mad — or what was this that possessed me? I leaped the churchyard wall and took the straight cut across the fields, led by the light from our windows. Just as I got over the first stile, a dark figure seemed to spring out of the ground. Mad still with that certainty of misfortune, I made for the thing that stood in my path, shouting. "Get out of the way, can't you!"

But my push met with a more vigorous resistance than I had expected. My arms were caught just above the elbow and held as in a vice, and the raw-boned Irish doctor actually shook me.

"Would ye?" he cried, in his own unmistakable accents, "would ye, then?"

"Let me go, you fool," I gasped. "The marble figures have gone from the church; I tell you they've gone."

He broke into a ringing laugh. "I'll have to give ye a draught tomorrow, I see. Ye've bin smoking too much and listening to old wives' tales."

"I tell you, I've seen the bare slabs."

"Well, come back with me. I'm going up to old Palmer's — his daughter's ill; we'll look in at the church and let me see the bare slabs."

"You go, if you like," I said, a little less frantic for his laughter; "I'm going home to my wife."

"Rubbish, man," said he. "D'ye think I'll permit that? As ye to go saying all yer life that ye've seen solid marble endowed with vitality, and me to go all me life saying ye were a coward? No sir—ye shan't do ut."

The night air—a human voice—and I think also the physical contact with this six feet of solid common sense, brought me back a little to my ordinary self, and the word "coward" was a mental shower bath.

"Come on, then," I said sullenly, "perhaps you're right."

He still held my arm tightly. We got over the stile and back to the church. All was still as death. The place smelt very damp and earthy. We walked up the aisle. I am not ashamed to confess that I shut my eyes: I knew the figures would not 121 be there. I heard Kelly strike a match.

"Here they are, ye see, right enough; ye've been dreaming or drinking, asking yer pardon for the imputation."

I opened my eyes. By Kelly's expiring vesta I saw two shapes lying "in their marble" on their slabs. I drew a deep breath, and caught his hand.

"I'm awfully indebted to you," I said. "It must have been some trick of light, or I have been working rather hard, perhaps that's it. Do you know, I was quite convinced they were gone."

"I'm aware of that," he answered rather grimly. "Ye'll have to be careful of that brain of yours, my friend, I assure ye."

He was leaning over and looking at the right-hand figure, whose stony face was the more villainous and deadly in expression.

"By Jove," he said, "something has been afoot here — this hand is broken.

And so it was. I was certain that it had been perfect the last time Laura and I had been there.

"Perhaps some one has *tried* to remove them," said the young doctor.

"That won't account for my impression," I objected.

"Too much painting and tobacco will account for that, well enough."

"Come along," I said, "or my wife will be getting anxious. You'll come in and have a drop of whiskey and drink confusion to ghosts and better sense to me."

"I ought to go up to Palmer's, but it's so late now I'd best leave it till the morning," he replied. "I was kept late at the Union, and I've had to see a lot of people since. All right, I'll come back with ye."

I think he fancied I needed him more than did Palmer's girl, so, discussing how such an illusion could have been possible, and deducing from this experience large generalities concerning ghostly apparitions, we walked up to our cottage. We saw, as we walked up the garden path, that bright light streamed out of the front door, and presently saw that the parlor door was open too. Had she gone out?

"Come in," I said, and Dr. Kelly followed me into the parlor. It was all ablaze with candles, not only the wax ones, but at least a dozen guttering, glaring tallow dips, stuck in vases and ornaments in unlikely places. Light, I knew, was Laura's remedy for nervousness. Poor child! Why had I left her? Brute that I was.

We glanced round the room, and

at first we did not see her. The window was open, and the draft set all the candles flaring one way. Her chair was empty and her handkerchief and book lay on the floor. I turned to the window. There, in the recess of the window, I saw her. Oh, my child, my love, had she gone to that window to watch for me? And what had come into the room behind her? To what had she turned with that look of frantic fear and horror? Oh, my little one, had she thought that it was I whose step she heard, and turned to meet—what?

She had fallen back across a table in the window, and her body lay half on it and half on the window seat, and her head hung down over the table, the brown hair loosened and fallen to the carpet. Her lips were drawn back, and her eyes wide, wide open. They saw nothing now. What had they seen last?

The doctor moved towards her, but I pushed him aside and sprang to her, caught her in my arms and cried:

"It's all right, Laura! I've got you safe, wifie."

She fell into my arms in a heap. I clasped her and kissed her, and called her by all her pet names, but I think I knew all the time that she was dead. Her hands were tightly

clenched. In one of them she held something fast. When I was quite sure that she was dead, and that nothing mattered at all any more, I let him open her hand to see what she held.

It was a gray marble finger.

3  The Bold Dragoons

My grandfather was a bold dragoon, for it's a profession, d'ye see, that has run in the family. All my forefathers have been dragoons and died upon the field of honor except myself, and I hope my posterity may be able to say the same; however, I don't mean to be vainglorious. Well, my grandfather, as I said, was a bold dragoon, and had served in the Low Countries. In fact, he was one of that very army, which, according to my uncle Toby, "swore so terribly in Flanders." He could swear a good stick himself; and, moreover, was the very man that introduced the doctrine Corporal Trim mentions, of radical heat and radical moisture; or, in other words, the mode of keeping out the damps of ditch water by burnt brandy. Be that as it may, it's nothing to the purport of my story. I only tell it to show you that my grandfather was a man not easily to be humbugged. He had seen service; or, according to his own phrase, "he had seen the divil"—and that's saying everything.

Well, gentlemen, my grandfather was on his way to England, for which he intended to embark at Ostend—bad luck to the place for one where I was kept by storms and head winds for three long days, and the divil of a jolly companion or pretty face to comfort me. Well, as I was saying, my grandfather was on his way to England, or rather to Ostend—no matter which, it's all the same. So one evening, towards nightfall, he rode jollily into Bruges. Very like you all know Bruges, gentlemen, a queer, old-fashioned Flemish town, once they say a great place for trade and money-making, in old times, when the Mynheers were in their glory; but almost as large and as empty as an Irishman's pocket at the present day. Well, gentlemen, it was the time of the annual fair. All Bruges was crowded; and the canals swarmed with Dutch boats, and the streets swarmed with Dutch merchants; and there was hardly any getting along for goods, wares, and merchandises, and peasants in big breeches, and women in half a score of petticoats.

My grandfather rode jollily along, in his easy, slashing way, for he was a saucy, sunshiny fellow — staring about him at the motley crowd, and the old houses with gable ends to the street and storks' nests on the chimneys; winking at the ya vrouws* who showed their faces at the windows, and joking the women right and left in the street; all of whom laughed and took it in amazing good part; for though he did not know a word of their language, yet he had always a knack of making himself understood among the women.

Well, gentlemen, it being the time of the annual fair, all the town was crowded; every inn and tavern full, and my grandfather applied in vain from one to the other for admittance. At length he rode up to an old rackety inn that looked ready to fall to pieces, and which all the rats would have run away from, if they could have found room in any other house to put their heads. It was just such a queer building as you see in Dutch pictures, with a tall roof that reached up into the clouds; and as many garrets, one over the other, as the seven heavens of Mahomet. Nothing had saved it from tumbling down but a stork's nest on the chimney, which always brings good luck to a house in the Low Countries; and at the very time of my grandfather's arrival, there were two of these long-legged birds of grace, standing like ghosts on the chimney top. Faith, but they've kept the house on its legs to this very day; for you may see it any time you pass through Bruges, as it stands there yet; only it is turned into a brewery—a brewery of strong Flemish beer; at least it was so when I came that way after the battle of Waterloo.

My grandfather eyed the house curiously as he approached. It might not altogether have struck his fancy, had he not seen in large letters over the door,

HEER VERKOOPT MAN
GOEDEN DRANK

My grandfather had learnt enough of the language to know that the sign promised good liquor. "This is the house for me," said he, stopping short before the door.

The sudden appearance of a dashing dragoon was an event in an old inn, frequented only by the peaceful sons of traffic. A rich burgher of Antwerp, a stately ample

125

* housewives

man, in a broad Flemish hat, and who was the great man and great patron of the establishment, sat smoking a clean long pipe on one side of the door; a fat distiller of Geneva from Schiedam sat smoking on the other, and the bottle-nosed host stood in the door, and the comely hostess, in crimped cap, beside him, and the hostess' daughter, a plump Flanders lass, with long gold pendants in her ears, was at a side window.

"Humph!" said the rich burgher of Antwerp, with a sulky glance at the stranger.

"Der duyvel!" said the fat little distiller of Schiedam.

The landlord saw with the quick glance of a publican that the new guest was not at all, at all, to the taste of the old ones; and to tell the truth, he did not himself like my grandfather's saucy eye. He shook his head—not a garret in the house but was full.

"Not a garret!" echoed the landlady.

"Not a garret!" echoed the daughter.

The burgher of Antwerp and the little distiller of Schiedam continued to smoke their pipes sullenly, eyed the enemy askance from under their broad hats, but said nothing.

My grandfather was not a man to be browbeaten. He threw the reins on his horse's neck, cocked his hat on one side, stuck one arm akimbo, — "Faith and troth!" said he, "but I'll sleep in this house this very night." — As he said this he gave a slap on his thigh, by way of emphasis — the slap went to the landlady's heart.

He followed up the vow by jumping off his horse, and making his way past the staring Mynheers into the public room. — Maybe you've been in the bar-room of an old Flemish inn — faith, but a handsome chamber it was as you'd wish to see; with a brick floor, and a great fireplace, with the whole Bible history in glazed tiles; and then the mantel-piece, pitching itself head foremost out of the wall, with a whole regiment of cracked tea-pots and earthen jugs paraded on it; not to mention half a dozen great Delft platters, hung about the room by way of pictures; and the little bar in one corner, and the bouncing barmaid inside of it, with a red calico cap, and yellow ear-drops.

My grandfather snapped his fingers over his head, as he cast an eye round the room, — "Faith, this is the very house I've been looking after," said he.

There was some further show of

resistance on the part of the garrison; but my grandfather was an old soldier, and an Irishman to boot, and not easily repulsed, especially after he had got into the fortress. So he blarneyed the landlord, kissed the landlord's wife, tickled the landlord's daughter, chucked the barmaid under the chin; and it was agreed on all hands that it would be a thousand pities, and a burning shame into the bargain, to turn such a bold dragoon into the streets. So they laid their heads together, that is to say, my grandfather and the landlady, and it was at length agreed to accommodate him with an old chamber that had been for some time shut up.

"Some say it's haunted!" whispered the landlord's daughter, "but you're a bold dragoon, and I dare say don't fear ghosts."

"The divil a bit!" said my grandfather, pinching her plump cheek; "but if I should be troubled by ghosts, I've been to the Red Sea in my time, and have a pleasant way of laying them, my darling!"

And then he whispered something to the girl which made her laugh, and give him a good-humored box on the ear. In short, there was nobody knew better how to make his way among the petticoats than my grandfather.

In a little while, as was his usual way, he took complete possession of the house; swaggering all over it—into the stable to look after his horse; into the kitchen to look after his supper. He had something to say or do with every one; smoked with the Dutchmen; drank with the Germans; slapped the men on the shoulders, tickled the women under the ribs—never since the days of Ally Croaker had such a rattling blade been seen. The landlord stared at him with astonishment; the landlord's daughter hung her head and giggled whenever he came near; and as he turned his back and swaggered along, his tight jacket setting off his broad shoulders and plump buckskins, and his long sword trailing by his side, the maids whispered to one another—"What a proper man!"

At supper my grandfather took command of the table d'hôte as though he had been at home; helped everybody, not forgetting himself; talked with every one, whether he understood their language or not; and made his way into the intimacy of the rich burgher of Antwerp, who had never been known to be sociable with any one during his life. In fact, he revolutionized the whole establishment, and gave it such a rouse, that the very house reeled with it. He outsat every one at table excepting the little fat distiller of Schiedam, who had sat soaking for a long time before he broke forth; but when he did, he was a very divil incarnate. He took a violent affection for my grandfather; so they sat drinking, and smoking, and telling stories, and singing Dutch and Irish songs, without understanding a word each other said, until the little Hollander was fairly swamped with his own gin and water, and carried off to bed, whooping and hiccuping, and trolling the burthen of a Low Dutch love song.

Well, gentlemen, my grandfather was shown to his quarters, up a huge staircase composed of loads of hewn timber; and through long rigmarole passages, hung with blackened paintings of fruit, and fish, and game, and country frolics, and huge kitchens, and portly burgomasters, such as you see about old-fashioned Flemish inns, till at length he arrived at his room.

An old-times chamber it was, sure enough, and crowded with all kinds of trumpery. It looked like an infirmary for decayed and superannuated furniture, where everything diseased and disabled was sent to nurse, or to be forgotten. Or rather, it might have been taken for a general congress of old legitimate movables, where every kind and country had a representative. No two chairs were alike; such high backs and low backs, and leather bottoms, and worsted bottoms, and straw bottoms, and no bottoms; and cracked marble tables with curiously carved legs, holding balls in their claws, as though they were going to play at ninepins.

My grandfather made a bow to the motley assemblage as he entered, and having undressed himself, placed his light in the fireplace, asking pardon of the tongs, which seemed to be making love to the shovel in the chimney corner, and whispering soft nonsense in its ear.

The rest of the guests were by this time sound asleep; for your Mynheers are huge sleepers. The housemaids, one by one, crept yawning to their attics, and not a female head in the inn was laid on a pillow that night without dreaming of the Bold Dragoon.

My grandfather, for his part, got into bed, and drew over him one of those great bags of down, under which they smother a man in the Low Countries; and there he lay, melting between two feather beds, like an anchovy sandwich between two slices of toast and butter. He was a warm-complexioned man, and this smothering played the very deuce with him. So, sure enough, in a little while it seemed as if a legion of imps were twitching at him, and all the blood in his veins was in fever heat.

He lay still, however, until all the house was quiet, excepting the snoring of the Mynheers from the different chambers; who answered one another in all kinds of tones and cadences, like so many bullfrogs in a swamp. The quieter the house became, the more unquiet became my grandfather. He waxed warmer and warmer, until at length the bed became too hot to hold him.

"Faith, there's no standing this any longer," says he; so he jumped out of bed and went strolling about the house.

Well, my grandfather had been for some time absent from his room, and was returning, perfectly cool, when just as he reached the door he heard a strange noise within. He paused and listened. It seemed as if some one was trying to hum a tune in defiance of the asthma. He recollected the report of the room's being haunted; but he was no believer in ghosts. So he pushed the door gently ajar, and peeped in.

Egad, gentlemen, there was a gambol carrying on within enough to have astonished St. Anthony.

By the light of the fire he saw a pale, weazen-faced fellow in a long flannel gown and a tall white nightcap with a tassel to it, who sat by the fire, with a bellows under his arm by way of bagpipe, from which he forced the asthmatical music that had bothered my grandfather. As he played, too, he kept twitching about with a thousand queer contortions; nodding his head and bobbing about his tasselled nightcap.

My grandfather thought this very odd, and mighty presumptuous and was about to demand what business he had to play his wind instruments in another gentleman's quarters, when a new cause of astonishment met his eye. From the opposite side of the room a long-backed, dandy-legged chair, covered with leather, and studded all over in a coxcomical fashion with little brass nails, got suddenly into motion; thrust out first a claw foot, then a crooked arm, and at length, making a leg, slid gracefully up to an easy chair of tarnished brocade, with a hole in its bottom, and led it gallantly out in a ghostly minuet about the floor.

The musician now played fiercer and fiercer, and bobbed his head and his nightcap about like mad. By degrees the dancing mania seemed to seize upon all the other pieces of

129

furniture. The antique, long-bodied chairs paired off in couples and led down a country dance; a three-legged stool danced a hornpipe, though horribly puzzled by its supernumerary leg; while the amorous tongs seized the shovel around the waist and whirled it about the room in a German waltz. In short, all the movables got in motion, capering about; pirouetting, hands across, right and left, like so many devils, all except the clothes-press, which kept curtseying and curtseying, like a dowager, in one corner, in exquisite time to the music—being either too corpulent to dance, or perhaps at a loss for a partner.

My grandfather concluded the latter to be the reason; so, being, like a true Irishman, devoted to the sex, and at all times ready for a frolic, he bounced into the room, calling to the musicians to strike up "Paddy O'Rafferty," capered up to the clothes-press and seized upon two handles to lead her out—when, whizz!—the whole revel was at an end. The chairs, tables, tongs, and shovel slunk in an instant as quietly into their places as if nothing had happened; and the musician vanished up the chimney, leaving the bellows behind him in his hurry. My grandfather found himself seated in the middle of the floor, with the clothes-press sprawling before him, and the two handles jerked off and in his hands.

Well, gentlemen, as the clothes-press was a mighty heavy body, and my grandfather likewise, particularly in the rear, you may easily suppose two such heavy bodies coming to the ground would make a bit of noise. Faith, the old mansion shook as though it had mistaken it for an earthquake. The whole garrison was alarmed. The landlord, who slept just below, hurried up with a candle to inquire the cause, but with all his haste his daughter had hurried to the scene of uproar before him. The landlord was followed by the landlady, who was followed by the bouncing barmaid, who was followed by the simpering chambermaids all holding together, as well as they could, such garments as they had first laid hands on; but all in a terrible hurry to see what the divil was to pay in the chamber of the Bold Dragoon.

My grandfather related the marvelous scene he had witnessed, and the prostrate clothes-press and the broken handles bore testimony to the fact. There was no contesting such evidence; particularly with a lad of my grandfather's complexion, who seemed able to make good every word either with sword or shillelah. So the landlord scratched his head and looked silly, as he was apt to do when puzzled. The landlady scratched—no, she did not scratch her head—but she knit her brow, and did not seem half pleased with the explanation. But the landlady's daughter corroborated it by recollecting that the last person who had dwelt in that chamber was a famous juggler who had died of St. Vitus's dance, and no doubt had infected all the furniture.

This set all things to rights, particularly when the chambermaids declared that they had all witnessed strange carryings on in that room—and as they declared this "upon their honors," there could not remain a doubt upon the subject.

4 The Canterville Ghost

I

When Mr. Hiram B. Otis, the American Minister, bought Canterville Chase, everyone told him he was doing a very foolish thing, as there was no doubt at all that the place was haunted. Indeed, Lord Canterville himself, who was a man of the most punctilious honor, had felt it his duty to mention the fact to Mr. Otis when they came to discuss terms.

"We have not cared to live in the place ourselves," said Lord Canterville, "since my grand-aunt, the Dowager Duchess of Bolton, was frightened into a fit, from which she never really recovered, by two skeleton hands being placed on her shoulders as she was dressing for dinner, and I feel bound to tell you, Mr. Otis, that the ghost has been seen by several living members of my family, as well as by the rector of the parish, the Rev. Augustus Dampier, who is a Fellow of King's College, Cambridge. After the unfortunate accident to the Duchess none of our younger servants would stay with us, and Lady Canterville often got very little sleep at night, in consequence of the mysterious noises that came from the corridor and the library."

"My lord," answered the Minister, "I will take the furniture and the ghost at a valuation. I come from a modern country, where we have everything that money can buy; and with all our spry young fellows painting the Old World red, and carrying off your best actresses and prima donnas, I reckon that if there were such a thing as a ghost in Europe we'd have it at home in a very short time in one of our public museums, or on the road as a show."

"I fear that the ghost exists," said Lord Canterville, smiling, "though it may have resisted the overtures of your enterprising impresarios. It has been well known for three centuries, since 1584 in fact, and always makes its appearance before the death of any member of our family."

"Well, so does the family doctor for that matter, Lord Canterville. But there is no such thing, sir, as a ghost, and I guess the laws of Nature are not going to be suspended for the British aristocracy."

"You are certainly very natural in America," answered Lord Canterville, who did not quite understand Mr. Otis's last observation, "and if you don't mind a ghost in the house, it is all right. Only you must remember I warned you."

A few weeks after this, the purchase was completed, and at the close of the season the Minister and his family went down to Canterville Chase. Mrs. Otis, who, as Miss Lucretia R. Tappan, of West 53rd Street, had been a celebrated New York belle, was now a very handsome, middle-aged woman, with fine eyes and a superb profile. Many American ladies on leaving their native land adopt an appearance of chronic ill-health, under the impression that it is a form of European refinement, but Mrs. Otis had never fallen into this error. She had a magnificent constitution, and a really wonderful amount of animal spirits. Indeed, in many respects she was quite English, and was an excellent example of the fact that we have really everything in common with America nowadays, except, of course, language. Her eldest son, christened Washington by his parents in a moment of patriotism, which he never ceased to regret, was a fair-haired, rather good-looking young man, who had qualified himself for American diplomacy by leading the German at the Newport Casino for three successive seasons, and even in London was well known as an excellent dancer. Gardenias and the peerage were his only weaknesses. Otherwise he was extremely sensible. Miss Virginia E. Otis was a little girl of fifteen, lithe and lovely as a fawn, and with a fine freedom in her large blue eyes. She was a wonderful Amazon, and had once raced old Lord Bilton on her pony twice round the park, winning by a length and a half, just in front of the Achilles statue, to the huge delight of the young Duke of Cheshire, who proposed for her on the spot, and was sent back to Eton that very night by his guardians, in floods of tears. After Virginia came the twins, who were usually called "The Stars and Stripes," as they were always getting swished. They were delightful boys, and with the exception of the worthy Minister the only true republicans of the family.

As Canterville Chase is seven miles from Ascot, the nearest railway station, Mr. Otis had telegraphed for a waggonette to meet them, and they started on their drive in high spirits. It was a lovely July evening, and the air was delicate with the scent of the pine-woods. Now and then they heard a wood pigeon brooding over its own sweet voice, or saw deep in the rustling fern, the burnished breast of the pheasant. Little squirrels peered at them from the beech trees as they went by, and the rabbits scudded away through the brush-wood and over the mossy knolls, with their white tails in the air. As they entered the avenue of Canterville Chase, however, the sky became suddenly overcast with clouds, a curious stillness seemed to hold the atmosphere, a great flight of rooks passed silently over their heads, and, before they reached the house, some big drops of rain had fallen.

Standing on the steps to receive them was an old woman, neatly dressed in black silk, with a white cap and apron. This was Mrs. Umney, the housekeeper, whom Mrs. Otis, at Lady Canterville's earnest request, had consented to keep on in her former position. She made them each a low curtsey as they alighted, and said, in a quaint, old-fashioned manner, "I bid you welcome to Canterville Chase." Following her, they passed through the fine Tudor hall into the library, a long, low room, panelled in black oak, at the end of which was a large stained-glass window. Here they found tea laid out for them, and, after taking off their wraps, they sat down and began to look round, while Mrs. Umney waited on them.

Suddenly Mrs. Otis caught sight of a dull red stain on the floor just by the fireplace and, quite unconscious of what it really signified, said to Mrs. Umney, "I am afraid something has been spilt there."

"Yes, madam," replied the old housekeeper in a low voice, "blood has been spilt on that spot."

"How horrid," cried Mrs. Otis; "I don't at all care for bloodstains in a sitting room. It must be removed at once."

The old woman smiled, and answered in the same low, mysterious voice, "It is the blood of Lady Eleanore de Canterville, who was murdered on that very spot by her own husband, Sir Simon de Canterville, in 1575. Sir Simon survived her nine years, and disappeared suddenly under very mysterious circumstances. His body has never been discovered, but his guilty spirit still haunts the Chase. The bloodstain has been much admired by tourists and others, and cannot be removed."

"That is all nonsense," cried Washington Otis, "Pinkerton's Champion Stain Remover and Paragon Detergent will clean it up in no time," and before the terrified housekeeper could interfere he had fallen upon his knees, and was rapidly scouring the floor with a small stick of what looked like a black cosmetic. In a few moments no trace of the bloodstain could be seen.

"I knew Pinkerton would do it," he exclaimed triumphantly, as he looked round at his admiring family; but no sooner had he said these words than a terrible flash of lightning lit up the somber room, a fearful peal of thunder made them all start to their feet, and Mrs. Umney fainted.

"What a monstrous climate!" said the American Minister calmly, as he lit a long cheroot. "I guess the old country is so over-populated that they have not enough decent weather for everybody. I have always been of opinion that emigration is the only thing for England."

"My dear Hiram," cried Mrs. Otis, "what can we do with a woman who faints?"

"Charge it to her like breakages," answered the Minister, "she won't faint after that," and in a few moments Mrs. Umney certainly came to. There was no doubt, however, that she was extremely upset, and she sternly warned Mr. Otis to beware of some trouble coming to the house.

"I have seen things with my own eyes, sir," she said, "that would make any Christian's hair stand on end, and many and many a night I have not closed my eyes in sleep for the awful things that are done here." Mr. Otis, however, and his wife warmly assured the honest soul that they were not afraid of ghosts, and, after invoking the blessings of Providence on her new master and mistress, and making arrangements for an increase of salary, the old housekeeper tottered off to her own room.

II

The storm raged fiercely all that night, but nothing of particular note occurred. The next morning, however, when they came down to breakfast, they found the terrible stain of blood once again on the floor. "I don't think it can be the fault of the Paragon Detergent," said Washington, "for I have tried it with everything. It must be the

135

ghost." He accordingly rubbed out the stain a second time, but the second morning it appeared again. The third morning also it was there, though the library had been locked up at night by Mr. Otis himself, and the key carried upstairs. The whole family were now quite interested; Mr. Otis began to suspect that he had been too dogmatic in his denial of the existence of ghosts. Mrs. Otis expressed her intention of joining the Psychical Society, and Washington prepared a long letter to Messrs. Myers and Podmore on the subject of the Permanence of Sanguineous Stains when connected with Crime. That night all doubts about the objective existence of phantasmata were removed for ever.

The day had been warm and sunny; and, in the cool of the evening, the whole family went out for a drive. They did not return home till nine o'clock, when they had a light supper. The conversation in no way turned upon ghosts, so there were not even those primary conditions of receptive expectation which so often precede the presentation of psychical phenomena. The subjects discussed, as I have since learned from Mr. Otis, were merely such as form the ordinary conversation of cultured Americans of the better class, such as the immense superiority of Miss Fanny Davenport over Sarah Bernhardt as an actress; the difficulty of obtaining green corn, buckwheat cakes, and hominy, even in the best English houses; the importance of Boston in the development of the world-soul; the advantages of the baggage check system in railway travelling; and the sweetness of the New York accent as compared to the London drawl. No mention at all was made of the supernatural, nor was Sir Simon de Canterville alluded to in any way. At eleven o'clock the family retired, and by half-past all the lights were out. Some time after, Mr. Otis was awakened by a curious noise in the corridor, outside his room. It sounded like the clank of metal, and seemed to be coming nearer every moment. He got up at once, struck a match, and looked at the time. It was exactly one o'clock. He was quite calm, and felt his pulse, which was not at all feverish. The strange noise still continued, and with it he heard distinctly the sound of footsteps. He put on his slippers, took a small oblong phial out of his dressing case, and opened the door. Right in front of him he saw, in the wan moonlight, an old man of terrible aspect. His eyes were as red burning coals; long gray hair fell over his shoulders in matted coils;

his garments, which were of antique cut, were soiled and ragged, and from his wrists and ankles hung heavy manacles and rusty gyves.

"My dear sir," said Mr. Otis, "I really must insist on your oiling those chains, and have brought you for that purpose a small bottle of the Tammany Rising Sun Lubricator. It is said to be completely efficacious upon one application, and there are several testimonials to that effect on the wrapper from some of our most eminent native divines. I shall leave it here for you by the bedroom candles, and will be happy to supply you with more should you require it." With these words the United States Minister laid the bottle down on a marble table, and, closing his door, retired to rest.

For a moment the Canterville ghost stood quite motionless in natural indignation; then, dashing the bottle violently upon the polished floor, he fled down the corridor, uttering hollow groans, and emitting a ghastly green light. Just, however, as he reached the top of the great oak staircase, a door was flung open. two little white-robed figures appeared, and a large pillow whizzed past his head! There was evidently no time to be lost, so, hastily adopting the Fourth Dimension of Space 137 as a means of escape, he vanished through the wainscoting, and the house became quite quiet.

On reaching a small secret chamber in the left wing, he leaned up against a moonbeam to recover his breath, and began to try and realize his position. Never, in a brilliant and uninterrupted career of three hundred years, had he been so grossly insulted. He thought of the Dowager Duchess, whom he had frightened into a fit as she stood before the glass in her lace and diamonds; of the four housemaids who had gone off into hysterics when he merely grinned at them through the curtains of one of the spare bedrooms; of the rector of the parish, whose candle he had blown out as he was coming late one night from the library, and who had been under the care of Sir William Gull ever since, a perfect martyr to nervous disorders; and of old Madame de Tremouillac, who, having wakened up one morning early and seen a skeleton seated in an arm-chair by the fire reading her diary, had been confined to her bed for six weeks with an attack of brain fever, and, on her recovery, had become reconciled to the Church, and broken off her connection with that notorious sceptic, Monsieur de Voltaire. He remembered the terrible night

when the wicked Lord Canterville was found choking in his dressing room, with the knave of diamonds halfway down his throat, and confessed, just before he died, that he had cheated Charles James Fox out of £50,000 at Crockford's by means of that very card, and swore that the ghost had made him swallow it. All his great achievements came back to him again, from the butler who had shot himself in the pantry because he had seen a green hand tapping at the window pane, to the beautiful Lady Stutfield, who was always obliged to wear a black velvet band round her throat to hide the mark of five fingers burnt upon her white skin, and who drowned herself at last in the carp pond at the end of the King's Walk. With the enthusiastic egotism of the true artist he went over his most celebrated performances, and smiled bitterly to himself as he recalled to mind his last appearance as "Red Reuben, or the Strangled Babe," his *début* as "Gaunt Gibeon, the Blood-sucker of Bexley Moor," and the *furore* he had excited one lovely June evening by merely playing ninepins with his own bones upon the lawn-tennis ground. And after all this, some wretched modern Americans were to come and offer him the Rising Sun Lubricator, and throw pillows at his head! It was quite unbearable. Besides, no ghosts in history had ever been treated in this manner. Accordingly, he determined to have vengeance, and remained till daylight in an attitude of deep thought.

III

The next morning when the Otis family met at breakfast, they discussed the ghost at some length. The United States Minister was naturally a little annoyed to find that his present had not been accepted. "I have no wish," he said, "to do the ghost any personal injury, and I must say that, considering the length of time he has been in the house, I don't think it is at all polite to throw pillows at him"—a very just remark, at which, I am sorry to say, the twins burst into shouts of laughter. "Upon the other hand," he continued, "if he really declines to use the Rising Sun Lubricator, we shall have to take his chains from him. It would be quite impossible to sleep, with such a noise going on outside the bedrooms."

For the rest of the week, however, they were undisturbed, the only thing that excited any attention being the continual renewal of the bloodstain on the library floor. This certainly was very strange, as the door was always locked at night by Mr. Otis, and the windows kept closely barred. The chameleon-like color, also, of the stain excited a good deal of comment. Some mornings it was a dull (almost Indian) red, then it would be vermilion, then a rich purple, and once when they came down for family prayers, according to the simple rites of the Free American Reformed Episcopalian Church, they found it a bright emerald green. These kaleidoscopic changes naturally amused the party very much, and bets on the subject were freely made every evening. The only person who did not enter into the joke was little Virginia, who, for some unexplained reason, was always a good deal distressed at the sight of the bloodstain, and very nearly cried the morning it was emerald green.

The second appearance of the ghost was on Sunday night. Shortly after they had gone to bed they were suddenly alarmed by a fearful crash in the hall. Rushing downstairs, they found that a large suit of old armor had become detached from its stand and had fallen on the stone floor, while, seated in a high-backed chair, was the Canterville ghost, rubbing his knees with an expression of acute agony on his face.

The twins, having brought their pea shooters with them, at once discharged two pellets on him, with that accuracy of aim which can only be attained by long and careful practice on a writing master, while the United States Minister covered him with his revolver, and called upon him, in accordance with Californian etiquette, to hold up his hands! The ghost started up with a wild shriek of rage, and swept through them like a mist, extinguishing Washington Otis's candle as he passed, and so leaving them all in total darkness. On reaching the top of the staircase he recovered himself, and determined to give his celebrated peals of demoniac laughter. This he had on more than one occasion found extremely useful. It was said to have turned Lord Raker's wig gray in a single night, and had certainly made three of Lady Canterville's French governesses give warning before their month was up. He accordingly laughed his most horrible laugh, till the old vaulted roof rang and rang again, but hardly had the fearful echo died away when a door opened, and Mrs. Otis came out in a light blue dressing gown. "I am afraid you are far from well," she said, "and have brought you a bottle of Dr. Dobell's tincture. If it is indi-

140

gestion, you will find it a most excellent remedy." The ghost glared at her in fury, and began at once to make preparations for turning himself into a large black dog, an accomplishment for which he was justly renowned, and to which the family doctor always attributed the permanent idiocy of Lord Canterville's uncle, the Hon. Thomas Horton. The sound of approaching footsteps, however, made him hesitate in his fell purpose, so he contented himself with becoming faintly phosphorescent and vanished with a deep churchyard groan, just as the twins had come up to him.

On reaching his room he entirely broke down, and became a prey to the most violent agitation. The vulgarity of the twins, and the gross materialism of Mrs. Otis were naturally extremely annoying, but what really distressed him most was that he had been unable to wear the suit of mail. He had hoped that even modern Americans would be thrilled by the sight of a Specter In Armor, if for no more sensible reason, at least out of respect for their national poet, Longfellow, over whose graceful and attractive poetry he himself had whiled away many a weary hour when the Cantervilles were up in town. Besides, it was his own suit. He had worn it with great success at the Kenilworth tournament, and had been highly complimented on it by no less a person than the Virgin Queen herself. Yet when he had put it on, he had been completely overpowered by the weight of the huge breastplate and steel casque, and had fallen heavily on the stone pavement, barking both his knees severely, and bruising the knuckles of his right hand.

For some days after this he was extremely ill, and hardly stirred out of his room at all, except to keep the bloodstain in proper repair. However, by taking great care of himself, he recovered, and resolved to make a third attempt to frighten the United States Minister and his family. He selected Friday, the 17th of August, for his appearance, and spent most of that day in looking over his wardrobe, ultimately deciding in favor of a large slouched hat with a red feather, a winding sheet frilled at the wrists and neck, and a rusty dagger. Towards evening a violent storm of rain came on, and the wind was so high that all the windows and doors in the old house shook and rattled. In fact, it was just such weather as he loved. His plan of action was this. He was to make his way quietly to Washington Otis's room, gibber at him from the foot of the bed, and stab himself three times in the throat to the sound of slow music. He bore Washington a special grudge, being quite aware that it was he who was in the habit of removing the famous Canterville bloodstain, by means of Pinkerton's Paragon Detergent. Having reduced the reckless and foolhardy youth to a condition of abject terror, he was then to proceed to the room occupied by the United States Minister and his wife, and there to place a clammy hand on Mrs. Otis's forehead, while he hissed into her trembling husband's ear the awful secrets of the charnel house. With regard to little Virginia, he had not quite made up his mind. She had never insulted him in any way, and was pretty and gentle. A few hollow groans from the wardrobe, he thought, would be more than sufficient, or, if that failed to wake her, he might grabble at the counterpane with palsy-twitching fingers. As for the twins, he was quite determined to teach them a lesson. The first thing to be done was, of course, to sit upon their chests, so as to produce the stifling sensation of nightmare. Then, as their beds were quite close to each other, to stand between them in the form of a green, icy-cold corpse, till they became paralyzed with fear, and finally, to throw off the wind-

ing-sheet and crawl round the room, with white bleached bones and one rolling eyeball in the character of "Dumb Daniel, or the Suicide's Skeleton," a *rôle* in which he had on more than one occasion produced a great effect, and which he considered quite equal to his famous part of "Martin the Maniac, or the Masked Mystery."

At half-past ten he heard the family going to bed. For some time he was disturbed by wild shrieks of laughter from the twins, who, with the light-hearted gaiety of school-boys, were evidently amusing themselves before they retired to rest, but at a quarter-past eleven all was still, and, as midnight sounded, he sallied forth. The owl beat against the window panes, the raven croaked from the old yew tree, and the wind wandered moaning round the house like a lost soul; but the Otis family slept unconscious of their doom, and high above the rain and storm he could hear the steady snoring of the Minister for the United States. He stepped stealthily out of the wainscoting, with an evil smile on his cruel, wrinkled mouth, and the moon hid her face in a cloud as he stole past the great oriel window, where his own arms and those of his murdered wife were blazoned in azure and gold. On and on he glided, like an evil shadow, the very darkness seeming to loathe him as he passed. Once he thought he heard something call, and stopped; but it was only the baying of a dog from the Red Farm, and he went on, muttering strange sixteenth-century curses, and ever and anon brandishing the rusty dagger in the midnight air. Finally he reached the corner of the passage that led to luckless Washington's room. For a moment he paused there, the wind blowing his long gray locks about his head, and twisting into grotesque and fantastic folds the nameless horror of the dead man's shroud. Then the clock struck the quarter, and he felt the time was come. He chuckled to himself, and turned the corner, but no sooner had he done so than, with a piteous wail of terror, he fell back, and hid his blanched face in his long, bony hands. Right in front of him was standing a horrible specter, motionless as a carven image, and monstrous as a madman's dream! Its head was bald and burnished; its face round, and fat, and white; and hideous laughter seemed to have writhed its features into an eternal grin. From the eyes streamed rays of scarlet light, the mouth was a wide well of fire, and a hideous garment, like to his own, swathed with

its silent snows the Titan form. On its breast was a placard with strange writing in antique characters, some scroll of shame it seemed, some record of wild sins, some awful calendar of crime, and, with its right hand, it bore aloft a falchion of gleaming steel.

Never having seen a ghost before, he naturally was terribly frightened, and, after a second hasty glance at the awful phantom, he fled back to his room, tripping up in his long winding-sheet as he sped down the corridor, and finally dropping the rusty dagger into the Minister's jackboots, where it was found in the morning by the butler. Once in the privacy of his own apartment, he flung himself down on a small pallet bed, and hid his face under the clothes. After a time, however, the grave old Canterville spirit asserted itself, and he determined to go and speak to the other ghost as soon as it was daylight. Accordingly, just as the dawn was touching the hills with silver, he returned toward the spot where he had first laid eyes on the grisly phantom, feeling that, after all, two ghosts were better than one, and that, by the aid of his new friend, he might safely grapple with the twins. On reaching the spot, however, a terrible sight met his gaze. Something   143 had evidently happened to the specter, for the light had entirely faded from its hollow eyes, the gleaming falchion had fallen from its hand, and it was leaning up against the wall in a strained and uncomfortable attitude. He rushed forward and seized it in his arms, when, to his horror, the head slipped off and rolled on the floor, the body assumed a recumbent posture, and he found himself clasping a white dimity bed-curtain, with a sweeping brush, a kitchen cleaver, and a hollow turnip lying at his feet! Unable to understand this curious transformation, he clutched the placard with feverish haste, and there, in the grey morning light, he read these fearful words:

YE OTIS GHOSTE.
Ye Onlie True and Originale Spook.
Beware of Ye Imitationes.
All others are Counterfeite.

The whole thing flashed across him. He had been tricked, foiled, and outwitted! The old Canterville look came into his eyes; he ground his toothless gums together; and, raising his withered hands high above his head, swore, according to the picturesque phraseology of the antique school, that when Chanticleer had sounded twice his merry horn, deeds of blood would be wrought, and Murder walk abroad with silent feet.

Hardly had he finished this awful oath when, from the red-tiled roof of a distant homestead, a cock crew. He laughed a long, low, bitter laugh, and waited. Hour after hour he waited, but the cock, for some strange reason, did not crow again. Finally, at half-past seven, the arrival of the housemaids made him give up his fearful vigil, and he stalked back to his room, thinking of his vain hope and baffled purpose. There he consulted several books of ancient chivalry, of which he was exceedingly fond, and found that, on every occasion on which his oath had been used, Chanticleer had always crowed a second time. "Perdition seize the naughty fowl," he muttered. "I have seen the day when, with my stout spear, I would have run him through the gorge, and made him crow for me an 'twere in death!" He then retired to a comfortable lead coffin, and stayed there till evening.

IV

The next day the ghost was very weak and tired. The terrible excitement of the last four weeks was beginning to have its effect. His nerves were completely shattered, and he started at the slightest noise. For

144

five days he kept his room, and at last made up his mind to give up the point of the bloodstain on the library floor. If the Otis family did not want it, they clearly did not deserve it. They were evidently people on a low, material plane of existence, and quite incapable of appreciating the symbolic value of sensuous phenomena. The question of phantasmic apparitions, and the development of astral bodies, was of course quite a different matter, and really not under his control. It was his solemn duty to appear in the corridor once a week, and to gibber from the large oriel window on the first and third Wednesday in every month, and he did not see how he could honorably escape from his obligations. It is quite true that his life had been very evil, but, upon the other hand, he was most conscientious in all things connected with the supernatural. For the next three Saturdays, accordingly, he traversed the corridor as usual between midnight and three o'clock, taking every possible precaution against being either heard or seen. He removed his boots, trod as lightly as possible on the old worm-eaten boards, wore a large black velvet cloak, and was careful to use the Rising Sun Lubricator for oiling his chains. I am bound to acknowledge that it was with a good deal of difficulty that he brought himself to adopt this last mode of protection. However, one night, while the family were at dinner, he slipped into Mr. Otis's bedroom and carried off the bottle. He felt a little humiliated at first but afterward was sensible enough to see that there was a great deal to be said for the invention, and, to a certain degree, it served his purpose. Still, in spite of everything, he was not left unmolested. Strings were continually being stretched across the corridor, over which he tripped in the dark, and on one occasion, while dressed for the part of "Black Isaac, or the Huntsman of Hogley Woods," he met with a severe fall, through treading on a butter slide, which the twins had constructed from the entrance of the Tapestry Chamber to the top of the oak staircase. This last insult so enraged him that he resolved to make one final effort to assert his dignity and social position, and determined to visit the insolent young Etonians the next night in his celebrated character of "Reckless Rupert, or the Headless Earl."

He had not appeared in this disguise for more than seventy years; in fact, not since he had so frightened pretty Lady Barbara Modish by means of it that she suddenly broke off her engagement with the present Lord Canterville's grandfather, and ran away to Gretna Green with handsome Jack Castleton, declaring that nothing in the world would induce her to marry into a family that allowed such a horrible phantom to walk up and down the terrace at twilight. Poor Jack was afterwards shot in a duel by Lord Canterville on Wandsworth Common, and Lady Barbara died of a broken heart at Tunbridge Wells before the year was out, so, in every way, it had been a great success. It was, however, an extremely difficult "make up," if I may use such a theatrical expression in connection with one of the greatest mysteries of the supernatural, or, to employ a more scientific term, the higher-natural world, and it took him fully three hours to make his preparations. At last everything was ready, and he was very pleased with his appearance. The big leather riding boots that went with the dress were just a little too large for him, and he could only find one of the two horse pistols, but, on the whole, he was quite satisfied, and at a quarter-past one he glided out of the wainscoting and crept down the corridor. On reaching the room occupied by the twins, which I should

146

mention was called the Blue Bed Chamber, on account of the color of its hangings, he found the door just ajar. Wishing to make an effective entrance, he flung it wide open, when a heavy jug of water fell right down on him, wetting him to the skin and just missing his left shoulder by a couple of inches. At the same moment he heard stifled shrieks of laughter proceeding from the four-poster bed. The shock to his nervous system was so great that he fled back to his room as hard as he could go, and the next day he was laid up with a severe cold. The only thing that at all consoled him in the whole affair was the fact that he had not brought his head with him, for, had he done so, the consequences might have been very serious.

He now gave up all hope of ever frightening this rude American family, and contented himself, as a rule, with creeping about the passages in list slippers, with a thick red muffler round his throat for fear of draughts, and a small arquebus, in case he should be attacked by the twins. The final blow he received occurred on the 19th of September. He had gone downstairs to the great entrance hall, feeling sure that there, at any rate, he would be quite unmolested, and was amusing himself by making satirical remarks on the large Saroni photographs of the United States Minister and his wife, which had now taken the place of the Canterville family pictures. He was simply but neatly clad in a long shroud, spotted with churchyard mold, had tied up his jaw with a strip of yellow linen, and carried a small lantern and a sexton's spade. In fact, he was dressed for the character of "Jonas the Graveless, or the Corpse Snatcher of Chertsey Barn," one of his most remarkable impersonations, and one which the Cantervilles had every reason to remember, as it was the real origin of their quarrel with their neighbor, Lord Rufford. It was about a quarter-past two o'clock in the morning, and, as far as he could ascertain, no one was stirring. As he was strolling toward the library, however, to see if there were any traces left of the bloodstain, suddenly there leaped out on him from a dark corner two figures, who waved their arms wildly above their heads, and shrieked out "Boo!" in his ear.

Seized with a panic, which, under the circumstances, was only natural, he rushed for the staircase, but found Washington Otis waiting for him there with the big garden syringe; and being thus hemmed in by his enemies on every side, and driven almost to bay, he vanished into the great iron stove, which, fortunately for him, was not lit, and had to make his way home through the flues and chimneys, arriving at his own room in a terrible state of dirt, disorder, and despair.

After this he was not seen again on any nocturnal expedition. The twins lay in wait for him on several occasions, and strewed the passages with nutshells every night to the great annoyance of their parents and the servants, but it was of no avail. It was quite evident that his feelings were so wounded that he would not appear. Mr. Otis consequently resumed his great work on the history of the Democratic Party, on which he had been engaged for some years; Mrs. Otis organized a wonderful clambake, which amazed the whole county; the boys took to lacrosse, euchre, poker, and other American national games; and Virginia rode about the lanes on her pony, accompanied by the young Duke of Cheshire, who had come to spend the last week of his holidays at Canterville Chase. It was generally assumed that the ghost had gone away, and, in fact, Mr. Otis wrote a letter to that effect to Lord Canterville, who, in reply, expressed his great pleasure at the news, and sent his best congratulations to the Minister's worthy wife.

147

The Otises, however, were deceived, for the ghost was still in the house, and though now almost an invalid, was by no means ready to let matters rest, particularly as he heard that among the guests was the young Duke of Cheshire, whose granduncle, Lord Francis Stilton, had once bet a hundred guineas with Colonel Carbury that he would play dice with the Canterville ghost, and was found the next morning lying on the floor of the card room in such a helpless paralytic state that though he lived on to a great age, he was never able to say anything again but "Double Sixes." The story was well known at the time, though, of course, out of respect to the feelings of the two noble families, every attempt was made to hush it up; and a full account of all the circumstances connected with it will be found in the third volume of Lord Tattle's *Recollections of the Prince Regent and His Friends*. The ghost, then, was naturally very anxious to show that he had not lost his influence over the Stiltons, with whom, indeed, he was distantly connected, his own first cousin having been married *en secondes noces* to the Sieur de Bulkeley, from whom, as everyone knows, the Dukes of Cheshire are lineally descended. Accordingly, he made arrangements for appearing to Virginia's little lover in his celebrated impersonation of "The Vampire Monk, or the Bloodless Benedictine," a performance so horrible that when old Lady Startup saw it, which she did on one fatal New Year's Eve, in the year 1764, she went off into the most piercing shrieks, which culminated in violent apoplexy, and died in three days, after disinheriting the Cantervilles, who were her nearest relations, and leaving all her money to her London apothecary. At the last moment, however, his terror of the twins prevented his leaving his room, and the little Duke slept in peace under the great feathered canopy in the Royal Bedchamber, and dreamed of Virginia.

V

A few days after this, Virginia and her curly haired cavalier went out riding in Brockley meadows, where she tore her habit so badly in getting through a hedge that, on her return home, she made up her mind to go up by the back staircase so as not to be seen. As she was running past the Tapestry Chamber, the door of which happened to be open, she fancied she saw someone inside, and thinking it was her mother's maid, who sometimes used to bring her work there, looked in to ask her to mend her habit. To her immense surprise, however, it was the Canterville Ghost himself! He was sitting by the window, watching the ruined gold of the yellowing trees fly through the air, and the red leaves dancing madly down the long avenue. His head was leaning on his hand, and his whole attitude was one of extreme depression. Indeed, so forlorn, and so much out of repair did he look, that little Virginia, whose first idea had been to run away and lock herself in her room, was filled with pity, and determined to try and comfort him. So light was her footfall, and so deep his melancholy, that he was not aware of her presence till she spoke to him.

"I am so sorry for you," she said, "but my brothers are going back to Eton tomorrow, and then, if you behave yourself, no one will annoy you."

"It is absurd asking me to behave myself," he answered, looking round in astonishment at the pretty little girl who had ventured to address him, "quite absurd. I must rattle my chains and groan through keyholes, and walk about at night, if that is what you mean. It is my only reason for existing."

"It is no reason at all for existing, and you know you have been very wicked. Mrs. Umney told us, the first day we arrived here, that you had killed your wife."

"Well, I quite admit it," said the ghost petulantly, "but it was a purely family matter, and concerned no one else."

"It is very wrong to kill any one," said Virginia, who at times had a sweet Puritan gravity, caught from some old New England ancestor.

"Oh, I hate the cheap severity of abstract ethics! My wife was very plain, never had my ruffs properly starched, and knew nothing about cookery. Why, there was a buck I had shot in Hogley Woods, a magnificent pricket, and do you know how she had it sent up to table? However, it is no matter now, for it is all over, and I don't think it was very nice of her brothers to starve me to death, though I did kill her."

"Starve you to death? Oh, Mr. Ghost, I mean Sir Simon, are you hungry? I have a sandwich in my case. Would you like it?"

"No, thank you, I never eat anything now; but it is very kind of you, all the same, and you are much nicer than the rest of your horrid, rude, vulgar, dishonest family."

"Stop!" cried Virginia, stamping her foot, "it is you who are rude, and horrid, and vulgar, and as for dishonesty, you know you stole the paints out of my box to try and furbish up that ridiculous bloodstain in the library. First you took all my reds, including the vermilion, and I couldn't do any more sunsets, then you took the emerald green and the chrome yellow, and finally I had nothing left but indigo and Chinese white, and could only do moonlight scenes, which are always depressing to look at, and not at all easy to paint. I never told on you, though I was very much annoyed, and it was most ridiculous, the whole thing; for who ever heard of emerald green blood?"

"Well, really," said the ghost rather meekly, "what was I to do? It is a very difficult thing to get real blood nowadays, and, as your brother began it all with his Paragon Detergent, I certainly saw no reason why I should not have your paints. As for color, that is always a matter of taste: the Cantervilles have blue blood, for instance, the very bluest in England; but I know you Americans don't care for things of this kind."

"You know nothing about it, and the best thing you can do is to emigrate and improve your mind. My father will be only too happy to give you a free passage, and though there is a heavy duty on spirits of every kind there will be no difficulty about the Custom House, as the officers are all Democrats. Once in New York, you are sure to be a great success. I know lots of people there who would give a hundred thousand dollars to have a grandfather, and much more than that to have a family ghost!"

"I don't think I should like America."

"I suppose because we have no ruins and no curiosities," said Virginia satirically.

"No ruins! No curiosities!" answered the ghost, "You have your navy and your manners."

"Good evening; I will go and ask papa to get the twins an extra week's holiday."

"Please don't go, Miss Virginia," he cried; "I am so lonely and so unhappy, and I really don't know what to do. I want to go to sleep and I cannot."

"That's quite absurd! You have merely to go to bed and blow out the candle. It is very difficult sometimes to keep awake, especially at church, but there is no difficulty at all about sleeping. Why, even babies know how to do that, and they are not very clever."

"I have not slept for three hundred years," he said sadly, and Virginia's beautiful blue eyes opened in wonder. "For three hundred years I have not slept, and I am so tired."

Virginia grew quite grave, and her little lips trembled like rose leaves. She came toward him, and kneeling down at his side looked up into his old withered face.

"Poor, poor Ghost," she murmured; "have you no place where you can sleep?"

"Far away beyond the pine woods," he answered, in a low dreamy voice, "there is a little garden. There the grass grows long and deep, there are the great white stars of the hemlock flower, there the nightingale sings all night long. All night long he sings, and the cold, crystal moon looks down, and the yew tree spreads out its giant arms over the sleepers."

Virginia's eyes grew dim with tears, and she hid her face in her hands.

"You mean the Garden of Death," she whispered.

"Yes, Death. Death must be so beautiful. To lie in the soft brown earth, with the grasses waving over one's head, and listen to silence. To have no yesterday, and no tomorrow. To forget time, to forgive life, to be at peace. You can help me. You can open for me the portals of Death's house, for Love is always with you, and Love is stronger than Death is."

Virginia trembled, a cold shudder ran through her, and for a few moments there was silence. She felt as if she was in a terrible dream.

Then the ghost spoke again, and his voice sounded like the sighing of the wind.

"Have you ever read the old prophecy on the library window?"

"Oh, often," cried the little girl, looking up: "I know it quite well. It is painted in curious black letters, and it is difficult to read. There are only six lines:

> When a golden girl can win
> Prayer from out the lips of sin,
> When the barren almond bears,
> And a little child gives away its
>   tears,
> Then shall all the house be still
> And peace come to Canterville.

But I don't know what they mean."

"They mean," he said sadly, "that you must weep for me for my sins, because I have no tears, and pray with me for my soul, because I have no faith, and then, if you have always been sweet, and good, and gentle, the Angel of Death will have mercy on me. You will see fearful shapes in darkness, and wicked voices will whisper in your ear, but

151

they will not harm you, for against the purity of a little child the powers of Hell cannot prevail."

Virginia made no answer, and the ghost wrung his hands in wild despair as he looked down at her bowed golden head. Suddenly she stood up, very pale, and with a strange light in her eyes. "I am not afraid," she said firmly, "and I will ask the Angel to have mercy on you."

He rose from his seat with a faint cry of joy, and taking her hand bent over it with old-fashioned grace and kissed it. His fingers were as cold as ice, and his lips burned like fire, but Virginia did not falter as he led her across the dusky room. On the faded green tapestry were embroidered little huntsmen. They blew their tasseled horns and with their tiny hands waved to her to go back. "Go back, Virginia," they cried, "go back!" but the ghost clutched her hand more tightly, and she shut her eyes against them. Horrible animals with lizard tails and goggle eyes blinked at her from the carven chimneypiece and murmured "Beware! little Virginia, beware! We may never see you again," but the ghost glided on more swiftly, and Virginia did not listen. When they reached the end of the room he stopped, and muttered some words

she could not understand. She opened her eyes and saw the wall slowly fading away like a mist and a great black cavern in front of her. A bitter cold wind swept round them and she felt something pulling at her dress. "Quick, quick," cried the ghost, "or it will be too late," and, in a moment, the wainscoting had closed behind them and the Tapestry Chamber was empty.

VI

About ten minutes later the bell rang for tea, and, as Virginia did not come down, Mrs. Otis sent up one of the footmen to tell her. After a little time he returned and said that he could not find Miss Virginia anywhere. As she was in the habit of going out to the garden every evening to get flowers for the dinner-table, Mrs. Otis was not at all alarmed at first, but when six o'clock struck, and Virginia did not appear, she became really agitated and sent the boys out to look for her, while she herself and Mr. Otis searched every room in the house. At half-past six the boys came back and said that they could find no trace of their sister anywhere. They were all now in the greatest state of excitement and did not know what to do, when Mr. Otis suddenly remembered that, some few days before, he had given a band of gypsies permission to camp in the park. He accordingly at once set off for Black-ell Hollow, where he knew they were, accompanied by his eldest son and two of the farm servants. The little Duke of Cheshire, who was perfectly frantic with anxiety, begged hard to be allowed to go too, but Mr. Otis would not allow him, as he was afraid there might be a scuffle. On arriving at the spot, however, he found that the gypsies had gone, and it was evident that their departure had been rather sudden, as the fire was still burning and some plates were lying on the grass. Having sent off Washington and the two men to scour the district, he ran home and despatched telegrams to all the police inspectors in the county, telling them to look out for a little girl who had been kidnapped by tramps or gypsies. He then ordered his horse to be brought round, and, after insisting on his wife and the three boys sitting down to dinner, rode off down the Ascot Road with a groom. He had hardly, however, gone a couple of miles when he heard somebody galloping after him, and, looking round, saw the little Duke coming up on his pony, with his face very flushed and no hat. "I'm awfully sorry, Mr. Otis," gasped out the boy, "but I can't eat any dinner as

long as Virginia is lost. Please don't be angry with me; if you had let us be engaged last year there would never have been all this trouble. You won't send me back, will you? I can't go! I won't go!"

The Minister could not help smiling at the handsome young scapegrace, and was a good deal touched at his devotion to Virginia, so leaning down from his horse he patted him kindly on the shoulders, and said, "Well, Cecil, if you won't go back I suppose you must come with me, but I must get you a hat at Ascot."

"Oh, bother my hat! I want Virginia!" cried the little Duke, laughing, and they galloped on to the railway station. There Mr. Otis inquired of the station master if any one answering the description of Virginia had been seen on the platform, but could get no news of her. The station master, however, wired up and down the line and assured him that a strict watch would be kept for her, and, after having bought a hat for the little Duke from a linen draper, who was just putting up his shutters, Mr. Otis rode off to Bexley, a village about four miles away, which he was told was a well-known haunt of the gypsies, as there was a large common next to it. Here they roused up the

153

rural policeman, but could get no information from him, and, after riding all over the common, they turned their horses' heads homeward, and reached the Chase about eleven o'clock, dead tired and almost heartbroken. They found Washington and the twins waiting for them at the gatehouse with lanterns, as the avenue was very dark. Not the slightest trace of Virginia had been discovered. The gypsies had been caught on Brockley meadows, but she was not with them, and they had explained their sudden departure by saying that they had mistaken the date of Chorton Fair and had gone off in a hurry for fear they might be late. Indeed, they had been quite distressed at hearing of Virginia's disappearance, as they were very grateful to Mr. Otis for having allowed them to camp in his park, and four of their number had stayed behind to help in the search. The carp pond had been dragged, and the whole Chase thoroughly gone over, but without any result. It was evident that, for that night at any rate, Virginia was lost to them; and it was in a state of the deepest depression that Mr. Otis and the boys walked up to the house, the groom following behind with the two horses and the pony. In the hall they found a group of frightened servants, and lying on a sofa in the library was poor Mrs. Otis, almost out of her mind with terror and anxiety, and having her forehead bathed with eau-de-cologne by the old housekeeper. Mr. Otis at once insisted on her having something to eat and ordered up supper for the whole party. It was a melancholy meal, as hardly any one spoke, and even the twins were awestruck and subdued, as they were very fond of their sister. When they had finished, Mr. Otis, in spite of the entreaties of the little Duke, ordered them all to bed, saying that nothing more could be done that night, and that he would telegraph in the morning to Scotland Yard for some detectives to be sent down immediately. Just as they were passing out of the dining room, midnight began to boom from the clock tower, and when the last stroke sounded they heard a crash and a sudden shrill cry; a dreadful peal of thunder shook the house, a strain of unearthly music floated through the air, a panel at the top of the staircase flew back with a loud noise, and out on the landing, looking very pale and white, with a little casket in her hand, stepped Virginia. In a moment they had all rushed up to her. Mrs. Otis clasped her passionately in her arms, the Duke smothered her with violent kisses, and the twins executed a wild war dance round the group.

"Good heavens! child where have you been?" said Mr. Otis, rather angrily, thinking that she had been playing some foolish trick on them. "Cecil and I have been riding all over the country looking for you, and your mother has been frightened to death. You must never play these practical jokes any more."

"Except on the ghost! Except on the ghost!" shrieked the twins, as they capered about.

"My own darling, thank God you are found; you must never leave my side again," murmured Mrs. Otis, as she kissed the trembling child, and smoothed the tangled gold of her hair.

"Papa," said Virginia quietly, "I have been with the ghost. He is dead, and you must come and see him. He had been very wicked, but he was really sorry for all that he had done, and he gave me this box of beautiful jewels before he died."

The whole family gazed at her in mute amazement, but she was quite grave and serious; and, turning round, she led them through the opening in the wainscoting down a narrow secret corridor, Washington following with a lighted candle which he had caught up from the table. Finally they came to a great oak door, studded with rusty nails. When Virginia touched it, it swung back on its heavy hinges, and they found themselves in a little low room, with a vaulted ceiling, and one tiny grated window. Imbedded in the wall was a huge iron ring, and chained to it was a gaunt skeleton that was stretched out at full length on the stone floor, and seemed to be trying to grasp with its long fleshless fingers an old-fashioned trencher and ewer that were placed just out of its reach. The jug had evidently been once filled with water, as it was covered inside with green mold. There was nothing on the trencher but a pile of dust. Virginia knelt down beside the skeleton, and, folding her little hands together, began to pray silently, while the rest of the party looked on in wonder at the terrible tragedy whose secret was now disclosed to them.

"Hallo!" suddenly exclaimed one of the twins, who had been looking out of the window to try and discover in what wing of the house the room was situated. "Hallo! the old withered almond tree has blossomed. I can see the flowers quite plainly in the moonlight."

"God has forgiven him," said Vir-

155

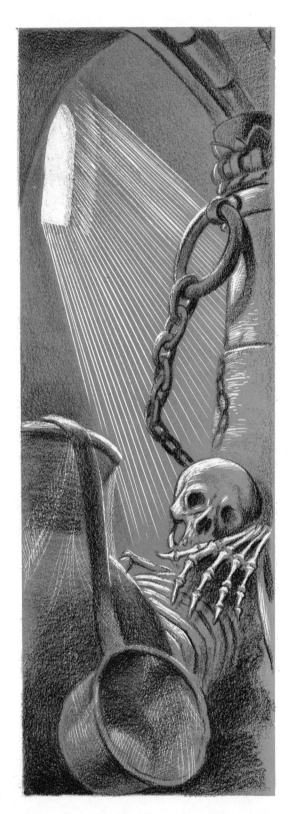

ginia gravely, as she rose to her feet, and a beautiful light seemed to illumine her face.

"What an angel you are!" cried the young Duke, and he put his arm round her neck and kissed her.

VII

Four days after these curious incidents, a funeral started from Canterville Chase at about eleven o'clock at night. The hearse was drawn by eight black horses, each of which carried on its head a great tuft of nodding ostrich plumes, and the leaden coffin was covered by a rich purple pall, on which was embroidered in gold the Canterville coat of arms. By the side of the hearse and the coaches walked the servants with lighted torches, and the whole procession was wonderfully impressive. Lord Canterville was the chief mourner, having come up specially from Wales to attend the funeral, and sat in the first carriage along with little Virginia. Then came the United States Minister and his wife, then Washington and the three boys, and in the last carriage was Mrs. Umney. It was generally felt that, as she had been frightened by the ghost for more than fifty years of her life, she had a right to see the last of him. A deep grave had been dug in the corner of the churchyard, just under the old yew-tree, and the service was read in the most impressive manner by the Reverend Augustus Dampier. When the ceremony was over, the servants, according to an old custom observed in the Canterville family, extinguished their torches, and, as the coffin was being lowered into the grave, Virginia stepped forward and laid on it a large cross made of white and pink almond-blossoms. As she did so, the moon came out from behind a cloud, and flooded with its silent silver the little churchyard, and from a distant copse a nightingale began to sing. She thought of the ghost's description of the Garden of Death, her eyes became dim with tears, and she hardly spoke a word during the drive home.

The next morning, before Lord Canterville went up to town, Mr. Otis had an interview with him on the subject of the jewels the ghost had given to Virginia. They were perfectly magnificent, especially a certain ruby necklace with old Venetian setting, which was really a superb specimen of sixteenth-century work, and their value was so great that Mr. Otis felt considerable scruples about allowing his daughter to accept them.

"My lord," he said, "I know that in this country mortmain is held to apply to trinkets as well as to land, and it is quite clear to me that these jewels are, or should be, heirlooms in your family. I must beg you, accordingly, to take them to London with you and to regard them simply as a portion of your property which has been restored to you under certain strange conditions. As for my daughter, she is merely a child, and has yet, I am glad to say, but little interest in such appurtenances of idle luxury. I am also informed by Mrs. Otis, who, I may say, is no mean authority upon Art—having had the privilege of spending several winters in Boston when she was a girl—that these gems are of great monetary worth, and if offered for sale would fetch a tall price. Under these circumstances, Lord Canterville, I feel sure that you will recognize how impossible it would be for me to allow them to remain in the possession of any member of my family; and, indeed, all such vain gauds and toys, however suitable or necessary to the dignity of the British aristocracy, would be completely out of place among those who have been brought up on the severe and I believe immortal principles of republican simplicity. Perhaps I should mention that Virginia is very anxious that you should allow her to retain the box as a memento of your unfortunate but misguided ancestor. As it is extremely old, and consequently a good deal out of repair, you may perhaps think fit to comply with her request. For my own part, I confess I am a good deal surprised to find a child of mine expressing sympathy with medievalism in any form, and can only account for it by the fact that Virginia was born in one of your London suburbs shortly after Mrs. Otis had returned from a trip to Athens.''

Lord Canterville listened very gravely to the worthy Minister's speech, pulling his gray moustache now and then to hide an involuntary smile, and when Mr. Otis had ended, he shook him cordially by the hand and said, ''My dear sir, your charming little daughter rendered my unlucky ancestor, Sir Simon, a very important service, and I and my family are much indebted to her for her marvelous courage and pluck. The jewels are clearly hers and, egad, I believe that if I were heartless enough to take them from her, the wicked old fellow would be out of his grave in a fortnight, leading me the devil of a life. As for their being heirlooms, nothing is an heirloom that is not so mentioned in a will or legal document, and the existence of these jewels has been quite unknown. I assure you I have no more claim on them than your butler, and when Miss Virginia grows up I daresay she will be pleased to have pretty things to wear. Besides, you forget, Mr. Otis, that you took the furniture and the ghost at a valuation, and anything that belonged to the ghost passed at once into your possession, as, whatever activity Sir Simon may have shown in the corridor at night, in point of law he was really dead, and you acquired his property by purchase.''

Mr. Otis was a good deal distressed at Lord Canterville's refusal, and begged him to reconsider his decision, but the good-natured peer was quite firm, and finally induced the Minister to allow his daughter to retain the present the ghost had given her, and when, in the spring of 1890, the young Duchess of Cheshire was presented at the Queen's first drawing room on the occasion of her marriage, her jewels were the universal theme of admiration. For Virginia received the coronet, which is the reward of all good little American girls, and was married to her boy-lover as soon as he came of age. They were both so charming and they loved each other so much, that every one was delighted at the match, except the old Marchioness of Dumbleton, who had tried to catch the Duke for one of her seven unmarried daughters, and had given no less than three expensive dinner parties for that purpose, and, strange to say, Mr. Otis himself. Mr. Otis was extremely fond of the young Duke personally, but, theoretically, he objected to titles and, to use his own words, "was not without apprehension lest, amid the enervating influences of a pleasure-loving aristocracy, the true principles of republican simplicity should be forgotten." His objections, however, were completely overruled, and I believe that when he walked up the aisle of St. George's, Hanover Square, with his daughter leaning on his arm, there was not a prouder man in the whole length and breadth of England.

The Duke and Duchess, after the honeymoon was over, went down to Canterville Chase, and on the day after their arrival they walked over in the afternoon to the lonely churchyard by the pine woods. There had been a great deal of difficulty at first about the inscription on Sir Simon's tombstone, but finally it had been decided to engrave on it simply the initials of the old gentleman's name, and the verse from the library window. The Duchess had brought with her some lovely roses, which she strewed upon the grave, and after they had stood by it for some time they strolled into the ruined chancel of the old abbey. There the Duchess sat down on a fallen pillar, while her husband lay at her feet smoking a cigarette and looking up at her beautiful eyes. Suddenly he threw his cigarette away, took hold of her hand, and said to her, "Virginia, a wife should have no secrets from her husband."

"Dear Cecil! I have no secrets from you."

"Yes, you have," he answered, smiling, "you have never told me what happened to you when you were locked up with the ghost."

"I have never told any one, Cecil," said Virginia gravely.

"I know that, but you can tell me."

"Please don't ask me, Cecil, I cannot tell you. Poor Sir Simon! I owe him a great deal. Yes, don't laugh, Cecil, I really do. He made me see what Life is, and what Death signifies, and why Love is stronger than both."

The Duke rose and kissed his wife lovingly.

"You can have your secret as long as I have your heart," he murmured.

"You always have had that, Cecil."

"And you will tell our children some day, won't you?"

Virginia blushed.

5  The Signalman

"Halloa! Below there!"

When he heard a voice thus calling to him, he was standing at the door of his box, with a flag in his hand, furled round its short pole. One would have thought, considering the nature of the ground, that he could not have doubted from what quarter the voice came; but instead of looking up to where I stood on the top of the steep cutting nearly over his head, he turned himself about and looked down the Line. There was something remarkable in his manner of doing so, though I could not have said for my life what. But I know it was remarkable enough to attract my notice, even though his figure was foreshortened and shadowed, down in the deep trench, and mine was high above him, so steeped in the glow of an angry sunset that I had shaded my eyes with my hand before I saw him at all.

"Halloa! Below!"

From looking down the Line, he turned himself about again and, raising his eyes, saw my figure high above him.

"Is there any path by which I can come down and speak to you?"

He looked up at me without replying, and I looked down at him without pressing him too soon with a repetition of my idle question. Just then there came a vague vibration in the earth and air, quickly changing into a violent pulsation, and an oncoming rush that caused me to start back, as though it had force to draw me down. When such vapor as rose to my height from this rapid train had passed me, and was skimming away over the landscape, I looked down again, and saw him refurling the flag he had shown while the train went by.

I repeated my inquiry. After a pause, during which he seemed to regard me with fixed attention, he motioned with his rolled-up flag toward a point on my level, some two or three hundred yards distant. I called down to him, "All right!" and made for that point. There, by dint of looking closely about me, I found a rough zigzag descending path notched out, which I followed.

The cutting was extremely deep,

and unusually precipitate. It was
made through a clammy stone that
became oozier and wetter as I went
down. For these reasons, I found
the way long enough to give me
time to recall a singular air of reluctance or compulsion with which
he had pointed out the path.

When I came down low enough
upon the zigzag descent to see him
again, I saw that he was standing between the rails on the way by which
the train had lately passed, in an
attitude as if he were waiting for
me to appear. He had his left hand
at his chin, and that left elbow
rested on his right hand, crossed
over his breast. His attitude was
one of such expectation and watchfulness that I stopped a moment,
wondering at it.

I resumed my downward way,
and stepping out upon the level of
the railroad, and drawing nearer to
him, saw that he was a dark, sallow
man, with a dark beard and rather
heavy eyebrows. His post was in as
solitary and dismal a place as ever
I saw. On either side, a dripping-
wet wall of jagged stone, excluding
all view but a strip of sky; the perspective one way only a crooked pro-
longation of this great dungeon; the
shorter perspective in the other direction terminating in a gloomy red
light, and the gloomier entrance to

a black tunnel, in whose massive architecture there was a barbarous, depressing, and forbidding air. So little sunlight ever found its way to this spot that it had an earthy, deadly smell; and so much cold wind rushed through it that it struck chill to me, as if I had left the natural world.

Before he stirred, I was near enough to him to have touched him. Not even then removing his eyes from mine, he stepped back one step, and lifted his hand.

This was a lonesome post to occupy (I said), and it had riveted my attention when I looked down from up yonder. A visitor was a rarity, I should suppose; not an unwelcome rarity, I hoped? In me, he merely saw a man who had been shut up within narrow limits all his life, and who, being at last set free, had a newly awakened interest in these great works. To such purpose I spoke to him; but I am far from sure of the terms I used; for, besides that I am not happy in opening any conversation, there was something in the man that daunted me.

He directed a most curious look toward the red light near the tunnel's mouth, and looked all about it, as if something were missing from it, and then looked at me.

That light was part of his charge? Was it not?

He answered in a low voice, "Don't you know it is?"

The monstrous thought came into my mind, as I perused the fixed eyes and the saturnine face, that this was a spirit, not a man. I have speculated since, whether there may have been infection in his mind.

In my turn I stepped back. But in making the action, I detected in his eyes some latent fear of me. This put the monstrous thought to flight.

"You look at me," I said, forcing a smile, "as if you had a dread of me."

"I was doubtful," he returned, "whether I had seen you before."

"Where?"

He pointed to the red light he had looked at.

"There?" I said.

Intently watchful of me, he replied (but without sound), "Yes."

"My good fellow, what should I do there? However, be that as it may, I never was there, you may swear."

"I think I may," he rejoined. "Yes; I am sure I may."

His manner cleared, like my own. He replied to my remarks with readiness, and in well-chosen words. Had he much to do there? Yes; that was to say, he had enough responsibility to bear; but exactness and watchfulness were what was required of him, and of actual work—manual labor—he had next to none. To change that signal, to trim those lights, and to turn this iron handle now and then, was all he had to do under that head. Regarding those many long and lonely hours of which I seemed to make so much, he could only say that the routine of his life had shaped itself into that form, and he had grown used to it. He had taught himself a language down here—if only to know it by sight, and to have formed his own crude ideas of its pronunciation, could be called learning it. He had also worked at fractions and decimals, and tried a little algebra; but he was, and had been as a boy, a poor hand at figures. Was it necessary for him when on duty always to remain in that channel of damp air, and could he never rise into the sunshine from between those high stone walls? Why, that depended upon time and circumstances. Under some conditions there would be less upon the Line than under others, and the same held good as to certain hours of the day and night. In bright weather, he did choose occasions for getting a little above these lower shadows; but, being at all times liable to be called by his electric bell, and at such times listening for it with redoubled anxiety, the relief was less than I would suppose.

He took me into his box, where there was a fire, a desk for an official book in which he had to make certain entries, a telegraphic instrument with its dial, face and needles, and the little bell of which he had spoken. On my trusting that he would excuse the remark that he had been well educated, and (I hoped I might say without offense) perhaps educated above that station, he observed that instances of slight incongruity in such wise would rarely be found wanting among large bodies of men; that he had heard it was so in workhouses, in the police force, even in that last desperate resource, the army; and that he knew it was so, more or less, in any great railway staff. He had been, when young (if I could believe it, sitting in that hut — he scarcely could), a student of natural philosophy, and had attended lectures; but he had run wild, misused his opportunities, gone down, and never risen again. He had no complaint to offer about that. He had made his bed, and he lay upon it. It

163

was far too late to make another.

All that I have here condensed he said in a quiet manner, with his grave dark regards divided between me and the fire. He threw in the word, "Sir," from time to time, and especially when he referred to his youth—as though to request me to understand that he claimed to be nothing but what I found him. He was several times interrupted by the little bell, and had to read off messages, and send replies. Once he had to stand without the door, and display a flag as a train passed, and make some verbal communication to the driver. In the discharge of his duties, I observed him to be remarkably exact and vigilant, breaking off his discourse at a syllable and remaining silent until what he had to do was done.

In a word, I should have set this man down as one of the safest of men to be employed in that capacity, but for the circumstance that while he was speaking to me he twice broke off with a fallen color, turned his face toward the little bell when it did NOT ring, opened the door of the hut (which was kept shut to exclude the unhealthy damp), and looked out toward the red light near the mouth of the tunnel. On both of those occasions, he came back to the fire with the inexplicable air upon him which I had remarked, without being able to define, when we were so far asunder.

Said I, when I rose to leave him, "You almost make me think that I have met with a contented man."

(I am afraid I must acknowledge that I said it to lead him on.)

"I believe I used to be so," he rejoined, in the low voice in which he had first spoken; "but I am troubled, sir, I am troubled."

He would have recalled the words if he could. He had said them, however, and I took them up quickly.

"With what? What is your trouble?"

"It is very difficult to impart, sir. It is very, very difficult to speak of. If ever you make me another visit, I will try to tell you."

"But I expressly intend to make you another visit. Say, when shall it be?"

"I go off early in the morning, and I shall be on again at ten tomorrow night, sir."

"I will come at eleven."

He thanked me, and went out at the door with me. "I'll show my white light, sir," he said, in his peculiar low voice, "till you have found the way up. When you have found it, don't call out! And when you are at the top, don't call out."

His manner seemed to make the

place strike colder to me, but I said no more than, "Very well."

"And when you come down to-morrow night, don't call out! Let me ask you a parting question. What made you cry 'Halloa! Below there!' tonight?"

"Heaven knows," said I, "I cried something to that effect—"

"Not to that effect, sir. Those were the very words. I know them well."

"Admit those were the very words. I said them, no doubt, because I saw you below."

"For no other reason?"

"What other reason could I possibly have?"

"You had no feeling that they were conveyed to you in any supernatural way?"

"No."

He wished me good night, and held up his light. I walked by the side of the down Line of rails (with a very disagreeable sensation of a train coming behind me) until I found the path. It was easier to mount than to descend, and I got back to my inn without any adventure.

Punctual to my appointment, I placed my foot on the first notch of the zigzag next night, as the distant clocks were striking eleven. He was waiting for me at the bottom, with his white light on. "I have not called out," I said, when we came close together. "May I speak now?" "By all means, sir." "Good night, then, and here's my hand." "Good night, sir, and here's mine." With that we walked side by side to his box, entered it, closed the door, and sat down by the fire.

"I have made up my mind, sir," he began, bending forward as soon as we were seated, and speaking in a tone but a little above a whisper, "that you shall not have to ask me twice what troubles me. I took you for someone else yesterday evening. That troubles me."

"That mistake?"

"No. That someone else."

"Who is it?"

"I don't know."

"Like me?"

"I don't know. I never saw the face. The left arm is across the face, and the right arm is waved, violently waved. This way."

I followed his action with my eyes, and it was the action of an arm gesticulating, with the utmost passion and vehemence, "For God's sake, clear the way!"

"One moonlight night," said the man, "I was sitting here, when I heard a voice cry, 'Halloa! Below there!' I started up, looked from that door, and saw this Someone 165 else standing by the red light near the tunnel, waving as I just now showed you. The voice seemed hoarse with shouting, and it cried, 'Look out! Look out!' And then again, 'Halloa! Below there! Look out!' I caught up my lamp, turned it on red, and ran towards the figure, calling, 'What's wrong? What has happened? Where?' It stood just outside the blackness of the tunnel. I advanced so close upon it that I wondered at its keeping the sleeve across its eyes. I ran right up at it, and had my hand stretched out to pull the sleeve away, when it was gone."

"Into the tunnel?" said I.

"No. I ran on into the tunnel, five hundred yards. I stopped, and held my lamp above my head, and saw the figures of the measured distance, and saw the wet stains stealing down the walls and trickling through the arch. I ran out again faster than I had run in (for I had a mortal abhorrence of the place upon me), and I looked all round the red light with my own red light, and I went up the iron ladder to the gallery atop of it, and I came down again, and ran back here. I telegraphed both ways. 'An alarm has been given. Is anything wrong?' The answer came back, both ways, 'All well.' "

Resisting the slow touch of a frozen finger tracing out my spine, I showed him how that this figure must be a deception of his sense of sight; and how figures, originating in disease of the delicate nerves that minister to the functions of the eye, were known to have often troubled patients, some of whom had become conscious of the nature of their affliction, and had even proved it by experiments upon themselves. "As to an imaginary cry," said I, "do but listen for a moment to the wind in this unnatural valley while we speak so low, and to the wild harp it makes of the telegraph wires."

That was all very well, he returned, after we had sat listening for a while, and he ought to know something of the wind and the wires —he who so often passed long winter nights there, alone and watching. But he would beg to remark that he had not finished.

I asked his pardon, and he slowly added these words, touching my arm:

"Within six hours after the appearance, the memorable accident on this Line happened, and within ten hours the dead and wounded were brought along through the tunnel over the spot where the figure had stood."

A disagreeable shudder crept

over me, but I did my best against it. It was not to be denied, I rejoined, that this was a remarkable coincidence, calculated deeply to impress his mind. But it was unquestionable that remarkable coincidences did continually occur, and they must be taken into account in dealing with such a subject. Though to be sure I must admit, I added (for I thought I saw that he was going to bring the objection to bear upon me), men of common sense did not allow much for coincidences in making the ordinary calculations of life.

He again begged to remark that he had not finished.

I again begged his pardon for being betrayed into interruptions.

"This," he said, again laying his hand upon my arm, and glancing over his shoulder with hollow eyes, "was just a year ago. Six or seven months passed, and I had recovered from the surprise and shock, when one morning, as the day was breaking, I, standing at the door, looked towards the red light, and saw the specter again." He stopped with a fixed look at me.

"Did it cry out?"

"No. It was silent."

"Did it wave its arm?"

"No. It leaned against the shaft of the light, with both hands before the face. Like this."

Once more I followed his action with my eyes. It was an action of mourning. I have seen such an attitude on stone figures on tombs.

"Did you go up to it?"

"I came in and sat down, partly to collect my thoughts, partly because it had turned me faint. When I went to the door again, daylight was above me, and the ghost was gone."

"But nothing followed? Nothing came of this?"

He touched me on the arm with his forefinger twice or thrice, giving a ghastly nod each time:

"That very day, as a train came out of the tunnel, I noticed, at a carriage window on my side, what looked like a confusion of hands and heads, and something waved. I saw it, just in time to signal the driver, Stop! He shut off, and put his brake on, but the train drifted past here a hundred and fifty yards or more. I ran after it, and, as I went along, heard terrible screams and cries. A beautiful young lady had died instantaneously in one of the compartments, and was brought in here, and laid down on this floor between us."

Involuntarily, I pushed my chair back as I looked from the boards at which he pointed, to himself.   167

"True, sir. True. Precisely as it happened, so I tell it to you."

I could think of nothing to say, to any purpose, and my mouth was very dry. The wind and the wires took up the story with a long lamenting wail.

He resumed. "Now, sir, mark this, and judge how my mind is troubled. The specter came back, a week ago. Ever since, it has been there, now and again, by fits and starts."

"At the light?"

"At the danger light."

"What does it seem to do?"

He repeated, if possible with increased passion and vehemence, that former gesticulation of "For God's sake, clear the way!"

Then he went on. "I have no peace or rest for it. It calls to me, for many minutes together, in an agonized manner, 'Below there! Look out! Look out!' It stands waving to me. It rings my little bell—"

I caught at that. "Did it ring your bell yesterday evening when I was here, and you went to the door?"

"Twice."

"Why, see," said I, "how your imagination misleads you. My eyes were on the bell, and my ears were open to the bell, and if I am a living man, it did NOT ring at those times. No, nor at any other time, except when it was rung in the natural course of physical things by the station communicating with you."

He shook his head. "I have never made a mistake as to that yet, sir. I have never confused the specter's ring with the man's. The ghost's ring is a strange vibration in the bell that it derives from nothing else, and I have not asserted that the bell stirs to the eye. I don't wonder that you failed to hear it. But *I* heard it."

"And did the specter seem to be there when you looked out?"

"It was there."

"Both times?"

He repeated firmly: "Both times."

"Will you come to the door with me, and look for it now?"

He bit his under lip as though he were somewhat unwilling, but arose. I opened the door, and stood on the step, while he stood in the doorway. There was the danger light. There was the dismal mouth of the tunnel. There were the high, wet stone walls of the cutting. There were the stars above them.

"Do you see it?" I asked him, taking particular note of his face. His eyes were prominent and strained, but not very much more so, per-

168

haps, than my own had been when I had directed them earnestly towards the same spot.

"No," he answered. "It is not there."

"Agreed," said I.

We went in again, shut the door, and resumed our seats. I was thinking how best to improve this advantage, if it might be called one, when he took up the conversation in such a matter of course way, so assumming that there could be no serious question of fact between us, that I felt myself placed in the weakest of positions.

"By this time you will fully understand, sir," he said, "that what troubles me so dreadfully is the question, 'What does the specter mean?' "

I was not sure, I told him, that I did fully understand.

"What is its warning against?" he said, ruminating, with his eyes on the fire, and only by times turning them on me. "What is the danger? Where is the danger? There is danger overhanging somewhere on the Line. Some dreadful calamity will happen. It is not to be doubted this third time, after what has gone before. But surely this is a cruel haunting of *me*. What can I do?"

He pulled out his handkerchief, and wiped the drops from his heated forehead.

"If I telegraph Danger, on either side of me, or on both, I can give no reason for it," he went on, wiping the palms of his hands. "I should get into trouble and do no good. They would think I was mad. This is the way it would work—Message: 'Danger! Take Care!' Answer: 'What Danger? Where?' Message: 'Don't know. But, for God's sake, take care!' They would displace me. What else could they do?"

His pain of mind was most pitiable to see. It was the mental torture of a conscientious man, oppressed beyond endurance by an unintelligible responsibility involving life.

"When it first stood under the danger light," he went on, putting his dark hair back from his head, and drawing his hands outward across and across his temples in an extremity of feverish distress, "why not tell me where that accident was to happen—if it must happen? Why not tell me how it could be averted —if it could have been averted? When on its second coming it hid its face, why not tell me, instead, 'She is going to die. Let them keep her at home'? If it came, on those two occasions, only to show me that its warnings were true, and so to prepare me for the third, why not

169

warn me plainly now? And I, Lord help me! a mere poor signalman on this solitary station! Why not go to somebody with credit to be believed, and power to act?"

When I saw him in this state, I saw that for the poor man's sake, as well as for the public safety, what I had to do for the time was to compose his mind. Therefore, setting aside all question of reality or unreality between us, I represented to him that whoever thoroughly discharged his duty must do well, and that at least it was his comfort that he understood his duty, though he did not understand these confounding appearances. In this effort I succeeded far better than in the attempt to reason him out of his conviction. He became calm; the occupations incidental to his post as the night advanced began to make larger demands on his attention: and I left him at two in the morning. I had offered to stay through the night, but he would not hear of it.

That I more than once looked back at the red light as I ascended the pathway, that I did not like the red light, and that I should have slept but poorly if my bed had been under it, I see no reason to conceal. Nor did I like the two sequences of the accident and the dead girl. I see no reason to conceal that either.

But what ran most in my thoughts was the consideration how ought I to act, having become the recipient of this disclosure? I had proved the man to be intelligent, vigilant, painstaking, and exact; but how long might he remain so, in his state of mind? Though in a subordinate position, still he held a most important trust, and would I (for instance) like to stake my life on the chance of his continuing to execute it with precision?

Unable to overcome a feeling that there would be something treacherous in my communicating what he had told me to his superiors in the Company, without first being plain with himself and proposing a middle course to him, I ultimately resolved to offer to accompany him (otherwise keeping his secret for the present) to the wisest medical practitioner we could hear of in those parts, and to take his opinion. A change in his time of duty would come round next night, he had apprised me, and he would be off an hour or two after sunrise, and on again soon after sunset. I had appointed to return accordingly.

Next evening was a lovely evening and I walked out early to enjoy it. The sun was not yet quite down when I traversed the field path near the top of the deep cutting. I would extend my walk for an hour, I said to myself, half an hour on and half an hour back, and it would then be time to go to my signalman's box.

Before pursuing my stroll, I stepped to the brink, and mechanically looked down, from the point from which I had first seen him. I cannot describe the thrill that seized upon me, when, close at the mouth of the tunnel, I saw the appearance of a man, with his left sleeve across his eyes, passionately waving his right arm.

The nameless horror that oppressed me passed in a moment, for in a moment I saw that this appearance of a man was a man indeed, and that there was a little group of other men, standing at a short distance, to whom he seemed to be rehearsing the gesture he made. The danger light was not yet lighted. Against its shaft a little low hut, entirely new to me, had been made of some wooden supports and tarpaulin. It looked no bigger than a bed.

With an irresistible sense that something was wrong—with a flashing self-reproachful fear that fatal mischief had come of my leaving the man there, and causing no one to be sent to overlook or correct

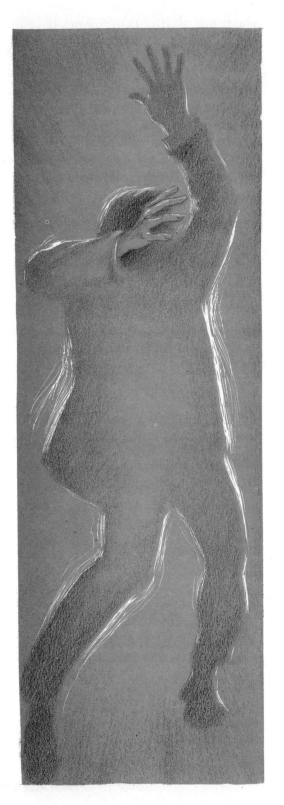

what he did — I descended the notched path with all the speed I could make.

"What is the matter?" I asked the men.

"Signalman killed this morning, sir."

"Not the man belonging to that box?"

"Yes, sir."

"Not the man I know?"

"You will recognize him, sir, if you knew him," said the man who spoke for the others, solemnly uncovering his own head, and raising an end of the tarpaulin, "for his face is quite composed."

"Oh, how did this happen, how did this happen?" I asked, turning from one to another as the hut closed in again.

"He was cut down by an engine, sir. No man in England knew his work better. But somehow he was not clear of the outer rail. It was just at broad day. He had struck the light, and had the lamp in his hand. As the engine came out of the tunnel, his back was toward her, and she cut him down. That man drove her, and was showing how it happened. Show the gentleman, Tom."

The man, who wore a rough dark dress, stepped back to his former place at the mouth of the tunnel.

"Coming round the curve of the tunnel, sir," he said, "I saw him at the end, like as if I saw him down a perspective glass. There was no time to check speed, and I knew him to be very careful. As he didn't seem to take heed of the whistle, I shut it off when we were running down upon him, and called to him as loud as I could call."

"What did you say?"

"I said, 'Below there! Look out! Look out! For God's sake, clear the way.'"

I started.

"Ah! it was a dreadful time, sir. I never left off calling to him. I put my arm before my eyes not to see, and I waved this arm to the last; but it was no use."

Without prolonging the narrative to dwell on any one of its curious circumstances more than on any other, I may, in closing it, point out the coincidence that the warning of the engine driver included, not only the words which the unfortunate signalman had repeated to me as haunting him, but also the words which I myself—not he—had attached, and that only in my own mind, to the gesticulation he had imitated.

The Water Ghost of Harrowby Hall

6

The trouble with Harrowby Hall was that it was haunted, and, what was worse, the ghost did not content itself with merely appearing at the bedside of the afflicted person who saw it, but persisted in remaining there for one mortal hour before it would disappear.

It never appeared except on Christmas Eve, and then as the clock was striking twelve, in which respect alone was it lacking in that originality which in these days is a *sine qua non* of success in spectral life. The owners of Harrowby Hall had done their utmost to rid themselves of the damp and dewy lady who rose up out of the best bedroom floor at midnight, but without avail. They had tried to stop the clock, so that the ghost would not know when it was midnight; but she made her appearance just the same, with that fearful miasmatic personality of hers, and there she would stand until everything about her was thoroughly saturated.

Then the owners of Harrowby Hall calked up every crack in the floor with the very best quality of hemp, and over this were placed layers of tar and canvas; the walls were made waterproof, and the doors and windows likewise, the proprietors having conceived the notion that the unexorcised lady would find it difficult to leak into the room after these precautions had been taken; but even this did not suffice. The following Christmas Eve she appeared as promptly as before, and frightened the occupant of the room quite out of his senses by sitting down alongside of him and gazing with her cavernous blue eyes into his; and he noticed, too, that in her long, aqueously bony fingers bits of dripping seaweed were entwined, the ends hanging down, and these ends she drew across his forehead until he became like one insane. And then he swooned away, and was found unconscious in his bed the next morning by his host, simply saturated with sea water and fright, from the combined effects of which he never recovered, dying four years

173

later of pneumonia and nervous prostration at the age of seventy-eight.

The next year the master of Harrowby Hall decided not to have the best spare bedroom opened at all, thinking that perhaps the ghost's thirst for making herself disagreeable would be satisfied by haunting the furniture, but the plan was as unavailing as the many that had preceded.

The ghost appeared as usual in the room—that is, it was supposed she did, for the hangings were dripping wet the next morning, and in the parlor below the haunted room a great damp spot appeared on the ceiling. Finding no one there, she immediately set out to learn the reason why, and she chose none other to haunt than the owner of the Harrowby himself. She found him in his own cozy room drinking whiskey—whiskey undiluted—and felicitating himself upon having foiled her ghostship, when all of a sudden the curl went out of his hair, his whiskey bottle filled and overflowed, and he was himself in a condition similar to that of a man who had fallen into a water-butt. When he had recovered from the shock, which was a painful one, he saw before him the lady of the cavernous eyes and the seaweed fingers. The sight was so unexpected and so terrifying that he fainted, but immediately came to, because of the vast amount of water in his hair, which, trickling down over his face, restored his consciousness.

Now it so happened that the master of Harrowby was a brave man, and while he was not particularly fond of interviewing ghosts, especially such quenching ghosts as the one before him, he was not to be daunted by an apparition. He had paid the lady the compliment of fainting from the effects of his first surprise, and now that he had come to, he intended to find out a few things he felt he had a right to know. He would have liked to put on a dry suit of clothes first, but the apparition declined to leave him for an instant until her hour was up, and he was forced to deny himself that pleasure. Every time he would move she would follow him, with the result that everything she came in contact with got a ducking. In an effort to warm himself up, he approached the fire, an unfortunate move as it turned out, because it brought the ghost directly over the fire, which immediately was extinguished. The whiskey became utterly valueless as a comforter to his chilled system, because it was by this time diluted to a proportion of ninety per cent of water. The only thing he could do to ward off the evil effects of his encounter he did, and that was to swallow ten two-grain quinine pills, which he managed to put into his mouth before the ghost had time to interfere. Having done this, he turned with some asperity to the ghost, and said:

"Far be it from me to be impolite to a woman, madam, but I'm hanged if it wouldn't please me better if you'd stop these infernal visits of yours to this house. Go sit out on the lake, if you like that sort of thing; soak the water-butt, if you wish; but do not, I implore you, come into a gentleman's house and saturate him and his possessions in this way. It is disagreeable."

"Henry Hartwick Oglethorpe," said the ghost, in a gurgling voice, "you don't know what you are talking about."

"Madam," returned the unhappy householder, "I wish that remark were strictly truthful. I was talking about you. It would be shillings and pence—nay, pounds, in my pocket, madam, if I did not know you."

"That is a bit of specious nonsense," returned the ghost, throwing a quart of indignation into the face of the master of Harrowby. "It may rank high as repartee, but as a comment upon my statement that you do not know what you are talking about, it savors of irrelevant impertinence. You do not know that I am compelled to haunt this place year after year by inexorable fate. It is no pleasure to me to enter this house, and ruin and mildew everything I touch. I never aspired to be a shower bath, but it is my doom. Do you know who I am?"

"No, I don't," returned the master of Harrowby. "I should say you were the Lady of the Lake, or Little Sallie Waters."

"You are a witty man for your years," said the ghost.

"Well, my humor is drier than yours will ever be," returned the master.

"No doubt. I'm never dry. I am the Water Ghost of Harrowby Hall, and dryness is a quality entirely beyond my wildest hope. I have been the incumbent of this highly unpleasant office for two hundred years tonight."

"How the deuce did you ever come to get elected?" asked the master.

"Through a suicide," replied the specter. "I am the ghost of that fair maiden whose picture hangs over the mantelpiece in the drawing room. I should have been your great-great-great-great-great-great-aunt if I had lived, Henry Hartwick Oglethorpe, for I was the own sister of your great-great-great-great-great-grandfather."

"But what induced you to get this house into such a predicament?"

"I was not to blame, sir," returned the lady. "It was my father's fault. He it was who built Harrowby Hall, and the haunted chamber was to have been mine. My father had it furnished in pink and yellow, knowing well that blue and gray formed the only combination of color I could tolerate. He did it merely to spite me, and with what I deem a proper spirit, I declined to live in the room; whereupon my father said I could live there or on the lawn, he didn't care which. That night I ran from the house and jumped over the cliff into the sea."

"That was rash," said the master of Harrowby.

"So I've heard," returned the ghost. "If I had known what the consequences were to be I should not have jumped; but I really never realized what I was doing until after I was drowned. I had been drowned a week when a sea nymph came to me and informed me that I was to be one of her followers forever afterwards, adding that it should be my doom to haunt Harrowby Hall for one hour every

Christmas Eve throughout the rest of eternity. I was to haunt that room on such Christmas Eves as I found it inhabited; and if it should turn out not to be inhabited, I was and am to spend the allotted hour with the head of the house."

"I'll sell the place."

"That you cannot do, for it is also required of me that I shall appear as the deeds are to be delivered to any purchaser, and divulge to him the awful secret of the house."

"Do you mean to tell me that on every Christmas Eve that I don't happen to have somebody in that guest chamber, you are going to haunt me wherever I may be, ruining my whiskey, taking all the curl out of my hair, extinguishing my fire, and soaking me through to the skin?" demanded the master.

"You have stated the case, Oglethorpe. And what is more," said the water ghost, "it doesn't make the slightest difference where you are; if I find that room empty, wherever you may be I shall douse you with my spectral pres——"

Here the clock struck one, and immediately the apparition faded away. It was perhaps more of a trickle than a fade, but as a disappearance it was complete.

"By Saint George and his Dragon!" ejaculated the master of Harrowby, wringing his hands. "It is guineas to hot cross buns that next Christmas there's an occupant of the spare room, or I spend the night in a bathtub."

But the master of Harrowby would have lost his wager had there been any one there to take him up, for when Christmas Eve came again he was in his grave, never having recovered from the cold contracted that awful night. Harrowby Hall was closed, and the heir to the estate was in London, where to him in his chambers came the same experience that his father had gone through, saving only that, being younger and stronger, he survived the shock. Everything in his room was ruined —his clocks were rusted in the works; a fine collection of water-color drawings was entirely obliterated by the onslaught of the water ghost; and, what was worse, the apartments below his were drenched with the water soaking through the floors, a damage for which he was compelled to pay, and which resulted in his being requested by his landlady to vacate the premises immediately.

The story of the visitation inflicted upon his family had gone abroad, and no one could be got to invite him out to any function save afternoon teas and receptions. Fath-

ers of daughters declined to permit him to remain in their houses later than eight o'clock at night, not knowing but that some emergency might arise in the supernatural world which would require the unexpected appearance of the water ghost in this on nights other than Christmas Eve, and before the mystic hour when weary churchyards, ignoring the rules which are supposed to govern polite society, begin to yawn. Nor would the maids themselves have aught to do with him, fearing the destruction by the sudden incursion of aqueous femininity of the costumes which they held most dear.

So the heir of Harrowby Hall re-   177

solved, as his ancestors for several generations before him had resolved, that something must be done. His first thought was to make one of his servants occupy the haunted room at the crucial moment; but in this he failed, because the servants themselves knew the history of the room and rebelled. None of his friends would consent to sacrifice their personal comfort to his, nor was there to be found in all England a man so poor as to be willing to occupy the doomed chamber on Christmas Eve for pay.

Then the thought came to the heir to have the fireplace in the room enlarged, so that he might evaporate the ghost at its first appearance, and he was felicitating himself upon the ingenuity of his plan, when he remembered what his father had told him—how that no fire could withstand the lady's extremely contagious dampness. And then he bethought him of steampipes. These, he remembered, could lie hundreds of feet deep in water, and still retain sufficient heat to drive the water away in vapor; and as a result of this thought the haunted room was heated by steam to a withering degree, and the heir for six months attended daily the Turkish baths, so that when Christmas Eve came he could himself

withstand the awful temperature of the room.

The scheme was only partially successful. The water ghost appeared at the specified time, and found the heir of Harrowby prepared; but hot as the room was, it shortened her visit by no more than five minutes in the hour, during which time the nervous system of the young master was well-nigh shattered, and the room itself was cracked and warped to an extent which required the outlay of a large sum of money to remedy. And worse than this, as the last drop of the water ghost was slowly sizzling itself out on the floor, she whispered to her would-be conqueror that his scheme would avail him nothing, because there was still water in great plenty where she came from, and that next year would find her rehabilitated and as exasperatingly saturating as ever.

It was then that the natural action of the mind, in going from one extreme to the other, suggested to the ingenious heir of Harrowby the means by which the water ghost was ultimately conquered, and happiness once more came within the grasp of the house of Oglethorpe.

The heir provided himself with a warm suit of fur underclothing. Donning this with the furry side in, he placed over it a rubber garment, tight-fitting, which he wore just as a woman wears a jersey. On top of this he placed another set of underclothing, this suit made of wool, and over this was a second rubber garment like the first. Upon his head he placed a light and comfortable diving helmet, and so clad, on the following Christmas Eve he awaited the coming of his tormentor.

It was a bitterly cold night that brought to a close this twenty-fourth day of December. The air outside was still, but the temperature was below zero. Within all was quiet, the servants of Harrowby Hall awaiting with beating hearts the outcome of their master's campaign against his supernatural visitor.

The master himself was lying on the bed in the haunted room, clad as has already been indicated, and then——

The clock clanged out the hour of twelve.

There was a sudden banging of doors, a blast of cold air swept through the halls, the door leading into the haunted chamber flew open, a splash was heard, and the water ghost was seen standing at the side of the heir of Harrowby, from whose outer dress there streamed rivulets of water, but whose own person deep down under the various garments he wore was as dry and as warm as he could have wished.

"Ha!" said the young master of Harrowby. "I'm glad to see you."

"You are the most original man I've met, if that is true," returned the ghost. "May I ask where did you get that hat?"

"Certainly, madam," returned the master, courteously. "It is a little portable observatory I had made just for such emergencies as this. But, tell me, is it true that you are doomed to follow me about for one mortal hour — to stand where I stand, to sit where I sit?"

"That is my delectable fate," returned the lady.

"We'll go out on the lake," said the master, starting up.

"You can't get rid of me that way," returned the ghost. "The water won't swallow me up; in fact, it will just add to my present bulk."

"Nevertheless," said the master firmly, "we will go out on the lake."

"But, my dear sir," returned the ghost, with a pale reluctance, "it is fearfully cold out there. You will be frozen hard before you've been out ten minutes."

"Oh, no, I'll not," replied the master. "I am very warmly dressed. Come!" This last in a tone of com-

179

mand that made the ghost ripple.

And they started.

They had not gone far before the water ghost showed signs of distress.

"You walk too slowly," she said. "I am nearly frozen. My knees are so stiff now I can hardly move. I beseech you to accelerate your step."

"I should like to oblige a lady," returned the master courteously, "but my clothes are rather heavy, and a hundred yards an hour is about my speed. Indeed, I think we would better sit down here on this snowdrift, and talk matters over."

"Do not! Do not do so, I beg!" cried the ghost. "Let me move on. I feel myself growing rigid as it is. If we stop here, I shall be frozen stiff."

"That, madam," said the master slowly, and seating himself on an ice cake, "that is why I have brought you here. We have been on this spot just ten minutes; we have fifty more. Take your time about it, madam, but freeze, that is all I ask of you."

"I cannot move my right leg now," cried the ghost in despair, "and my overskirt is a solid sheet of ice. Oh, good, kind Mr. Oglethorpe, light a fire, and let me go free from these icy fetters."

"Never, madam. It cannot be. I have you at last."

"Alas!" cried the ghost, a tear trickling down her frozen cheek. "Help me, I beg. I congeal."

"Congeal, madam, congeal!" returned Oglethorpe coldly. "You have drenched me and mine for two hundred and three years, madam. Tonight you have had your last drench."

"Ah, but I shall thaw out again, and then you'll see. Instead of the comfortably tepid, genial ghost I have been in my past, sir, I shall be iced water," cried the lady threateningly.

"No, you won't, either," returned Oglethorpe; "for when you are frozen quite stiff, I shall send you to a cold-storage warehouse, and there shall you remain an icy work of art forever more."

"But warehouses burn."

"So they do, but this warehouse cannot burn. It is made of asbestos and surrounding it are fireproof walls, and within those walls the temperature is now and shall forever be 416 degrees below the zero point; low enough to make an icicle of any flame in the world—or the next," the master added, with an ill-suppressed chuckle.

"For the last time let me beseech

180

you. I would go on my knees to you, Oglethorpe, were they not already frozen. I beg of you do not doo——"

Here even the words froze on the water ghost's lips and the clock struck one. There was a momentary tremor throughout the ice-bound form, and the moon, coming out from behind a cloud, shone down on the rigid figure of a beautiful woman sculptured in clear, transparent ice. There stood the ghost of Harrowby Hall, conquered by the cold, a prisoner for all time.

The heir of Harrowby had won at last, and today in a large storage house in London stands the frigid form of one who will never again flood the house of Oglethorpe with woe and sea water.

As for the heir of Harrowby, his success in coping with a ghost has made him famous, a fame that still lingers about him, although his victory took place some twenty years ago; and so far from being unpopular with the fair sex, as he was when we first knew him, he has not only been married twice, but is to lead a third bride to the altar before the year is out.

Dracula

by Bram Stoker

adapted by Rosalie Kershaw

illustrated by Harry Borgman

One

Jonathan Harker's ordeal of terror began most innocently. He left England for Transylvania by train on the first of May, 1897. It was to be a brief business trip for the young lawyer — a visit to the Castle of an unheard-of nobleman — a Count Dracula.

"Just complicated real estate dealings," Jonathan explained to his new bride Mina, "I'll be back in a few weeks."

Thus he embarked on the most unbelievable, horrifying six months of his young life. In that time, Jonathan's brown hair would turn white from fear and Mina would be on the threshold of the world of the Un-Dead.

Even the trip through the wild, beautiful Hungarian countryside would have been a warning to anyone less carefree than Jonathan. Although the Castle Dracula was near the town of Bistritz, high in the Carpathian Mountains, no map showed its location. As the train drew closer to his destination, Jonathan found his sleep troubled by all sorts of queer dreams. These he blamed upon the cramped sleeping car berth and the motion of the train.

Or perhaps it was all the unaccustomed sights and sounds. During the day, the train hurtled through a country which was full of beauty on every side. Sometimes he saw little walled towns or turreted castles on top of steep hills—scenes such as he had admired in the paintings in museums.

At every station there were groups of people in all sorts of costumes. Some of the women wore layers of skirts with bright ribbons and flowers sewn to them. There were peasant cowboys with trousers tucked into high boots. Around their waists they fastened heavy leather belts, nearly a foot wide, studded over with brass nails.

It was almost twilight when the express train reached Bistritz, an old, historically noteworthy town. Count Dracula had sent instructions for Jonathan to stay overnight at the Golden Krone Hotel.

To his delight, it proved to be a busy, old-fashioned sort of place. Set in the middle of the wide entrance room was a great, whitewashed clay fireplace that served to warm travelers who sat about it on a circular bench. The fireplace was taller than a man and shaped like a beehive.

Jonathan moved closer and held out his hands to the glowing fire. A cheery-looking elderly woman in peasant dress stepped up to him.

"You are Mr. Harker, the Englishman?" she inquired.

"Yes, I have just arrived. I am a guest of Count Dracula."

At this, the woman's expression completely changed. She glanced at Jonathan in a frightened way. Reaching into her apron pocket she drew out a letter on heavy, crested stationery and thrust it into Jonathan's hand.

"My husband and I are at your service. I hope your stay at our Inn will be a long and pleasant one." The old woman rushed her welcoming speech so that the words tangled together in her hurry to be done. Then she bustled off to her husband's side where the two stood whispering together in a most agitated way.

Taking a seat on the curved bench, Jonathan opened the envelope and read:

My Friend,

Welcome to Transylvania. I am anxiously expecting you. Sleep well tonight. At three tomorrow afternoon the coach will make its weekly trip to the border. It will stop at the Borgo Pass where my horses and carriage will await you. I trust you will enjoy your stay in my country.

Signed "Count Dracula."

As Jonathan looked up from the letter, he noticed the hotel keeper and his wife watching intently.

"Do you know Count Dracula?" he asked in a friendly voice. "Perhaps you could tell me something about him and the location of his castle."

The old couple crossed themselves and shook their heads. The wife abruptly went back to sweeping off the front steps. Her husband picked up Jonathan's bags and led the way to the rooms reserved for him. It was all very peculiar and not too comforting.

In the morning, Jonathan was once more aware of the strange glances he drew from the servants in the hotel. As he ate lunch, it seemed the serving girl crossed herself whenever she turned from his table. No. It was simply that he had slept badly again. Was it a dream or had he truly heard wolves howling outside his window?

He was repacking when the hotel's proprietress knocked softly and entered his room. She seemed almost hysterical: "The coach is here and taking on passengers. Oh, young sir, must you go?"

Jonathan saw how agitated the old woman was and quietly interrupted her. "I am here on important business, madam. Of course I must take the coach, as Count Dracula requested."

"But do you know what day it is?" the innkeeper's wife whispered. "It is the eve of St. George's Day. Tonight when the clock strikes midnight, all the evil things in the world will have full sway. Do you know where you are going? Do you understand, sir?"

She was in such obvious distress that Jonathan tried to comfort her, but without effect. Finally she fell to her knees and begged him to wait at least a few days before starting. Such superstition made the young Englishman very uncomfortable. But there was no question that he had to fulfill his duty to his client. He thanked her for her concern and taking her arm, led the trembling peasant to the door.

Looking intently at Jonathan, the old woman took a small gold chain with a cross from her neck and placed it over his head. "Wear this — if only for your mother's sake," and she rushed out.

"It is not a pleasant beginning to my journey," Jonathan thought. He was made even more uneasy by the stir caused when he approached the coach filled with travelers. Its four horses whinnied and pranced as the coachman held his reins in one hand and made a sign in the air with two fingers pointed upwards.   189

He then tipped his hat toward his new fare.

"What did all that mean," Jonathan asked a man resting against the luggage rack. The man shrugged but by repeating the question Jonathan elicited the explanation that it was the way local peasants guarded against the devil or the evil eye.

"These are old fashioned people," the man growled. "If you are not a believer in their ways then ignore them," and he walked away.

The driver cracked his whip, signaling passengers to take their seats. As the carriage pulled away from the hotel's courtyard, Jonathan glanced back and was touched by the sorrowful yet sympathetic faces of the old couple and the people standing with them. Many crossed themselves repeatedly as they watched the coach leave Bistritz.

Soon all ghostly suspicions were forgotten. The road ahead went through mountainous, ever-changing land. The countryside was full of forests and woods, with here and there steep hills crowned with orchards in blossom and thatched farmhouses.

Gradually the farmland was left behind. The forests became more dense and dark. Pinewoods ran down to the highway like tongues of flame. Here and there were pointed crags and jagged rocks white with the foam of rushing rivers.

"Look, look, God's seat," one of the men called out, and he touched Jonathan's arm to direct his gaze to a lofty, snow-covered mountain peak that rose before them.

Now the way became so steep that the horses could only go slowly. Jonathan suggested that everyone get out and walk to make the burden less for the panting animals. But the driver would not hear of it.

"No sir, we must not walk here," he said. "There are fierce wolves in the forests," and then he added, "and you may have enough of such matters before you sleep tonight."

The others in the coach nodded in agreement. The only stop made was a moment's pause to light the lamps.

As the sun sank lower, the scenery melted into mist. The road was rugged, but the driver skimmed over it with feverish haste. Darkness closed down upon the travellers and they urged the coachman to greater and greater speed. Their excitement was visibly mounting. The coach rocked on its great leather springs like a boat tossed on a stormy sea.

It grew cold and Jonathan's earlier grim thoughts and uneasiness returned. One by one, several of his fellow passengers pressed upon him gifts of an odd and varied kind: a branch of wild rose, a bulb of garlic cloves, a medallion with a saint's picture. Each was urged upon the astonished Englishman with a kind word or a blessing or that strange sign against the evil eye. Evidentally, something worrisome was in the air, but no one would offer the slightest explanation.

Now the Borgo Pass through the mountains loomed up ahead. The air had a sense of thunder. Jonathan peered through the darkness looking for the lamps of the conveyance that was to take him to Castle Dracula. Suddenly the horses began to neigh and plunge wildly. The riders gasped and crossed themselves as a gleaming buggy with four coal black horses drew alongside. They were reined in by a tall man wearing a cape and a deep hat that hid his face. Only his eyes glittered in the darkness. They held a red glow that Jonathan blamed on the lamplight.

"You are early," he said to the coachman.

"The Englishman was in a hurry," stammered the driver.

"You cannot deceive me," sneered the stranger. "I know too much and my horses are too swift." He smiled and showed a hard mouth with very red lips and sharp teeth as white as ivory.

Then the stranger reached into the coach and with a grip of remarkable strength, grasped Jonathan's arm, almost lifting him to the ground. Without a word, he took the luggage from the rack and placed it behind the black horses. No sooner had Jonathan stepped towards the buggy, than the frightened coachman snapped his whip and raced through the pass, leaving his passenger and the tall driver alone in the night.

A chill swept over the young man. With foreboding he heard the driver urge him to hurry. "The night is cold, Mr. Harker. Let us be on our way. Count Dracula eagerly awaits you."

At that moment, Jonathan wished to be anywhere else on earth. He hunched back in his seat 191 and watched deepening forests and outcroppings of rock rush past. The buggy went at a fast pace and Jonathan must have dozed off. Somewhere a dog or wolf began to howl. The sound was taken by another and then another. The sleeper awakened with a pounding heart to the chorus of mournful sounds.

Jonathan struck a match and looked at his watch. Midnight! The horses had stopped.

Probably the general superstition about midnight had disturbed him after all. He waited, breathless, a sick feeling of suspense between his ribs. Howling echoed somewhere far down the road, a long, agonized wailing that was unearthly. This was taken up by another, then an-

other, till a wild chorus emerged from all around through the gloom of the night.

Just then the moon, sailing through dark clouds, appeared behind a jagged precipice. Its light illumined a ring of wolves with bared fangs and long shaggy fur. They were a hundred times more horrible in their grim silence than they had been when howling. Jonathan was frozen with fear. Only when a man comes face to face with such a sight can he understand its true impact.

The terrified horses reared back upon their hind legs. But their driver calmly tied the reins and stepped from his perch. His voice sounded forth in a tone of command. Before Jonathan's shocked sight, he swept his arm across the road and the wolves cringed back. Another cloud obscured the moon. When it passed, the wolves were gone. Taking his reins, the driver resumed the journey.

A dreadful fear possessed Jonathan. He could not speak or move. Time seemed endless before he heard the wheels grate against stone paving. They had pulled into the courtyard of a vast ruined Castle from whose tall windows came no ray of light. Broken battlements showed a jagged line against the moonlit sky.

As soon as they stopped, the driver sprang out to assist Jonathan. Again the exhausted passenger could not help noticing the man's amazing strength. His grasp felt like a vise of steel.

The baggage was deposited at the threshold of a huge wooden door, old and studded with iron nails and set in a doorway of massive stone. Even in the dim light, it could be seen that the stone was ornately carved but the details had been worn down by time and weather.

Before he could ask the driver to signal their arrival, the horses started forward and trotted out of sight down one of the many vaulted archways.

Jonathan stood in silence for he did not know what to do. Of bell or knocker there was no sign. What sort of place was this, and what kind of people? On what grim adventure had he embarked?

Perhaps this was a nightmare. He was simply an English lawyer arranging the purchase of a London estate to a foreign nobleman. Surely he would soon awake in his own bed to find his wife Mina opening the curtains and letting in the morning light.

Jonathan pinched himself to see if he were truly dreaming. The sound of steps echoed somewhere behind the great door. Through the chinks in the stone a wavering light glimmered. There was the sound of clanking bolts drawn back. A key turned with the loud grating noise of long disuse and the portal swung open.

193

Two

A gaunt old man clad in black from head to foot stood in the doorway. Not a single speck of color showed on him anywhere — except his face, which was deathly white. In his hand a silver lamp flickered, throwing long quivering shadows.

"Welcome to my house! Enter freely and of your own will." The old man gestured Jonathan to step across the doorsill. Then he grasped Jonathan's hand with a strength that almost hurt. The hand was as cold as ice—more like that of the dead than the living.

"Count Dracula?" ventured Jonathan.

The old man bowed in courtly manner. "I am Dracula. Come in, Mr. Harker. The night air is chill and you must need to eat and rest. Let me see to your comfort. It is late and my servants are not here."

Before Jonathan could protest, the Count picked up the luggage and strode swiftly up a great winding stair and along a stone passageway. At its end he threw open a heavy door. Jonathan rejoiced to see a well-lit room in which a table was spread for supper. On the mighty hearth a fire of tree-sized logs flamed and flared. Beyond was another high-ceilinged room — a bedroom, warmed by another fire. Fresh logs sent a hollow roar up the wide chimney.

Light and warmth and the courteous welcome dispelled Jonathan's doubts and fears. Now he realized how hungry he was.

"I pray you, be seated and eat. You will excuse me that I do not join you, but I have dined already."

As his guest ate, the Count asked many questions about his wife, himself, and his country. Then Jonathan handed over documents and maps dealing with the property in London which the Count planned to purchase. While the nobleman glanced over these papers, Jonathan observed him in a some detail.

Count Dracula's face was very strong. The eyebrows were massive, almost meeting over the arched bridge of the nose. His hair was rather long and white. Under a

195

heavy mustache, the mouth seemed hard with peculiar, sharp white teeth. Although the general effect was of an extraordinarily pale man, his lips were too red and youthful for one of his age.

When his eyes fell upon the Count's hands, Jonathan could not suppress a shudder. Both backs and palms were covered with hair and the nails came to long points.

Noticing his guest's intent gaze, the Count smiled. His eyes gleamed. "Listen," and he turned towards the high, narrow windows.

From the valley came the howling of wolves. "What music they make." The first light of dawn penetrated the room.

Hurriedly the Count strode to the door. "You must be tired. Sleep as late as you will. I must be away till late."

Alone with his troubled thoughts, Jonathan decided to begin a diary that would keep accurate note of everything that happened. He did not go to bed until he had written the details of his journey and the meeting with Count Dracula.

In the morning, Jonathan discovered breakfast had been set out for him. Nowhere was there a bell to ring for servants. How extraordinary in a Castle with such evidence of wealth. The table service was of solid gold. The curtains and chairs and bed linens were costly fabrics. Yet in no room was there a mirror. In order to shave, Jonathan had to prop the little mirror from his toilet case upon a table.

Once he had dressed and eaten, Jonathan ventured into the vaulted hallway. He had not expected such silence. Not a voice or footstep to indicate even a caretaker or chambermaid. He tried the door oppo-

196

site his but found it locked. The handle of the next door turned, however, and led into a private library. To his delight, the shelves were filled with English books as well as those in many foreign languages. On a table was a pile of books relating to English life and customs.

The remainder of the afternoon passed quickly among the books and he did not realize it had grown dark until Count Dracula entered.

"I am glad you found your way to my library. As you see, I have been studying much about your country. I wish to know it thoroughly, to share its life, its death, and all that make it what it is. Only then will I feel that I may be at home on the estate you have found for me."

"Indeed," Jonathan replied, "you speak English very well."

"Not so. But you shall, I trust, stay here with me awhile so that I learn from you."

Jonathan's heart constricted at that invitation. But he smiled politely. "I will be glad to help you in the time I have left. I hope you did not mind my exploring a bit."

"Certainly not," his host said. "Go anywhere you wish in the cas-tle except where the doors are locked. There is reason that things here are as they are. In Transylvania our ways are not your ways. Much shall be strange to you."

Jonathan said nothing. The two sat down before the large sheaf of legal papers on the desk. Jonathan described the estate his client was buying.

"The place is called Carfax. It is by the seashore, not far from London and contains some twenty acres surrounded by a solid stone wall. The house is large and rambling, though somewhat neglected. I believe it dates back to medieval times, for there are few windows and these are high up. There are many trees on it, which makes it in places rather gloomy.

"Only one house is nearby, and that is a very big building of the Victorian period. It has recently been enlarged and somewhat modernized and formed into a private lunatic asylum. It is very well guarded, however, and not at all visible from the grounds of the property you plan to purchase.

"Carfax also contains a ruined chapel or church. It is part of the foundation of the mansion and adjoins an overgrown cemetery which is so neglected that I could not even make out the markers on the graves."

Count Dracula nodded approvingly during this account. When the lawyer had finished, he said, "I am glad that this Carfax is old and big. I myself am of an old family and would not be comfortable in a new house. As for the cemetery, we Transylvanian nobles know how few days go to make up a century. We are at home among the dead. My own castle has its burial chambers and I am fond of shade and shadow."

Although these words were spoken softly, Jonathan felt that the Count's expression was sly and ominous. He listened carefully as the Count continued.

"We of the house of Dracula have a right to be proud of the past, for in our veins flows the blood of many brave nations who fought as the lion fights, for lordship.

"Not only European blood, but that of the tribes of Iceland who bore down on this country and the shores of Asia and Africa too, till the people thought that the werewolves themselves had come. From them we took the fighting spirit of Thor and Wodin.

"The Huns swept over this earth too, like a living flame, and those lands that fell to their armies held that in their veins ran the blood of witches who had mated with devils. Fools! Fools! What devil or witch was ever so great as Attila the Hun whose own history is in these veins?" He held up his arms. "Is it any wonder that we were a proud and conquering race ourselves, with such an inheritance?

"The Magyar and the Turk added to the mixture of our blood. It was one of my own house of Dracula who threw off the yoke of those who would enslave us. We Draculas were the leaders that crossed rivers of dead to beat the foe back.

"What other noble family in all Europe has the brave history of the house of Dracula? Yet now look at our domain."

An expression of contempt entered his tone. "Our castle in ruins, our subjects, who were once armies that spread terror by their very name, now superstitious peasants."

A pause, and then, "Ah, but the world has not yet heard the last of the Draculas!"

All at once there sounded the crow of a cock and morning showed

harry Borgman

through the library windows. Dracula jumped to his feet. "Why, it is morning again. I have kept you up too long." And with a slight bow he quickly departed.

Jonathan recorded every detail of his conversation before he allowed himself to go to sleep.

Two more days passed in the same way. During the day Jonathan was alone. Only at night would Count Dracula appear to talk away the evening, rushing off at dawn. Not once did the host join his guest for a meal. In fact, at no time did Jonathan see him eat or drink.

It was now clear that there was no one else in the castle. Somehow the Count himself must manage the simple meals Jonathan always found waiting on his table. Surely, the Count was the driver that had brought Jonathan to Castle Dracula.

What a terrible thought. If so, it meant that he could control wolves by merely waving his hand over their heads. And what was the meaning of the gifts the peasants had given Jonathan? The wild rose, the garlic, the sign for evil eye. He touched the gold cross at his neck and silently thanked the good woman who had put it there.

Late in the afternoon, as Jona-

than was shaving by the small mirror he'd hung near the window, he felt a hand on his shoulder. "Good evening," came the Count's voice. Startled, Jonathan cut himself slightly and looked again in the mirror. Though the Count was standing directly behind him, there was no reflection of the man in the mirror!

Jonathan lay down the razor and turned around. Abruptly Count Dracula's eyes came ablaze with demonic fury. He grabbed at the spot where a few drops of blood had trickled on Jonathan's chin. The startled fellow drew away and instead the Count's hand touched the cross hanging at his neck. He flinched as though he had touched flame.

"Take care," he warned, "to cut yourself is more dangerous than you think." Then seizing the shaving mirror he muttered, "And this wretched thing is a foul bauble of man's vanity. Away with it!" He dashed the mirror out the window where it shattered into a thousand pieces on the flagstones far below. Then he left without another word.

Jonathan looked out to the mountains beyond. The castle was on the edge of a high precipice. As far as he could see were tree tops

200

and silver threads where distant rivers ran. But he had no taste for this beauty. Unscalable heights on the outside. Locked doors inside. It was clear now that the castle was a prison and he the prisoner.

The following day Count Dracula was intent upon discussing business and practicing English, as always. At one point he asked if Jonathan had sent any letters to England since arriving.

"While at the Golden Krone," Jonathan answered, "I wrote to my wife and to friends."

"Then my young companion," the Count smiled, "write again to your wife. Please say that you shall stay with me until a month from now."

"You wish me to stay so long?" Jonathan gasped. His heart grew cold at the thought.

"I desire it much. In fact, I will take no refusal. Surely you came realizing that my needs must be satisfied before you left."

What could Jonathan do but agree? Everything in Count Dracula's bearing made him realize there was no choice. He must pretend that all was normal and not infuriate this terrifying man.

Jonathan wrote only the most formal, brief note. Perhaps Mina would understand how unlike him such a letter was. As he handed over the envelope, he saw the cruel smile exposing sharp, white teeth and Jonathan knew that no envelope could shut out those penetrating eyes.

"I must leave you again," the Count apologized. "But let me warn you with all seriousness not to roam too far. Above all, do not go to sleep in any other part of the castle. It is old and has many memories. Be warned. There are bad dreams for those who sleep unwisely."

Jonathan felt the net of gloom and mystery closing tightly. In an hour, not hearing any sound, he left his room and walked down the long hallway. A narrow window looked out over a beautiful moonlit scene. Bathed in the soft yellow light, it was almost as clear as day.

The fresh air was calming and Jonathan leaned from the window. Something was moving on the level below and to the left. What he saw was the Count's head emerging from a window. Then the whole body slowly appeared and began to crawl down the castle wall. His cloak spread out around him like great wings. First, Jonathan could not believe his eyes. But it was no illusion. The fingers and toes

grasped the corners of the stones
and moved just as a lizard moves
down a wall.

What manner of creature was
this? Jonathan was gripped by terrors he did not dare admit even to
himself.

Three

On the following night, Jonathan again saw the Count go out in his lizard fashion. Moving downward in a sidelong way, he vanished into an archway at the base of the precipice upon which the castle was built. Now there was an opportunity for Jonathan to explore some avenue of escape. He took the lamp from his room and descended the stone staircase. At the great door in the entrance hall, the bolts moved back easily enough, but a huge padlock could not be budged. Its key must be in the Count's room. Which could that be?

Along the entrance corridor were many small rooms. Their doors opened to show nothing but furniture dusty with age. One door seemed to be stuck but with a little pressure it pushed open.

This part of the castle must have been occupied by ladies in bygone days. Wispy curtains fluttered from windows. Even under the dust the furniture showed pretty flowers.

Loneliness overcame Jonathan. It replaced the grip of fear that was constantly with him. He sat upon the worn couch and leaned back, thinking of his wife, Mina. Sleep crept upon him. In his dream he was not alone. Standing in the moonlight were three young women. Two were dark and had piercing eyes much like the Count. One was fair with masses of golden hair. All had oddly pointed white teeth and dark, dark red lips. Their eyes glinted almost red in the reflection of light from the window. Though beautiful, something about these women inspired deadly fear.

They whispered together and laughed — a hard silvery laugh such as could never come through human lips. The fair girl shook her head and the two others urged, "Go on. You are first. We shall follow."

One added, "He is young and strong. There is enough for us all."

The fair girl advanced and bent so close to Jonathan he could feel her breath. Although he tried, he could not raise his eyelids. As she bent down she licked her lips like an animal. The skin on his throat

203

tingled and his heart pounded. At that instant a voice thundered out. It was Count Dracula.

"How dare you touch him, any of you?" Through his opening eyes Jonathan saw a strong hand grasp the neck of the fair woman and hurl her to the floor. Never had Jonathan imagined such fury and evil as in her expression.

With the same fierce sweep of his hand as had driven back the wolves, the Count sent the young women cringing to a corner. "You must wait your turn," the Count threatened. "I have work to do with him. I promise that when I am done and in England you shall have him in your power. Now go."

All that was implicit in that promise shocked Jonathan. He sank into unconsciousness.

Awaking in his own bed, the young lawyer instantly felt his pocket. Thank God, the diary was still there, wrapped with the cross. He took his pen and wrote: "As I look around this room, although it is full of fear, it is still a sanctuary. Here at least I am safe from those awful women who I now know are waiting to drink my blood. My only hope is to prolong my opportunities. Something may occur which will give me a chance to escape."

From the courtyard below came the sound of carriage wheels and voices. After so many days of silence, Jonathan could not believe his ears. He raced to the window. There stood a group of gypsy men and a half dozen wagons. They were talking to Count Dracula in a language Jonathan had never heard.

Paper. Paper and pen. He must get a letter smuggled out of the castle. But the Count had already anticipated this action. Every scrap of paper was gone along with the legal documents for the purchase of the estate in England.

Perhaps in the library. Jonathan dashed to his door. It was locked.

Fortunately, the innkeeper's cross had protected his diary. The desperate man wrote his plea on a page torn from this book, sealing it with candle wax. On the outside he penned the word "HELP."

Going to the window again, Jonathan awaited his chance. The Count was spilling a mound of gold coins into the hand of one of the gypsies. Then he disappeared into the castle.

A pebble thrown from Jonathan's window caused the men in the courtyard to look up. Wrapping a few English coins in his message, Jonathan tossed it to their feet. One of the brightly costumed men picked up the paper, smiled, and tipped his cap.

Results came sooner than Jonathan had dreamed possible. Barely a half hour later there was a scraping at the base of his door. Jonathan looked down to see his message, torn in pieces, pushed over the threshold.

Taking a moment to gather his wits, Jonathan went to the window again. He called out to the gypsies in desperate words, hoping the urgency of his voice would penetrate the barrier of no common language. The gypsies only pointed up at him and laughed. The leader bent low in a mocking bow. Then he touched his head and the others laughed again.

It was obvious, they assumed he was mad.

Once more the Count had outwitted his captive.

Hours passed, with Jonathan sitting in his chair stunned by hopelessness and despair. The sound of a shutter opening beneath the level of his own room brought him back to the window. He was just in time to see the Count balanced outside the sill of his apartments, struggling to lift a cloth sack past the shutters. Something in the bag squirmed and moved, making the task difficult.

Finally the Count tossed his burden into the room and climbed in after it. Listening carefully, with his heart pounding, Jonathan heard the soft laughter of women's voices. No others but the three ghoulish sisters could have such lifeless, metallic sound.

Then came a half-smothered cry, a wail, and silence. Jonathan covered his mouth with his hand to prevent his own terrified cry from escaping.

When a few hours had passed another noise came up from the courtyard. This time it was the cry of a woman. Jonathan peered out into the night. There was a peasant woman, holding her hands over her heart as if trying to quiet its beating. She was shaking the bars of the locked gate with all her might.

Looking up towards the windows of the castle, she shouted, "Monster, give me my child."

Over and over she cried the same words in a way which wrung Jonathan's very soul. Finally, she threw herself forward and he could hear the pounding of her hands against the bolted lock.

Somewhere, high overhead, probably on a tower, the voice of Count Dracula came in a harsh command. His call was answered from nearby with the howling of wolves. In moments, a pack of the shaggy gray beasts poured into the courtyard. There was no cry from the woman and only a growling and

gnashing of teeth from the wolves. Before long, they streamed away, one at a time, licking their lips.

Jonathan could not pity the woman for he knew what had become of her child — and both were better dead.

With morning, Jonathan embarked upon a daring plan. It was clear only he could save himself. No one else could help him.

207

During the bright hours of day, Jonathan had the run of the castle. Between twilight and dawn were the hours that he had been in fear or in danger. Obviously, the Dracula household slept when others were awake that they might be awake while others sleep.

In daylight Jonathan must find a way to the Count's room. Surely the key to the massive front door was hidden there. With his own room locked, only the window would provide passage to that part of the castle. It was a desperate chance. It could mean a fall to the rocks and certain death. Between that and the ghostly sisters, Jonathan chose the risk of death.

While courage was still fresh, he crawled out upon the narrow stone window ledge. The roughly shaped blocks of the castle's face provided a precarious hold for his hands and feet. Jonathan knew the direction of the Count's window, having watched the fearful man exiting from that spot on his gruesome errands. It was important not to look down to the rocks below the castle wall. He must not get dizzy and lose his grip.

In less time than he believed possible, the brave soul found himself

standing on the sill of the room he sought. Fortunately, it was empty. The room was barely furnished — not even a bed. Simply a desk, some dusty chairs, and in one corner a great heap of gold. The coins were very old and from all parts of Europe. Most were musty and stained as if they had lain long in the ground.

The key that Jonathan needed was nowhere. But there was a trap door cut into the floor. One sharp tug and it yawned open. Perhaps this was the route to freedom!

The door opened on a stone passageway. Thence, a circular staircase descended steeply. Through the dark tunnel at the bottom came an odor of old earth and decay.

Finally a ruined chapel came into view. Burial vaults lined the sides of the cobwebbed chamber. Ground had recently been dug up and several dozen new wooden boxes were filled with earth from the chapel.

Jonathan walked from one to the other. They were roughly coffin-shaped, with lids resting lightly upon them. However, in one, standing within a shadowy crypt, Jonathan made a discovery which froze his heart. There, on a pile of freshly shoveled earth lay Dracula!

Was he dead or asleep? The eyes were open and stony. Yet the lips were red with the warmth of life in that unliving face. No other sign of life — no breath, no beating of the heart.

With loathing Jonathan bent to search for the keys. Accidentally, he touched the corpse-like cheek and with sudden shock he saw in the eyes such a look of cruelty that he fled. Leaving the Count's room through the window, Jonathan edged his way up the castle wall and gained his own quarters. Panting from exhaustion and terror, the prisoner threw himself upon his bed and tried to think.

As the sun faded, the sound of a key turning in his lock brought Jonathan to his feet. The corpse had returned to the world of the living. From the Count's sincerity, there was no hint of anything but friendship. Jonathan doubted his own sanity.

"Tomorrow, my friend, we must part. I shall begin a long journey and you, I am sure, have your law books and sweet wife awaiting. When morning comes the gypsies

will see me on my way. My carriage shall then bear you once again through the Borgo Pass."

Determined to test the words of his tormentor, Jonathan demanded, "Why may I not go tonight? Our legal dealings are completed."

"Because, kind guest, my coachman and horses are away on a mission."

"But I would walk with pleasure."

Dracula laughed diabolically and walked to the window. Throwing the shutters wide he pointed. Close at hand came the howling of many wolves. Their voices sprang up at the raising of his hand as an orches-

tra leaps to life under the baton of its conductor.

"Stop them. Stop them. I will wait till morning!" Jonathan cried. He covered his face with his hands to hide tears of frustration.

The last he saw of Count Dracula was such a red glow of triumph in his eyes that the devil in Hell might be proud.

Alone again, Jonathan heard low voices in the hallway. He pressed against the door to listen. The Count was whispering, "Your time has not yet come. Have patience. Tomorrow he is yours." There was a low ripple of laughter. In a rage, Jonathan threw open the door. Outside were the three terrible women, their pointed teeth bared like bloodthirsty animals. Before Jonathan's unbelieving eyes they turned into three wide-winged bats and flew out into the moonlight.

Terror possessed him and Jonathan threw himself on his knees. "Is the end then so near? Tomorrow! Tomorrow! Lord, help me and those to whom I am dear."

Sleepless, Jonathan spent the night writing in his diary. He had determined that death would not seize him without a struggle. With dawn he made his way again to the

Count's room. From there he retraced his steps along the dark passage to the chapel. Finding the key to the courtyard door was his only hope.

The huge boxes were still there. Yet while the others had their lids nailed shut, one was only partly covered. What Jonathan saw there filled his soul with horror. Dracula lay back upon the musty earth looking as if youth had been half renewed. The white hair was changed to dark iron grey. The cheeks were fuller and the mouth more red than ever, for on the lips drops of fresh blood trickled down to the chin.

He was a human leech. Jonathan trembled, realizing he himself might be a banquet for the dreaded sisters.

All his nerve was needed to search for the key, but there was no sign of it anywhere in the casket. The mocking expression on Dracula's bloated face drove Jonathan to madness. This was the monster he was helping transfer to England. Perhaps for centuries to come it would pray upon the helpless. How could he rid the world of this madness?

Jonathan seized a shovel which the workmen had used to fill the boxes. Lifting it high, he brought it down with all his might upon the hated fiend. At that instant, the blazing eyes turned upon Jonathan. The sight paralyzed him and the shovel fell from his hand, merely grazing Dracula's forehead.

A sound of booted feet echoed down the courtyard. His heart pounding, Jonathan fled up the stairs to his prison. In the courtyard, the gypsies began loading the heavy boxes onto the wagons.

The chapel doors creaked closed. The gate was unbolted and then locked again. A shout to the horses and the wagons began to roll along the mountain trail.

Jonathan sat down to make one last entry in his diary: "I am alone in this castle with those unGodly women. This cannot be what fate has planned for me. Rather than remain with these demons I shall try to scale the castle wall to its foundation.

"My pockets are filled with gold from the Count's room so that by wit or by money I may find a way from this dreadful place. Though the precipice is steep, any risk is preferable to another night here. If this is my last word, then goodbye, Mina, my dear wife."

Four

A week after her husband had left on his business trip to Transylvania, Mina Harker received a letter from Castle Dracula. Her disappointment at its message brought tears to her eyes.

"One whole month more," she thought. "He will be gone so much longer than we planned. And such a brief little note. How unlike Jonathan."

Determined not to allow her spirits to impede her husband's work, Mina answered by return post. She would be spending the month at the home of her friend Lucy Westenra.

She had been invited to prepare for Lucy's wedding. And Lucy's mother could use some help. Poor Mrs. Westenra's heart had not been strong since her own husband's death. The widow and her daughter would be delighted by Mina's visit.

Of course, Mina's letter was never delivered to Jonathan.

The recent bride and the bride-to-be were like sisters. Mina and Lucy had known each other since school days. Their joy at being together was marred only by the lengthening time with no mail from Jonathan.

Nevertheless, Mina did her best not to let her own worries detract from Lucy's excitement. It was easy to see why Lord Arthur Holmwood had fallen in love with her friend. Cheerful, rosy-faced Lucy was prettier than ever.

The handsome English nobleman often took both girls walking on the cliffs above the nearby seashore. While he was busy talking to his fiancée, Mina would gaze far over the water.

"Come Mina, you cannot see all the way to Transylvania from here," Lucy would tease.

"Your husband is probably on his way home this very minute," Lord Holmwood might add. "You can't imagine how a man's work sometimes makes him forget everything else."

Although Mina tried to agree, uneasiness was growing in her spirit. To make things worse, the fine 213

A little after dark, with the wind booming across the cliffs and waves rising in fury, the schooner plunged across the harbor and was carried over the sand flats. As the onlookers rushed down to the water's edge, an immense shaggy animal sprang up on deck from below. Running forward, it jumped from the ship's bow to the beach. When it reached the cliffs, the creature disappeared into darkness.

"What a huge dog," the startled Mina commented.

"Oh no," Lucy said. "It was a wolf, I'm sure."

"The lady's right," an old sailor agreed, "though I'm sure I can't see a wolf running free on a schooner."

The Harbor Master was summoned from his cottage and boarded the beached ship with the aid of rope ladders. On deck he found a hollow-eyed captain and three crew members, all near collapse.

They reported that the vessel was from Finland carrying cargo from river ports in Transylvania. Most of the voyage had been calm and farm goods had been unloaded at two ports. With only one more load to be delivered in England, the ship ran into violent storms.

These are the words in which the

weather had changed. Each morning found the seas stormier and the skies filled with dark, boiling clouds.

During an afternoon stroll, the two young ladies saw a crowd watching a ship struggle to make port. Fishermen had already beached their boats in the face of threatening seas. They stood by, ready to rush to the aid of the vessel which had lowered its sails and was trying to steer to shore.

captain described his uncanny voyage:

"On the morning of our second stormy day at sea, my chief mate reported that one of the crew was missing. We could not account for it. He had been relieved of his watch at eight bells that night. But he never got down to his bunk.

"The men were very uneasy. These were all steady fellows. They had sailed with me before and I could trust them for common sense and level heads. But now they said something was not right with the ship. They didn't know what — just something.

"I feared trouble was coming.

"Later, one of the mates came to my cabin. In a dumbfounded way he confided to me that he thought there was a stowaway aboard. He said that he had been smoking his pipe behind the deckhouse, taking shelter from the rain, when he saw a tall, thin man come up the companion way and go along the forward deck. My mate followed cautiously, but when he reached the bow he found no one and all the hatchways were closed.

"He was in a panic of superstition. You know how sailors are. So I decided to solve the problem be-fore the panic spread to the rest of the lads.

"I called the whole crew together and told them that, since there was talk of a stowaway, we would search from stem to stern. The first mate said it was foolish to yield to the men's imaginings. He said he would take care of any troublemakers with a handspike.

"I sent him to take the helm and just keep out of trouble. Then we began a thorough search of the ship, carrying lanterns high to light up every corner.

"Since our hold was filled with the last of the cargo, there were not many corners for hiding anyway. Did I tell you what the cargo is? No? We have there twenty-four big wooden crates. I even had them pry the cover off one of the boxes. It was filled almost to the top with some foul-smelling earth. Fancy, shipping dirt halfway across the continent! Who would be doing such a thing?

"Well, the men were much relieved when the search was over and they went back to work cheerfully.

"But there seemed to be some doom over this ship. Another man was lost during the night watch. Like the first, he was seen heading for his bunk—and then—vanished!

"My crew was in a state of fear. Two hands short and the wind blowing up a tempest. No one had time to sleep and I don't know that anyone would be able to sleep, anyway.

"Despite all our precautions, the first mate also fell prey to whatever curse was with us. We searched everywhere for him without luck. From then on, every man on board was ordered to carry a weapon at all times.

"By the time we sighted England, only four of my crew were left. Still the worst was yet to come. Heavy fog settled over the English Channel. Here we had hoped to signal for help or to make shore somewhere, but not a sail was sighted.

"We had to drift wherever the tides took us. I dozed off and was awakened by a scream. One of my men was on deck with his neck bleeding and full of claw marks. He claimed a wolf jumped him and tried to get its fangs in his throat.

"After that, my crew was beyond fear. They worked constantly to keep their minds off whatever curse we had on board.

"One midnight, I went to relieve the man at the wheel and found him

in a faint. He looked so wild-eyed I feared his reason had given way. He came close to me and whispered hoarsely, with his mouth to my ear, as though fearing the very air might hear: 'It is here. I know it now. I saw It, like a man — tall and thin and ghostly pale. It was in the bow looking to sea. I crept behind It and gave It my knife. But the knife went straight through It, empty as the air.' And as he spoke, he took his knife and drove it savagely into space.

"Then he said to me, 'But It is here and I'll find It. Maybe It hides

in one of them boxes in the hold. I'll unscrew them one by one.'

"He was raving mad and it was no use my trying to stop him. He couldn't hurt those crates full of dirt. I could only wait and pray for the fog to clear so that I could make harbor — any harbor.

"From my station on deck I heard him knocking away at the boxes and I hoped he would come out calmer. Work is good for a man when his mind is troubled.

"Instead there came up the hatchway a scream which made my blood run cold. He ran up on deck with his eyes rolling and his face all twisted with fear. 'Save me! Save me!' he was yelling. Seeing that I made no move, he said, 'You had better come too, Captain, before it it too late. I know the secret now. The sea will save us. That's our only hope.' And before I could say a word or move towards him he deliberately threw himself into the sea.

"The rest of the crew wanted to lower a lifeboat and get away. Maybe the wind heard them because the weather shifted and the fog blew off. Fearful winds came up and it took all of us to lower the sails and tie down the steering wheel.

"We never had a chance to see what it was in the hold. We just had to keep the ship afloat. But last night, the lads said they heard a wolf howling. I told them it was only the howling of the storm. But I could hear it myself. And that is the truth, I swear it on my honor as a Captain.

"If we had not made shore today, the last of my crew would surely have mutineed. Storm or no storm, they would have gone over the side in a lifeboat."

The Harbor Master and some of the fishermen with him had heard many a story of cursed ships. But none had ever listened to as honestly told a tale as this.

"Your mate was right," the Harbor Master said. "Somehow a wolf *was* on board. I saw it jump ashore myself. It headed right up the cliffs and through the town cemetery there at the top of the overhang.

"By now it's probably far into the woods outside of town. And that's where it belongs. I will warn the hunters to keep an eye out for the beast.

"As for the bit about the tall, thin man, I wouldn't set store by that. Your mate was out of his mind by then. Crazy. He was seeing things that don't exist.

217

"We'll get you unloaded and call in some of the boys from the shipyard to check out your vessel. Don't worry, we'll have her set to rights in no time.

"Meanwhile, you and your crew get some rest and food in town. One of these men here will show you the way."

Arrangements were made to have the cargo picked up by a delivery cart. The consignment was addressed to Carfax, an estate not far inland — an abandoned property recently sold to a foreign nobleman.

Customs reports listed the cargo as two dozen coffin-shaped boxes containing, they said, gardening earth.

All these peculiar events Mina described in a letter to Jonathan after Lucy had gone to bed. She would mail it the next day, although she had not received a reply to any of her messages for over a month.

Tears filled Mina's eyes as she went upstairs to the bedroom she shared with Lucy. In the darkened room she was startled by the sight of Lucy sitting at the window in her nightgown.

"It's much too chilly to sit there," Mina scolded and went to close the window. To her surprise, she saw that Lucy was asleep but with her eyes wide open. Mina glanced into the garden. Below stood the huge animal they had seen running from the ship. Its eyes, fastened upon Lucy, glowed evilly red. An ominous howl filled the air and the wolf's pointed fangs glinted in the moonlight before it turned and loped away.

No amount of shaking would waken Lucy. She almost seemed hypnotized. Finally Mina walked her over to the bed and covered her tightly with the quilt. Restless,

Mina fancied she heard the sound of howling until daybreak.

During the following nights, Lucy began walking in her sleep quite frequently. Mina would lie quietly in bed until she heard her room-mate's steady breathing. Then she would lock the doors and shutters so no harm could come to the sleepwalker. She dared not tell Mrs.

Westenra about her daughter's strange habit. The widow's heart was weak and worry about Lucy could be dangerous. Instead, Mina waited for Arthur Holmwood to return the following weekend for a visit to his fiance. Then Mina could unburden her secret.

Worry about Lucy added to concern about Jonathan's long silence wore Mina down. One night she fell asleep while reading before she locked the door. As the oil lamp sputtered and burned out, Mina woke. Lucy's bed was empty and the door was open.

Snatching her cape from its hook, Mina ran silently downstairs. The front door creaked to and fro in the breeze. Fear choked Mina's heart as she darted into the garden. Not there! Down the path to the cliffs where Lucy loved to walk. The clock was striking two in the churchyard as she reached the cliff where their favorite bench overlooked the harbor.

A full moon with heavy wind-driven clouds threw the scene into weird shadows. For a moment, Mina saw nothing. Then as a cloud passed, the silvery light struck a seated figure, snowy white. Something dark leaned above the white

219

form. Whether man or beast, Mina could not tell. Though her knees trembled, she called "Lucy, Lucy," and ran forward.

The dark figure stood upright exposing a white face and gleaming red eyes. Again a dark cloud obscured the moon. When Mina reached her friend's side, she was quite alone. Not a sign of any other living thing prevailed. Had it been a trick of the shadows?

Lucy sat fast asleep upon the bench. She was breathing in long, heavy gasps. Mina threw her own cloak over the white nightgown and fastened it with a pin. As she did so, Lucy wakened and clutched her throat.

"Oh Lucy, I must have pricked you with the pin," Mina cried. For on Lucy's neck were two little red points and a drop of blood. She moaned softly and leaning upon Mina's shoulder, allowed herself to be led home like a child.

During the next few nights all was peaceful. Mina wore the bedroom key on a ribbon around her wrist. She waited impatiently for the weekend so that Lord Holmwood might offer his advice. Although Lucy ate well and slept well, she was very pale.

After dinner one evening Lucy went to bed early. Mrs. Westenra simply blamed it on her daughter's nervousness about the coming wedding. The widow and Mina strolled in the garden. But when the sun set, Mrs. Westenra hurried indoors. Lately she had seen a bat flying about and preferred not to encounter it.

Mina walked alone awhile. The chill of the night air finally turned her towards the house where she spied Lucy resting by the open bedroom window. "She must be watching for me," Mina thought and waved. Lucy gave no sign whatever. Just then a bat flew up from the sill where it had perched without Mina noticing.

The alarmed girl raced upstairs. Lucy was fast asleep. Her hand was at her throat as if to protect it from the cold. Mina distinctly heard Lucy murmur, "Those red eyes again. They are always the same."

While drawing up the covers, Mina noted that the little pricks on her friend's neck had not healed. If anything, they were a trifle larger. Perhaps a doctor should be called. Yet Mina dared not upset the ailing Mrs. Westenra. Tomorrow Lord Holmwood was arriving. Together they would decide.

Joy! Joy! At 10 A.M. Arthur

Holmwood came with a letter given him by the village postman. At last, news of Jonathan. The letter was written by a Sister Agatha of the Budapest Hospital in Hungary. It read:

Dear Mrs. Harker,

"I write by desire of your husband who is not strong enough yet to do so himself, though progressing well, thanks to God. He has been under our care for nearly two weeks suffering from a brain fever. He wishes me to convey his love.

Mr. Harker has had some fearful shock. In his delirium, his ravings were dreadful — words such as wolves, blood, vampires and I dare not say what else. The doctor says there must be nothing to excite him for a long time.

We would have written earlier but knew nothing of his origin. He came by train from Transylvania. The conductor reports that he rushed into the station shouting for a ticket to England. Seeing his agitated manner, they

brought him to our hospital.

Be assured your husband is well cared for. No doubt he will be ready to travel in a few weeks. Blessings to you both.

Of course, nothing could keep Mina from her husband's side. Arrangements were made to meet the next boat train departing for the Channel. Lord Holmwood wished to drive her to the station in his carriage. Seeing how pale his fiancée was, he insisted Lucy remain at home. At last Mina had an opportunity to tell Arthur of Lucy's odd behavior.

At first he could not believe the stories. However, he promised to look at the mark on Lucy's neck without arousing her suspicion. If it seemed necessary, he would then call upon Professor Van Helsing. The Professor was an old friend of Lord Holmwood's father. He had been a famous surgeon in Amster-dam but lived now in retirement near the sea he loved. His house was not more than a half-hour ride from the Westenra's.

For the first time in months, Mina's mind was at ease. She boarded the train happily. Now everything would be all right, with Jonathan safe and Lucy's welfare in the strong hands of her husband-to-be.

Five

Arthur Holmwood quickly realized that Mina had good reason for concern. His fiancée was very weak. With the excuse that he wanted her to meet a dear friend of his family, Arthur tucked Lucy into his carriage that very day and took her to visit Professor Van Helsing.

A housekeeper met them at the door of the neat white cottage.

"If you wish to see the Professor, please wait in the living room."

As they stepped inside she went on talking in a cheerful, friendly fashion. "He spends a few afternoons each week at the insane asylum. You see he is writing a book about diseases of the mind. There is a new patient who interests him very much. Poor thing, the Professor says he is a very difficult case."

The slam of the entry door caused her to stop. "Ah, here he comes now," she announced.

"Dr. Van Helsing, there are some lovely young people to see you. That should be a relief after the asylum, now shouldn't it?"

A pleasant-faced elderly man entered. His once-red hair was almost all gray and behind his glasses, humorous, steady brown eyes appraised the visitors.

What he saw was his old friend's son, the younger Lord Holmwood, casting worried glances at a pale, drawn looking young woman who nevertheless had a quick smile and charming ways.

"Professor Van Helsing, this is my fiancee, Lucy Westenra," Arthur said". She lives so near here that I was determined not to let another day pass without you two meeting."

The doctor was delighted to have two young visitors. He instructed his housekeeper to serve tea and cakes and settled with them in the comfortable living room.

Seeing that the young lady was somewhat nervous, Professor Van Helsing decided to distract her by speaking of what interested him so much at the moment, the new patient at the lunatic asylum.

"This man is a puzzle to me," the Professor began. "His name is Renfield — a person of great physical strength. Most of the time he is rather quiet but he can become very excited. I am sure he could be quite dangerous for I have studied others of similar personality, though none as difficult to understand.

"He is very secretive. As yet, I have not been able to get at the reason. At the moment, his hobby is collecting insects. First it was flies. When I went to see him last week he had such a huge quantity I suggested he release them before it became unhealthy. He thought for a moment, then promised to clear them away in no more than three days. Of course, that was good enough to satisfy me.

"Next he turned his mind to spiders. He kept feeding them the flies, and you can well imagine that his fly population fell very quickly. Soon I could see that Renfield's spiders were becoming as much of a nuisance as the flies had been. So again I insisted that he get rid of them. He very cheerfully said he would and promptly picked several out of a box and popped them in his mouth."

Lucy gasped in distress.

"Dear young miss, I am sorry if I upset you," Professor Van Helsing said. "I understand. I was equally horrified by such actions. But let me tell you a little more. It is not just an old man prattling aimlessly on, for while I give you this description I am also sorting out my own thoughts on this complicated matter.

"When I scolded Renfield for eating the spiders, he argued with me in a very serious and constructive manner. His idea was that they are good and wholesome to eat because they give him their life forces. This, he insisted, was far better than any other kind of nourishment.

"Evidently he has some plan, because he keeps a little notebook in which he is always jotting down markings. Whole pages are filled with masses of figures, generally single numbers added up and then these totals are added up together again."

Hours had passed listening to the Professor's fascinating account before anyone realized night had come. As the moon rose, Lucy became more and more restless and walked back and forth from the window. Suddenly the two men heard a noise like the beating of a bird's wings against the glass. They jumped up in time to see a bat

ing her. She told them of her sleep-walking and showed the doctor the wound on her neck. His eyes grew wide with concern.

"Tell me about the first night you went sleepwalking, the night you received this mark on your neck. Nothing is unimportant," the doctor instructed, "give me every detail no matter how small."

Lucy began thoughtfully, "I knew I was dreaming that night as I rose from my bed, yet I didn't quite dream. It all seemed to be real. I only knew I wanted to get to the cliffs by the sea. I don't know why.

"I remember passing through the streets and over the bridge towards the water. I remember a silvery fish leaping and I heard a lot of dogs howling. The whole town seemed as if it must be full of dogs all howling at once.

"Then I have a vague memory of something approaching me — something that spoke in a soft but frightening voice. It had red eyes and I was compelled to look into them even though I tried to turn away.

"My mouth seemed filled with bitterness and I felt as if I were sinking into deep water. There was a singing in my ears, as I have heard happens to drowning sailors. My

swirling into the air and then diving again towards the window. Lucy shuddered and fell to the floor in a faint.

She awoke on Professor Van Helsing's couch. The concern of the kind and fatherly man caused Lucy's mask of cheerfulness to relax. Tears rolled down her cheeks as she said, "Professor Van Helsing, I dread worrying those I love. Still, I must confess to you and Arthur that I have been very troubled."

The poor girl then confided that terrifying nightmares were torment-

225

soul seemed to leave my body and I felt so lost — so alone and lost.

"When Mina began shaking me to wake me, it had the sharpness of an earthquake."

Lucy looked at Professor Van Helsing with confusion. Tears filled her blue eyes.

"Arthur," the Professor said, "you will leave this patient and her doctor alone for a little while. I shall examine your Lucy and find out why she is so pale."

That evening's entry in the doctor's record book read:

"Miss Westenra is somewhat bloodless although there is no apparent reason for this condition. Her health is otherwise vigorous despite the fact that she sleepwalks and has frightening dreams. I also observed a strange mark on her throat. It has the appearance of a puncture by some two-fanged viper. But the patient reports it is a pin prick. This calls for careful observation. I shall keep in close contact with Miss Westenra."

At the same time, the kind doctor's attention was also busy with the unusual case of Renfield, at the asylum. Renfield had a new pet. By placing crumbs between the bars of his window sill, the patient had managed to coax a sparrow to come to his hand and eat. It had then been a simple matter to tame the bird. In this fashion Renfield rid his room of the excess supply of spiders, which the sparrow far preferred to dry crumbs.

Those spiders that did remain, however, also were fed well, for he still caught flies and kept them handy in a small box.

During one of Professor Van Helsing's visits, Renfield ran up to the doctor and insisted that he must ask a very great favor.

"I must have a kitten, a nice little playful kitten that I can play with and teach and feed — and feed — and feed."

Professor Van Helsing was not surprised by this request. But he had no intention of allowing the growing collection of tame sparrows to be wiped out in the same manner as the flies and spiders. It was obvious that Renfield meant to feed the birds to the cat, therefore he said it would not be possible to bring a kitten into the asylum at that time.

Renfield's face contorted in such anger that one of the asylum attendants rushed to the doctor's side. The patient then threw himself on

226

his knees before them and implored the doctor to give him a cat. Professor Van Helsing was firm, however, and told him that it was against the rules of the asylum to permit patients to keep pets.

That this was the correct action became clear to the professor when shortly after, a messenger came to his home to report that Renfield was violently ill. At the asylum, the doctor discovered his patient's pillow had several specks of blood upon it. The sparrows were gone and several feathers were on the floor.

Obviously, Renfield had eaten the birds. Professor Van Helsing administered some medicine to put him to sleep and took Renfield's notebook to see if it might offer some explanation of this odd behavior.

The columns of numbers appeared to list how many flies were fed to each spider, and how many spiders to the birds. By eating the sparrows in turn, Renfield had written, he had absorbed thousands of lives into his body.

Why would the man have dreamed up such a scheme? The puzzle of Renfield became ever more challenging.

In addition to his work at the asylum, Professor Van Helsing kept his word to Arthur Holmwood. Every few days he stopped by to see Lucy Westenra. Lucy's health began to improve and plans for the wedding cheered her greatly.

No small part of the good spirits at the Westenra household was due to the arrival of Quincey Morris. He was an American from Texas. Together he and Arthur Holmwood had spent a year exploring for oil in Arab lands. Their adventures had made them as close as brothers. It was only natural he should arrive to be best man at the wedding.

Even the delicate health of elderly Mrs. Westenra responded to the

warm friendliness of Quincey Morris. He entertained them all with jokes and tall tales about life in Texas. For a while, the nightmares were banished from Lucy's dreams. However, once she came to breakfast and asked, "Did anyone hear a wolf howling during the night?" Another day she asked, "Did you notice a big bat flapping about the roof?"

Quincey interested them with stories about bats. He knew of many species near his ranch in the West. Most were harmless creatures, he explained. They did much good eating insects and rodents that destroy farm crops. But one type had been known to kill cattle and horses. These were ferocious creatures that ignorant people called Vampire Bats. Lucy looked frightened at this, but Quincey assured her that none existed in England.

Professor Van Helsing suggested that both young men quit their lodgings at the village inn and move to the Westenra's guest room. "It would be better for Lucy to know you are nearby. You see how color is returning to her complexion? She is sure to sleep restfully with you here to protect her."

Arthur and Quincey agreed to move the following day. Lucy went to bed feeling better than in many weeks. Nonetheless, once the lamp was dimmed, her old fears kept her awake.

Outside in the shrubbery sounded a sort of howl, like a dog's but more fierce. Lucy looked out of her window but saw nothing.

Mrs. Westenra walked into her daughter's room. "I heard you moving about, darling, and came to see if you are all right." The two sat upon the bed and drew the warm quilt over them. They talked drowsily, until the stillness was shattered by a rattling at the window.

"What is that?" Mrs. Westenra asked.

Lucy quieted her mother but she could hear the poor woman's heart pounding. After a moment, the howl echoed again, then a crash at the window. The shutters blew open and a gaunt gray wolf leaped in.

Mrs. Westenra screamed in fright and clutched wildly at her daughter. There was a choking sound and the terrified woman fell back.

Lucy could not move. It was as if a spell had turned her to stone. She slumped over her mother's body.

In such a state did Professor Van

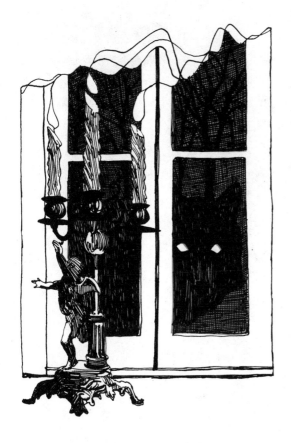

her mother was dead. The sun's rays showed the ravages of the girl's experience. She was hardly able to turn her head. In whispers she told of the wolf's intrusion. Shattered glass upon the rug showed that this was not merely another nightmare.

At times she slept. The three men noticed how much stronger she appeared at those moments. Awake she was haggard. When her pale lips were drawn back, her teeth seemed longer and sharper than normal.

All night Quincey and Arthur took turns sitting near her. Once she became very restless and in the full moon's light, Arthur saw a great bat wheeling around. Every now and again it struck the window with its wings and the sound caused Lucy to moan in her sleep.

The following day Quincey brought with him a huge mastiff dog. It belonged to the cemetery's caretaker who had let the American borrow it for a small fee.

"We'll lock the gate and let him run loose in the garden during the night," Quincey said. "Mastiffs are powerful fighters and fine guard dogs. No wolf would dare come near an animal of this size. I'll keep my own rifle handy too. I sure

Helsing find them when he came to call in the morning. On the bed lay the two women. Mrs. Westenra was covered with a white sheet, the edge of which framed her face — ghostly, drawn, with a look of terror fixed on it. By her side was Lucy, even more white and drawn. Her throat was bare, showing the two little wounds with a trickle of her life's blood still staining the fair neck.

A maid was sent to summon Lord Holmwood. By the time he and Quincey Morris arrived, the doctor had managed to revive Lucy. But

229

would like to get my sights trained on that mad animal."

For the second night, the young men sat watch over the sick girl. Professor Van Helsing remained downstairs reading from a pile of old books he had brought with him. He could be heard turning the pages. Once in a while he would mutter "God help her" when he thought no one heard.

Worn out by his vigil, Arthur dozed off. He was awakened by Professor Van Helsing's footsteps. When the doctor approached Lucy he drew in his breath sharply.

"Raise the blind. I need light," he commanded. He bent down and looked at her closely. "Good Heavens!" The wounds on Lucy's throat had completely disappeared.

Down in the garden, the mastiff lay dead with its head bitten almost completely off. What savage, powerful jaws did it take to destroy a dog of that great size?

The doctor put his arm about Lord Holmwood's shoulder. "She is dying. It will not be long."

Arthur covered his face with his hands and shook with grief. It was fortunate that he did not watch Lucy. It was as if two women lay dying. First she seemed sweet and angelic. Then her face became harsh and vicious. Her sharp teeth clamped together and her eyes were hard. Then sweetness again. She opened her eyes. They were all softness. "My true friends," she sighed, "please guard me and give me peace!"

Unable to answer, Arthur wept. Professor Van Helsing took her hand, "I swear it." Then Lucy's breathing stopped.

Quincey Morris led his friend from the room. "At least there is peace for her at last," he murmured.

The doctor turned towards them with solemnity, "Not so, alas, not so. It is only the beginning."

Quincey asked what he meant. He only shook his head and responded, "We can do nothing as yet. Wait and see."

Six

Nothing more could be done at the Westenra household. Wearily, Professor Van Helsing decided to look in on his patient at the asylum.

There had been a peculiar change in Renfield. The man, who had always been so talkative, was stubbornly silent. But he paced his room with the restlessness of an animal in a cage.

Upon seeing his doctor, Renfield turned his back angrily. "I don't want to talk to you. You don't matter anymore. The master is at hand."

He would explain no further but a veiled look came into his eyes which Professor Van Helsing recognized as a sign of possible trouble. Renfield stopped pacing and sat down on his bed.

"How are your spiders getting along?" the doctor asked. Once more the patient had begun collecting these creatures and the notebook was again filling up with columns of small figures.

"I don't care a pin about spiders now," Renfield responded. "There are more important sources of life than spiders you know." He then remained obstinately still and would not explain any further.

Leaving Renfield's room the Professor instructed the attendant on duty to keep a careful watch. Something was brewing in Renfield's mind. He was unpredictable.

Professor Van Helsing's thoughts turned to Lucy. Sadly he walked down the stairs of the asylum and into the library. There were similar cases to hers though they were not described in medical histories. Other books must be searched and studied — books dealing with superstition and mystery.

The attendant burst into the library as the Professor sat lost in thought. "Renfield has just escaped," he shouted. "I opened the door to check up on him and he pushed past me."

Both men hurried out of the building and searched the grounds. At the end of a line of trees they saw a running figure scale the high wall separating the asylum from a long-deserted neighboring estate called Carfax.

Professor Van Helsing signaled the attendant to follow silently, and the two climbed the wall after Renfield. They could see the patient just disappearing behind a corner of the eerie, neglected mansion on the estate. They crept up behind him. Renfield was standing pressed close against the ironbound oak door of an old chapel attached to the house. He was talking to something or someone he evidentally believed was within the chapel.

"I am here to do your bidding, master. I am your slave and I have worshiped you long from far off. I have been waiting for you to come. I knew you would not fail me. Now you will reward me, master, will you not? I await your commands and you will not pass me by, will you, master? You will share with me the things you take?"

Turning at last, Renfield saw that he had been discovered. Instead of running away, as they expected, the madman strolled back towards the asylum, smiling happily. After he had been locked in his room, he looked out the window toward the mansion at Carfax and called, "I shall be patient, master.

I know you are coming. Now I can wait."

For forty-eight hours Renfield sat silently in his room. He did not sleep, saying he was not tired, and refused to eat, saying food did not tempt him.

Professor Van Helsing, trying to draw him into conversation, asked if he was still unhappy at not being allowed to keep a kitten. Renfield sneered, "I don't want a kitten anymore. I have more important plans. I am waiting."

The Professor decided to allow Renfield to escape again in hope of gaining some clue to his new behavior. The door was left unlocked all day. Not until the sun began to sink behind the wall of the asylum did he attempt to leave.

This time two attendants followed with the doctor. The madman returned along the same route he had first taken through the overgrown gardens of the mansion. He went straight to the old chapel and pressed himself against the door. "Master, master, why haven't you come? Please don't forget me. I have been waiting for you so long."

Wheeling about, Renfield saw Professor Van Helsing and his aides. He was furious, throwing

233

himself upon the doctor as if he would kill him. The attendants seized him and were about to force on a restraining jacket when an odd change took place.

Renfield grew calm. He looked up at the top of the dark windowed mansion. Over the gabled roof, against the moonlit sky, a tremendous bat flapped its wings. Bats usually wheel and flit about but this one dropped to the branch of a nearby tree and sat watching the group by the chapel. Unblinking red eyes stared down at them from the bat's face.

"You needn't tie me," Renfield said. "I shall go quietly now."

Without struggle he went back to the asylum. But Professor Van Helsing felt something ominous in his calmness and could not forget the events of that night. He was sure now that the bat at Carfax was the same one which had pursued Lucy. That the bat had unnatural powers was obvious. Yet who would believe this?

Quincey Morris and Arthur Holmwood were waiting in the Professor's study when he awoke the next morning. Lucy's funeral was arranged and the young men came to accompany Professor Van Helsing to the undertakers.

All the mourners who had come to view the casket were amazed at the dead girl's appearance. Death had erased all traces of her suffering. She was as beautiful as in life. Many could not believe they were looking at a corpse.

"Can she really be dead?" Arthur kept repeating in his grief.

After the last visitor left, the Professor carried a small bag over to the casket. From it he took a handful of wild garlics and scattered them about the coffin. He placed wild rose branches at her head.

Finally he lay a small gold cross on Lucy's lips.

"You must trust me," he said to Arthur and Quincey as they looked on in surprise. "I have been reading in books that deal with sicknesses such as doctors cannot cure."

"This looks as if you are trying to put off some evil spell," Quincey commented.

"I have reasons for all I do," the doctor answered. "You saw how Lucy pleaded with me with her beautiful dying eyes. Did you not hear me promise to protect her? And she died grateful? Yes? There are terrible days before us. Will you have faith in me?"

The two men each grasped his hand in turn. Though mystified, they trusted the Professor completely.

All agreed to meet in several hours when the coffin lid was to be permanently closed. Arthur and Quincey arrived after the Professor. They found him in a state of great distress.

"Look," he groaned pointing to the coffin. "It is too late!" At first the young men did not understand. Then they saw that the garlic, the roses, and the cross were gone.

"But who took them?"

"Excuse me, sirs," the undertaker interrupted, "it was her uncle who took them."

"What uncle? Lucy had no uncle!" Lord Holmwood almost shouted.

"Excuse me, gentlemen," the undertaker said, "a tall, imposing gent came shortly after you left. He said he was the late Miss Westenra's uncle. In fact, he had the air of a nobleman. I must say, sirs, he somewhat frightened me with his ways. His face was as white as anyone in my coffins and his eyes had a most peculiar glow. I didn't dare question him."

"Of course not," Professor Van Helsing nodded. "How were you to know? How is anyone to know?"

Lucy was laid to rest alongside her mother in the family crypt not far from the cliffs she had once strolled along. As soon as the funeral was over, Lord Holmwood and Quincey Morris left for London. Professor Van Helsing insisted they go away from the sad surroundings for a while. "You must remain strong and ready if I should need you back here," he warned.

Although the men did not understand his meaning, they did as he wished.

235

* * *

These were the unhappy events that greeted Mina and Jonathan Harker upon their return from Transylvania. Jonathan had made remarkable progress in his recovery from the moment his wife arrived. She had barely unpacked when he began insisting that they go home to London. Even the doctors agreed. Home would be a healing place for the Englishman.

But London was not to provide peace. A letter awaited the couple:

My dearest friends,

You will be grieved to hear that Mrs. Westenra died five days ago and that our beloved Lucy died the day before yesterday. They are in the cemetery at the edge of the village. I regret to be the one to mar your return with such tidings. Signed, Arthur Holmwood.

Lord Holmwood came to visit the Harkers shortly after their arrival. He knew Mina would prefer hearing about Lucy's last days from another who loved her. With him came Professor Van Helsing.

"You must forgive my intruding," the silver-haired doctor said. "Arthur tells me you were with Miss Westenra when she first showed her strange symptoms. Will you do a curious scientist the favor of telling every detail? Many pieces of this puzzle must be fitted together before Lucy rests peacefully as she deserves."

It took hours for Mina to recount the whole story. During the telling she was alarmed by the expression of her husband's face. Was he still too ill to hear such a tragic tale?

In turn, Lord Holmwood told Mina of what had happened during her absence.

At last it was over. Jonathan Harker rose to his feet unsteadily. "Wolves," he echoed, "bats — and the man who defiled Lucy's coffin had fiery eyes?"

He didn't wait for an answer. Instead he reached into his desk and brought out a small book. This he handed to Mina. "I have not told you before of my own adventures. I was sure no person would believe me. Now, I see the threads of my life and Lucy's death were woven together. Here is the diary I kept while I was in Count Dracula's castle. I am sure he and Lucy's so-called uncle are the same. Please read this aloud."

All the listeners were stunned by Jonathan's journal. Professor Van

236

Helsing spoke first: "Miss Mina, your husband is a good and brave man. My life has been so full of work that I have not had much time for friendships. But all of you are close to my heart. I will gladly do anything to make your lives safe and happy. What I learned tonight opens the gate to me. This darkness will be conquered."

As Professor Van Helsing paced to and fro while speaking his eyes were caught by a newspaper on the table. Color faded from his face. Reading intently, the doctor moaned, "My God. So soon. So soon."

Following is the story he read:

SEASIDE MYSTERY

For the third day, this seaside village has been distressed by the disappearance of small children. In all cases, the children were found after a night of absence. They were too young to give any proper account of themselves. Each has spoken, however, of a pale lady in white who kissed them.

It is always late evening when these children are missed. No harm seems to have come to them except for a small loss of blood. All subjects had tiny punctures on the throat. Police believe these were made by a snake or rodent.

Parents are advised not to let children out of sight until the animal has been captured.

Quincey Morris turned to Professor Van Helsing. "Could those children have been attacked by a bat, doctor? If so, we would at last understand how a healthy young woman like Lucy was slowly drained of blood and died."

"You are a clever man, Quincey," the Professor acknowledged. "Yet you do not look beyond your own experience. Some things cannot be explained logically.

"Ah, it is the fault of our science that it wants to explain all that occurs in life. If it cannot explain, why then it says there is nothing to explain. Tell me then, for I am a student of man's brain, how can you explain hypnotism or the fact that some can read the thoughts of others?

"There have always been mysteries in life. Let me tell you, my friends, that experiments are done

237

today in electricity which would not so long ago have caused the inventors to be burned as wizards.

"What I am trying to tell you is that you must keep your minds open to what you once thought was impossible. I want you to believe — to believe in things that your senses tell you are not to be believed. Do not let the little bit of truth you know block the entrance to truths you have not learned yet.

"I see in your expressions that you trust me. You have taken the first step. So I will test your understanding.

"You think those punctures on the children's throats were made by the same creature that made the wound on Lucy's neck?"

"I suppose so," Quincey said.

"Then you are wrong. I wish it were so, but no. It is far worse."

"In God's name, what do you mean?" Lord Holmwood demanded.

"Those punctures were made by Miss Lucy. Tomorrow I will prove it. Do you dare to come with me?"

The following evening found Arthur, Quincey and Professor Van Helsing in the churchyard. With some difficulty, because of darkness, they located the Westenra family tomb. Arthur Holmwood's hand shook as he unlatched the creaking door. Once inside they dared to light a candle.

The musty crypt was dank with the scent of faded floral wreaths. Quincey went to work immediately, unscrewing the coffin lock. As the last bolt was drawn out, the Professor raised the heavy lid. To their horror, the coffin was empty!

"Come," the Professor beckoned. He motioned the others to close the casket and lock the tomb. They then concealed themselves behind some headstones in the churchyard and waited. It was a lonely vigil. How slowly the hours dragged. Not until a cock crowed before dawn did some movement attract their attention.

A white figure drifted out of the shadows. Without a blade of grass bending or the creak of the door, it passed through the wall of the tomb. All was silent.

Sunlight came at last and warmed the coldness in the hearts of the three men. Again they unlocked the crypt and lifted the coffin lid. There lay Lucy, just as she had been at her funeral. If possible she was more beautiful than ever. How could she be dead? Her lips were

so red. This was not the corpse of someone buried more than a week!

"Are you convinced now?" asked the Professor. He parted the lips. Her teeth were as sharp as an animal's. "This is how the little children were bitten. She is not dead. She is Un-Dead. It is for us to help her die."

Lucy was already lost to the world of the living, but still the young men shuddered at those words. They waited for Professor Van Helsing to continue. "She has not yet taken anyone else's life. And she is not long enough a vampire to create more vampires, as Dracula does. But that will come in time if we do not act now."

"Then we must do whatever you direct, Professor," Quincey said. "I will speak for Arthur, too. Now he is too shocked to know what is right. But we will follow wherever you lead."

At a quarter before midnight, the three returned to the graveyard. The night was dark and they kept close together, with the Professor striding impatiently ahead. By the light of a shaded lantern he unlocked the tomb door. Again Quincey undid the lid of the leaden coffin. Though they already knew what to expect, they recoiled on seeing the empty velvet-lined interior.

Professor Van Helsing opened his medical bag and removed a long garland of garlic bulbs. These he proceeded to hang over the tomb's door. At its threshold he lay branches of blossoming wild rose. On the coffin itself, he put a small Bible.

Closing the door quietly, the group hid behind gravestones nearby and scanned the shadows of the churchyard.

Never did stone grave markers appear so menacing. The cypress and yews seemed the embodiment of gloom. Far away, the howling of dogs in their kennels sent a woeful echo through the night.

There was a long spell of silence. Then, far down the avenue of trees they saw a dim white figure advance. Something dark was held close in its arms.

The figure stopped and a ray of moonlight showed a young woman dressed in the garments of the grave. They could not see the face, for it was bent over what seemed to be a child. There was a pause, then a little cry, such as a baby gives in its sleep while dreaming. Arthur and

Quincey started to step forward, but the Professor's warning glance kept them back.

As they watched, the white figure stood up and moved forward once more. Hearts grew as cold as ice as the features of Lucy Westenra became visible.

How she had changed. The sweetness had turned to cruelty and the pure smile had become a greedy grimace.

Professor Van Helsing stepped out and Arthur and Quincey followed, forming a line in front of the tomb's door. Quincey raised the lantern and in the light that fell on Lucy's face, they could see that her lips were stained with fresh blood.

The men shuddered with horror. Even Professor Van Helsing's iron nerve failed. If Quincey had not seized his arm and held him up, he would have fallen.

When Lucy saw them, she drew back with an angry snarl, such as a cat gives when taken unaware. Her eyes blazed with unholy light. There was a cold-bloodedness in her gaze which caused Arthur to groan aloud.

She advanced toward Arthur and stretching out her arms said,

"Come to me, Arthur. Leave these others and come with me. We were meant to be together. Come now, of your own will."

There was something devilishly inviting in her speech — like little silver bells — ringing and hypnotizing. Arthur seemed under a spell. He put out his hands and moved toward her open arms.

Lucy smiled triumphantly and reached to embrace Arthur when Professor Van Helsing leaped forward and held between them his small, gold cross. Lucy recoiled.

Her face was distorted with rage and she sprang back as if to enter the tomb.

Within a foot or two of the door, however, she stopped, arrested by some irresistible force. Never did a face show such malice. The eyes seemed to throw out sparks of fire. The bloody mouth opened in a snarl.

Seconds became an eternity before Arthur moaned, "Let her go. Let her get into that infernal casket. I can't bear it."

He rushed to the door of the tomb and ripped off the garland of garlic and the rose blossoms. The white-robed vampire passed through the solid stone wall as if walking through fog.

With understanding and sorrow, the Professor gazed at Arthur. "Answer me, my friend, shall we proceed with our work?"

Arthur clenched his fists in an ef-fort to control his tear-filled voice. "Do as you must. There can be no horror ever that is worse than this. We must stop her."

The doctor calmly replaced the garlic and roses on the door. When this was done he lifted the sleeping child and walked towards the cemetery gate. "Come now, we can do no more. A funeral is scheduled to take place this morning. I would prefer that no one meet us here. We shall return in late afternoon, before the sun sets and that tormented Un-Dead awakes.

"Right now we must return this child to the village. Not much harm has been done. Lucy is not yet that dangerous. The infant will not even know what truly happened.

"By this time tomorrow our ordeal will be finished. Then you will look back and see that all our trials were necessary."

Seven

An hour before sunset, Arthur and Quincey called for the Professor. Together, they went to the cemetery. Entering the tomb, they closed the door behind them and lit their lanterns.

Despite his knowing what they would find, Arthur turned ashen when the coffin was open and Lucy was revealed in her unnatural beauty. He asked, almost of himself, "Is this really my Lucy or only a demon in her shape?"

"It is her body but it is not Lucy. Wait a while and you shall see her as she was and really is." The Professor took out of his bag a round wooden stake.

"This is made of a branch of the wild rose," he explained. "But before we begin, let me tell you this. I have been studying the lore and experience of the ancients. They knew the true powers of the Un-Dead. When they become such, they have the curse of immortality thrust upon them. They cannot die, but must go on, century after century, adding new victims and mul-

tiplying their evil, for all those who die from the efforts of the Un-Dead, become themselves Un-Dead.

"So the circle goes, ever-widening, like ripples from a stone thrown into water.

"Friend Arthur, if you had accepted the embrace of this vampire, as she wished you to last night, you would in time have become like her. The career of this unhappy lady has just begun. Those children whose blood she drank were not hurt seriously. But if she keeps on with her vile prowling, her power is such that she can call them to her whenever she wishes.

"When we put an end to her half-death, the wounds on their throats will disappear and they will go back to their play completely free of her spell. And most blessed of all, when she is made to rest as true dead, then the soul of that dear lady whom we love shall at last be free."

Looking steadily at Arthur, the Professor went on. "You must be brave a little longer. Yours should be the blessed hand that releases

Lucy from this curse. Take this stake and drive it into her heart. It will be a fearful ordeal, but we, your true friends, will pray for you."

Once Lord Holmwood set his mind upon the action, his hand never wavered. He struck the stake in with all his might. The thing in the coffin writhed. A hideous screech came from the bright lips. The face twisted and the sharp ivory teeth ground together.

The body shook and quivered and thrashed in wild contortions. But Arthur did not falter. His face was set in blind determination. The

sight of it gave courage to the Professor and Quincey, who stood by reading the prayer for the dead from their missal.

As the final blow was struck, Arthur reeled and would have collapsed if Quincey had not caught him. Great drops of sweat sprang from his forehead and his breath came in broken gasps. If he had not been forced to this task by more than human considerations, he could never have completed it.

At last the terrible moment was over. In the coffin no longer lay the awful vampire threatening destruction. Once more Lucy looked as sweet as she had in life. True there were traces of her illness and suffering. But her calmness spread like sunshine within the tomb.

Arthur walked over to the bier. A glad expression filled his eyes and he bent to kiss her. "Her soul is free. She no longer belongs to that demon."

The Professor placed his Bible in the coffin and laid garlic bulbs at her head and feet. Then the lid was sealed forever.

* * *

Jonathan and Mina Harker had remained behind in London. Professor Van Helsing warned them that Jonathan's health could not yet stand the experience of a difficult mission.

Their relief was enormous when, after several days of waiting, they received a telegram from the three friends announcing:

"We have accomplished our work. Lucy rests in peace as she was meant to. We are not yet free of responsibility. Must have your help in next, and we hope final, chapter of this task. Please come by train at your earliest convenience."

Mina looked at Jonathan as he read the telegram aloud. His jaw was set in a determined way that could only mean they would be leaving for the seaside village immediately. She packed their bags and in only a few hours they were seated in a horse-drawn cab, bound for the railway station.

The train was not due for another hour, so the young couple found seats near the window of the station tearoom. From there they could watch the parade of travelers. Mina's attention was drawn to a beautiful girl in a pink flowered hat.

"Oh Jonathan," she commented, "Do you see that lovely hat?"

Jonathan turned to follow her gaze. Suddenly he clutched Mina's arm so tightly that she gasped. He had turned very pale and his eyes were round with terror and amazement.

"My God, Mina, do you see him? Can that really be him?"

Mina scanned the people in front of the tearoom. Jonathan was staring at a tall, thin man with an arched nose and pointed moustache. The man did not notice the Harkers, since he in turn was staring at the pretty girl with the flowered hat.

From her vantage point Mina saw that the man's face was unusually white with a hard and cruel quality. Between his parted lips, pointed white teeth protruded slightly.

It came to Mina with a shock that this could be the face of none other than Count Dracula.

"Jonathan, why is he here in London? What shall we do?"

The question was answered for Mina when the Count turned around and caught sight of the two awestruck faces peering at him. His expression was transformed to one of livid hatred. If a glance could destroy, Dracula's glare of malice and viciousness would surely have shattered the Harkers.

Instead, he swirled away into the crowds, dark cape flapping about his

245

shoulders like beating wings. Instantly he was lost to their sight.

Both Mina and Jonathan reached for the other's hand.

"He is even more terrifying than I dreamed," Mina exclaimed. "But he is much younger than you described in your diary."

Jonathan kept looking at the spot on the sidewalk where his tormentor had been only a minute before. Mina could barely hear him answer. "Yes, much, much younger. Who knows whose youth was sacrificed to give him that appearance."

Hours later when their story was related in Professor Van Helsing's study, it already seemed that the incident was unreal.

"He is real enough," Arthur Holmwood said bitterly. "Yes, we know that now. It might even have been my own dear Lucy who returned his youth to him so that he might seek out others as his prey."

"There is the task we have set for ourselves," the Professor announced, "to find the author of this tragedy and stamp him out. This devil is more cunning than mortal man and as strong as twenty. He is not human and not beast. He can appear in many forms — the wolf, the bat, even a moth. He throws no shadow and commands wild animals. If he is threatened, he can vanish like a fog.

"How then are we to destroy him?" the Professor went on. "How shall we find his whereabouts, and having found it, how can we conquer such a foe?

"My friends, this is a terrible chore we undertake. If we lose the fight, we lose more than our lives. We lose our hearts and our souls. I am old. I cannot say no to this challenge. I do not have many years left. But you others are young. Some have seen sorrow but there are fair days in store for all of you."

"We have no choice," Mina replied. "It is upon our consciences now. There is no safety while he walks the earth."

"Remember, to fail is worse than death," Jonathan warned. "We would become like him, foul things of the night, Un-Dead and without peace.

"I believe that I can lead you to his hiding place," Jonathan said, "for I drew up the documents that made it his. The mansion at Carfax must be where he keeps his coffins of earth. It is no more than five miles from here."

246

"Unbelievable," the Professor mused, "that it never occurred to me that the house adjoining the asylum might be the Count's hiding place. I cannot forgive myself. Surely, I had enough clues from the conduct of my patient, Renfield."

"Now we understand," Quincey added. "He needs earth from his own ancestral graveyard as a refuge. He probably plans to hide those boxes all over England. Then he will be free to roam anywhere at will, simply returning to his own grave from sunrise to sunset. Find the boxes and destroy them and we will have found and destroyed Dracula."

"I am with you," said Lord Holmwood, "for Lucy's sake if for no other reason."

"I answer for Mina and myself," Jonathan said. "I was in part responsible for bringing that monster to England. Therefore, I am morally obliged to drive him out."

"Count me in," Quincey Morris announced in his usual forthright manner.

"Then we are agreed," Professor Van Helsing said with determination.

The little band of companions stood and joined their hands together. So was their solemn compact sworn.

Professor Van Helsing turned to his guests and spoke with the authority of a teacher.

"You know what we have to contend with. Yet, we, too, are not without strength. We have on our side the resources of science. We are free to act and think and are not driven by unnatural forces. The hours of the day and the night are ours equally while the power of the Un-Dead ceases, as does that of all such evil, at the sun's rising.

"The vampire can live on and does not die by mere passing of time. He can flourish and even grow younger from the blood of the living. But he cannot survive without this diet. He does not eat as others do. Even Jonathan, who lived under his roof for weeks, never did see him eat, never!

"He is more of a prisoner than the madman in his cell. There are things which afflict him so that he has no power: The garlic plant stops him like an iron shield. A branch of wild rose on his coffin keeps him locked within it. A silver bullet fired into his grave forever destroys it as his refuge. The same bullet fired into his body or a stake

247

of the wild rose driven through his heart will make him truly dead.

"Take courage. Goodness is on our side. Now think about what we have spoken here tonight," the Professor concluded. "As soon as you are rested we must begin the search for Dracula. Time is now on his side — we must allow him as little of this time as possible."

After a brief nap for the exhausted men, it was agreed that Jonathan would lead them to Carfax. Meanwhile, Mina would accompany Professor Van Helsing on his visit to the insane asylum. In that way, she would not be left wait-

ing alone and worrying. Also, the mansion at Carfax was near enough to the asylum for the Professor to be summoned should his help be needed.

"Tell me," Mina asked, "is your patient dangerous?"

"He is generally quite calm," the Professor answered. "But he has an unpredictable nature."

"What you have told us about Mr. Renfield has interested me very much. Do you think I might meet him while I am in your hospital today?"

Mina looked so earnest and serious that the doctor could not refuse her. With an attendant accompanying them, no harm would come to Mina, he was sure. Perhaps a visit from a sympathetic lady would encourage Renfield to reveal more of his philosophy. Any clue to the mystery of the man's mind would be welcome.

The Professor entered Renfield's room alone at first and told him that a lady would like to meet him, to which he simply asked, "Why?"

"She is spending the day here as my guest," the doctor replied, "and hopes to meet some of the patients."

"Oh, very well," Renfield said, "let her come in."

He sat down on the edge of his

bed, watching warily. Mina walked in with an easy gracefulness. Her natural manner reassured the doctor since he knew that calmness and ease were qualities a mad person most respects. She stepped over to Renfield and held out her hand.

"Good evening, Mr. Renfield," Mina smiled pleasantly. "You see I know you, for Dr. Van Helsing has spoken a little about you. I am Mrs. Harker."

Cautiously Renfield asked, "Are you a doctor, too?"

"Oh, no," Mina said.

"Then what are you doing here?"

"My husband and I are staying at Dr. Van Helsing's home for a while."

"Then don't stay any longer!"

"But why?"

Renfield tightened his lips and remained quiet.

Mina tried to coax him from his silence. "The doctor tells me you are very good at taming birds. I am interested in them myself. We have several cages of songbirds at home in London."

Haltingly, at first, a conversation began about the ways of winning a bird's trust. To the Professor's amazement, Mina Harker's presence touched some deep chord in Renfield's personality, for he spoke with the gifts of a polished gentleman.

In a tone that had the most complete sanity, he brought the subject around to himself.

"I have always loved all living things both of the insect and animal world. My respect for them turned into a strange belief. Indeed, it was no wonder that my friends were alarmed and insisted on my being confined to an asylum. I used to fancy that life could be passed from one creature to another. At one point, I held the conviction that by eating living things — even insects — I could lengthen my own life indefinitely."

Renfield's expression became thoughtful, then sorrowful. Abruptly he stood up and made a courtly bow.

"Goodbye, Mrs. Harker."

Mina shook his hand, saying pleasantly, "Goodbye. I hope I may someday see you in more happy surroundings."

"No," Renfield answered sharply, "I pray to God that I may never see your sweet face again. May He bless you and keep you!"

Mina was very touched by the incident. She and the Professor went to the asylum's library to talk and await her husband's return.

249

The sun had been down for more than an hour when Jonathan, Quincey, and Arthur reached the asylum. They had an eerie tale to tell.

The three had planned to arrive at Carfax by early afternoon. But on nearing the estate, their horses began acting queerly. Quincey dismounted to calm them, whereupon they reared up, threw the riders, and galloped wildly off into the forest.

By walking, the four gained Carfax just as the sun went down. Jonathan still had a master key to the property. The door of the great stone house creaked open on rusty hinges. Light from their lamps illuminated a huge hall, thick with dust. Spiders' webs hung like torn draperies from the ceilings.

"There is a family burial chamber beneath the house," Jonathan explained. "I am sure we must go there."

After a few wrong turns, they found a low arched door ribbed with iron bands. It pushed open with some effort.

A strong smell of decay filled the grim chamber. But the boxes were indeed there. Obviously, Dracula had not yet found time to conceal them.

The darkness, dust, and loathesome air oppressed the men. Jonathan was fighting to overcome a dizziness that left him weak. He walked to the vaulted door to breathe a little more freely. In the dark passage beyond, concealed by shadow, he saw the outlines of what appeared to be a face — the ridge of a nose, red eyes, bright lips set in a deadly pallor. The vision lasted a few seconds and then it was gone.

As he turned, Jonathan found Lord Holmwood staring over his shoulder as though bewitched.

"What a fright," the nobleman said, "I almost thought I saw a face. But it was only the play of the shadows." He turned back to his inspection of the boxes.

Jonathan decided to say nothing and joined his companions. The men were going from one coffin to the other. First, they fired a silver bullet into each coffin. Then they lifted the cover. Each in turn proved empty.

"At least we know Dracula will never again be able to sleep in these coffins," Quincey said.

Jonathan reached the final box. He uttered a cry of disappointment. "There are only twenty-three. I counted twenty-four when the

250

gypsies carried them from the castle."

"You are right," Arthur Holmwood replied. "I checked with the Harbor Master. Twenty-four were unloaded from the ship."

Wind caught the chapel door. It slammed shut and the men jumped with fright. All at once the chapel became alive with rats. They swarmed over the floor and clawed at the men's boots. Lamplight shining on their squirming dark bodies and glittering eyes made the room look like a band of earth alive with fireflies. Their squeaking and scratching was deafening.

It was as if an evil presence suddenly filled the room. The men forced the door open again and fled into the cool night air.

Professor Van Helsing and Mina listened to the story with avid interest. "So far, no harm has come to you," the Professor said. "And we have been successful in sterilizing twenty-three of Dracula's hiding places. When we find the twenty-fourth we will face our most dangerous struggle."

Eight

Stopping at the asylum the following day, Professor Van Helsing found Renfield in a very excited state. Despite this, his speech and thinking appeared totally sane.

"Doctor, you must release me at once and let me return home," Renfield said.

There was such dignity and determination in the man's manner that Professor Van Helsing was astonished. Experience had taught him that a patient's character could not change overnight. The Professor suggested it might be better to wait a few days before making such an important decision. He acknowledged that Renfield seemed to be improving very rapidly but it would take time to be sure.

This did not satisfy Renfield. "But I fear that you don't understand. I must go at once — now — this very hour. Could you look into my heart, doctor, you would approve of my purpose. I am not free to explain them, but I swear to you my reasons are sound and unselfish and spring from the highest sense of duty."

Professor Van Helsing looked at him earnestly. "You try to impress me with your complete recovery, sir, yet you will not even say why you must leave so suddenly. How can I be sure you are to be trusted?"

Renfield shook his head. "Doctor, if I were able to speak I would. But I am not my own master in this matter. Please believe me. If you refuse," he concluded ominously, "the responsibility for whatever happens will be on your head!"

The Professor rose from his chair. Frantically, Renfield held out his arm to stop him. He spoke with deepest emotion. "Let me beg you, doctor, to release me at once. You don't know what you do by keeping me here. Can't you understand that I am no lunatic in a mad fit but a sane man fighting for his soul? There is a way for me to make up for all my mistakes of the past and to stop the tragedy of the future. I must save my soul from guilt. Let me go! Let me go!"

Fearful that the man would become even wilder, the doctor took him by the arm and led him to his

253

bed. "Without an honest explanation from you of your behavior there is no way for me to release you now. Calm yourself and we shall work together for your complete recovery."

As he closed the door, Professor Van Helsing heard Renfield say, "Do not forget that I did what I could to convince you."

In the quiet of his home after dinner, the Professor thought about the interview with Renfield. He was troubled and worried by the man's desperation.

Jonathan and Mina had gone up to their room. Arthur and Quincey sat near the lamp, poring over maps of the area, hoping to find some other likely spots where the last of Count Dracula's coffins might be hidden.

The clock chimed midnight when an attendant from the asylum came with an urgent message. Renfield had been found half dead in his room by the night watchman.

"I think, sir, he will not live very long. He looks as if he had been attacked by some very strong person. I can't understand. His door was locked from the outside and the window bars are all in place."

Quincey and Arthur insisted on coming along with the Professor. They could see that he was badly shaken by the news.

Renfield had indeed suffered some terrible injuries. He had been lifted from the floor, where he had been found, and laid upon his bed. His breathing was slow and painful. Hearing the doctor's voice, he lifted his head.

"Give me some water," he said, "my throat is dry and I must tell you . . . I had a dream . . ."

Professor Van Helsing moistened the parched lips and the patient revived a bit.

"It was no dream. I cannot deceive myself. I am dying and you must hear me. Do you remember when I asked you to let me go?"

"Yes," the doctor nodded.

"When you left I sat here in a state of misery for hours. My tired brain cooled down by evening, though. I heard a wolf howling somewhere on the grounds. And I knew my master had come. When you were with me earlier, I dreaded to see him again. But when I finally saw his face, I was happy to give my mind over to him."

"Where did you see this master of yours?" Professor Van Helsing asked.

rats. Hundreds of them. Then dogs to eat them. All with years of life to give to me.

"While I watched he held up his hands and they all disappeared. It was his way of saying, 'I will give you all these lives, and many more even greater, if you will worship me.' Then he showed me Mrs. Harker, asleep."

Quincey and Arthur who had been sitting and listening, stiffened and leaned forward, alarm widening their eyes.

Renfield continued with great effort. "It made me angry to think he would want to drink up her life. She was a kind and pretty lady. I didn't want him to force her — to make her become — like his others.

"So when he moved close to me I grabbed at his throat. That urge for freedom came back to me, just as when I spoke to you earlier. I felt I could stop him.

"I am quite strong, you know. He struggled but I held tight. I thought I was going to win until I saw his eyes. Those piercing eyes. They turned my strength into water and he lifted me up and hurled me to the floor with all his might." The voice began fading.

Professor Van Helsing jumped

"Oh, he came up to the window in a mist. But he was solid enough when I saw him. He was laughing with his red mouth. And his sharp teeth were real enough, all right. And he began promising me things, not just by words but by making them appear in this very room."

"What things?"

"First moths and spiders. Then

up. "We know the worst now. Dracula was here and we know his purpose. It must not be too late. There is not an instant to spare."

Leaving the dying Renfield with his aides, the Professor, Quincey, and Arthur raced to their carriage. They drove the horses at full gallop to the Professor's cottage.

During the panicked drive, none spoke. They dared not put their thoughts into words though they all shared the same sense of dread.

Silence greeted them when they reached the house.

"Mina and Jonathan must be sleeping," Quincey said.

Bounding up the stairs three at a time, he turned the door handle to their room. It did not yield.

"Mina," he called while pounding at the door, "Jonathan. We are back. Open up."

Not a sound.

Arthur's voice shook. "Put your shoulders to the door. Push it open. God knows if we are not too late already."

They threw themselves against the door and almost fell headlong into the room. What they saw appalled them. On the bed lay Mina Harker in a stupor. Bent over her was a tall, thin figure clad in a dark cape. He had just lifted his face. A thin trickle of blood dripped from his mouth. On Mina's throat was the horrible mark of two fangs.

Count Dracula leaped towards the window, his eyes flaming red, the sharp teeth bared like those of a wild beast. Although they were four and he only one, the men shrank back for just an instant. It was too long. Dracula's form changed into the shape of a bat and he streaked out into the night.

From the bed came a scream so shattering, so despairing, that it would ring in their ears till the day they died. Mina was ghostly white, her eyes mad with terror. Dr. Van Helsing rushed to her. With soft words he calmed her. Antiseptic and a bandage quickly covered the marks on her throat. He took a gold cross from his watch chain and hung it about her nightdress.

"Do not fear, my dear. We are here and will not leave you. With this you are safe." Only then did he turn to Jonathan, who had collapsed at the foot of the bed.

In the glow of the freshly lit lamp, all could see that his brown hair had turned white!

Precious hours passed before Mina could at last describe her or-

deal. The tale she told intensified the small band's understanding of their danger:

"After you left for the asylum I sat sewing while Jonathan read aloud. Since you might not return for a long while, we decided to go to bed. My dreams were full of horrible fancies. I awoke out of fear. At the foot of my bed was a tall thin man. I knew him instantly — the deathly pallor, the glowing eyes, the sharp teeth. For an instant my heart stopped beating. I would have screamed, but could not.

"He spoke in an icy voice saying, 'Silence! If you make a sound I shall dash your husband's brains out before your eyes.' Then he said mockingly, 'So you and the others would try your wits against mine. You would frustrate me in my design. You shall be sorry, each one of you. Tonight I will claim you as I claimed your friend Lucy. My revenge is just begun.

" 'You think you have left me without a place to rest. But I have one more place in England. And more still in my own country. I have waited for centuries. Time is on my side and I shall be back.' "

Mina shuddered at the memory but went bravely on. "Then he

bent over me with his terrible fangs bared. I could do nothing. I could not even lift my hand. And Jonathan lay helpless beside me. He had that look of being asleep with his eyes open — that same look I remember seeing in poor Lucy's eyes."

She burst into sobs and hid her face in Jonathan's arms.

"We have learned something that can lead us to the finish of Dracula," Lord Holmwood said. "Notwithstanding his threats, Count Dracula fears us. His words to Mina make it clear that we have driven him to leave England and return to Transylvania."

Quincey pondered, "But how? What means has he for transporting that last box of earth? Without it he has no where to hide during daylight hours." He paused. Then, striking the table with his fist, Quincey answered his own question. "I am sure he will try to get that coffin on a ship in order to reach his castle."

The next move was clear. Arthur and Quincey made a survey of vans for hire in town. The third carter they located, a certain Mr. Sam Bloxam of the Hampstead Carting Company, held the clue they needed. For a few shillings he was persuaded to reveal that a "foreign gentleman" paid for a box to be delivered to a ship in the harbor.

"It was a peculiar heavy box, gents," Mr. Bloxam complained. "But he paid me five pieces in gold to get it on board ship before sun up. Had to drive all the way past the insane asylum, I did. The box was stored in an old house. Lucky he drew me a map or I'd never of found the spot.

"That house felt haunted to me. You couldn't get me back there for ten crowns. And Lord was that box heavy. Took four men to load it, it did."

Arthur interrupted, "But what was the name of the ship, Mr. Bloxam, can you tell us that?"

"No," the ruddy faced carter said. "I'm not much good at remembering foreign words. But it was a Russian ship. That much I recall."

Gaining the waterfront in barely an hour, the two scanned the posted list of sailings. Only one ship, a fast four-rigger named *Czarina Catherine* was scheduled for the Black Sea and thence to ports along the Danube River in Hungary. Lord Holmwood and Quincey Mor-

ris raced their horses to the wharf.

Too late. The *Czarina Catherine* had already raised anchor. Her sails were silhouetted against the distant seas.

There was no need for a discussion. Their only hope was to reach the Danube before the *Czarina Catherine* put in to shore. In front of the warming fire in Professor Van Helsing's study, Jonathan Harker studied timetables spread out before him.

"Dracula will doubtlessly disembark at the port of Budapest. If we take the boat train from London at

259

the end of this week, we should win the race. In Paris we can secure places on the Orient Express. With luck we will be waiting a full two days before the *Czarina Catherine* drops anchor."

Mina and Professor Van Helsing agreed to stay behind. The doctor was too old for such a journey and Mina was still weakened by her shock.

"Of course we shall go armed," Lord Holmwood said, "armed against evil that is spiritual as well as physical."

Here Quincey Morris added, "I brought with me from Texas several repeating rifles. I propose we take them since I hear the Count comes from wolf country."

"Good fellow," Professor Van Helsing said. "And I will give you the charms that superstition has taught us to use against the Un-Dead. When you board that ship, find the box and fasten a branch of wild rose upon the lid. That way, none can emerge. Then when no one is near to interfere, open the demon's coffin and deal with him."

Too soon for Mina, it was time to say goodbye and see her husband leave with the others on their dangerous mission. In the excitement,

none but Professor Van Helsing noticed the change that had been coming over her. His experienced eyes watched her grow pale and restless. She ate less and less. In fact, food appeared to become distasteful to her.

Dracula had planted his poison well. The doctor alone realized that her teeth were growing a bit more pointed each day. She was in grave danger.

Count Dracula's cleverness was still not fully appreciated. When the three arrived in Budapest, they discovered that the *Czarina Catherine* had changed course. The shipping company's agent informed them that a message had arrived from the Captain of the *Czarina Catherine*. He would be putting in to the port of Galatz before proceeding to Budapest. There had been trouble on board and two sailors had disappeared on night watches.

Arthur looked at his companions knowingly. The strange history of the ship that first brought Dracula's boxes to England was known to all of them.

The agent explained. "The Captain's wireless informed me that he was heading off course in order to pick up some new crew and discharge those he thought might start a mutiny. He was close to Galatz after sailing past the Bosphorus, so that's where he put in."

Jonathan startled the others with his next question. "Tell me, was any cargo unloaded at Galatz?"

The agent turned some pages in his record book.

"Well, sir, and how did you know?" he asked in surprise. "It so happens that an hour after anchoring, the Captain reports a man came aboard with an order written to him from England. He had papers permitting him to receive a wooden crate marked for one Count Dracula. His papers were proper all right and he left with the shipment right then and there."

Only one train made connections to Galatz. More precious time would be lost. Exhausted as they were, the three travelers could not sleep during the journey. They had the address of the man who had signed for Dracula's evil freight. Would they be able to find him in this busy foreign port?

The man they were seeking was Petrof Skinsky. Yes, the cab driver waiting for fares at the railroad station certainly could take them to Mr. Skinsky's place of business. But when the men reached their destination, they found they were again too late.

Policemen were bending over the body of a bearded, black-haired man. It was Petrof Skinsky. His throat had been torn as if by a wild animal.

"Perhaps a wolf," one of the policemen guessed.

"What would a wolf be doing in the middle of the town?" his sergeant scoffed. "No, it was something unnatural. Look, there is hardly any blood in the poor man." And he made the sign of the evil eye that Jonathan remembered so well.

From the police, he learned that the only visitors seen at Mr. Skinsky's shop had been some gypsies. There was nothing unusual about that. His business had been supplying gypsies and peddlers with imported goods that they would sell to peasants in the villages. The gypsies had been seen leaving with a big wooden box shortly before sunset, yesterday. Mr. Skinsky had been alive then. His neighbors saw him smoking his pipe and watching the gypsies as they drove their wagon down the street.

261

Arthur shook his head bitterly as they walked back to the waiting cab. "Why would he kill the man?"

Jonathan frowned. "We know it was after sunset when the gypsies picked up their box. It would have been nothing for the Count to slip out of the box, remain behind, kill Skinsky and then return to his coffin again before sunrise. He could easily have run in the form of a wolf or fly as a bat to catch up with the wagon.

"As for why. Perhaps he knows we are following closely. He has uncanny powers to read men's intentions. Perhaps he thought he would blot out his traces by murdering the poor devil."

"Or," Quincey added, "he might have needed the strength of Skinsky's body for the journey he is undertaking."

"Then we must leave for Transylvania tonight," Jonathan said. "At Bistritz we can hire fast horses. A heavily loaded wagon cannot outdistance riders at full gallop. We shall stop him before he gains the Borgo Pass."

Nine

Snow had been falling in the Carpathian Mountains. The village of Bistritz was shrouded in white. Although the innkeepers at the Golden Krone Hotel looked at Jonathan with curiosity, they did not seem to remember him. Not even six months had passed since he first arrived at their inn. Now he had white hair and a worn face.

No one in town knew of a gypsy caravan passing through. That was a good sign. The trio decided to ride immediately to the Borgo Pass. They allowed themselves only one night of rest. Refreshed, they hired frisky young horses and a quantity of warm clothes and fur covers.

Hard riding brought them to a high point near the Pass. Here they lit a fire in a protected cove and set up camp. Two would keep watch while a third slept.

Following Professor Van Helsing's instructions, they drew a wide ring in the snow around themselves. This they sprinkled with some of the garlic he had packed in their bags.

The air was heavy and gray. As the skies darkened, the horses began to whinny and paw the ground. Presently, they started rearing and tearing at their tethers. Quincey moved out of the circle to quiet them.

Mists appeared from the snow flurries. Gradually these took on the shape of three women with trailing garments. They smiled and reached out with ensnaring arms.

"Come to us. Come! Come!" they called. They laughed a low, horrid laugh that had the ring of metal against glass. Their ghostly forms swayed toward Quincey, their bright cruel eyes gleaming and dark lips pulled back over sharp ivory teeth.

"Quincey, back into the circle, hurry," Jonathan shouted. He ran forward and pulled the American back towards the fire. "The three vampires — didn't you see them?"

"No," Quincey admitted, "the snow blinded me."

Jonathan shivered, remembering the golden-haired vampire's icy

breath on his own throat. So few months had passed since his ordeal at the Castle Dracula. Who could have guessed that he would be returning this soon?

The men peered through the whirling mist and snow. The sisters had vanished as silently as they had arrived. Stillness and soft flurries of white covered the scene.

No one could sleep until dawn brought the end of the storm. High on the mountain, above the encampment, towered the Castle Dracula. This was the first glimpse of the grim castle for Arthur and Quincey. Even the sun's glow could not dispel its gaunt and ominous aspect. It rose in decayed grandeur, perched a thousand feet high on the summit of a sheer precipice. Jonathan's description had not prepared them for such a dismal, threatening sight.

Watch was kept throughout the morning into the darkening afternoon. Lord Holmwood scanned the landscape with his binoculars. He had found a perfect vantage point, a natural hollow in a rock, which formed a doorway between two boulders. Protected from the weather, he could see for great distances. This was also a strategic point, where the little group would be less exposed in case of attack.

Suddenly he called, "Look, they are coming!"

Outlined against the snow not far below was a band of mounted gypsies. In their midst, a horse-drawn cart kept sliding from side to side on the icy road. Sweeping his binoculars over the countryside, Arthur saw dots moving in twos and threes towards the Pass.

The wolves were gathering to welcome their master.

Every instant seemed an age while they waited. Wind blew in harsh bursts, swirling fresh snow into their faces. Closer and closer the gypsies marched. Their leader, a splendid-looking man, sat his horse like a prince. He gave orders in a fierce voice as his followers rode toward the Pass.

All at once Jonathan sprang out from the rock sheltering his companions. The two others dashed to his side. "Halt!" he commanded. The gypsies may not have known the language, but there was no mistaking the tone.

The leader rose in his stirrups. Instantly, every man in the gypsy caravan drew his knife, sword, or pistol and held himself in readiness to attack.

The three friends charged towards the cart, their rifles raised. Jonathan's wild look of determination seemed to awe the guards surrounding the box. He leaped upon the cart and with superhuman strength, shoved it to the ground.

The force of the fall smashed the top of the box. Earth spilled upon the snow, revealing the form of Count Dracula within the coffin. He was as white as a waxen image, and his red eyes glared with hatred.

Everyone drew back in horror. Obviously, the gypsies had not known what freight they were carrying. As the gypsies made the sign of the evil eye, the snow gleamed golden in the rays of the setting sun. The look in those Un-Dead eyes turned to triumph.

Quincey aimed the gun with its silver bullet. At that moment, a huge gray wolf jumped from the rock ledge above him. Quincey dropped to the ground with the wolf's teeth in his throat.

A gypsy fell upon the wolf, slashing away with his curved dagger. Lord Holmwood and Jonathan drew their rifles. Before Dracula could free himself from his coffin, they fired their silver bullets into his heart. As quick as the drawing of a breath, the whole body crumbled into dust and blew from sight.

A sad procession made its way to the Castle Dracula. The gypsies had lifted Quincey's lifeless form to their wagon. Jonathan and Arthur flanked it, leading the riderless horse behind them.

There was yet one more piece of work to be done.

Dismounting in the castle courtyard, the gypsies and the Englishmen set up camp for the night. The gypsy leader refused to let them take shelter inside the castle. Repeatedly he made the sign of the evil eye and shook his head.

With first light of dawn, Jonathan and Lord Holmwood entered the decayed chapel. There were three graves to find.

The air was oppressive with the dust of centuries. First, it made the men dizzy. Then came a roaring in their ears that dissolved into the mournful howl of wolves. But they were resolved to keep on despite the hammering of their hearts.

In a dark corner they found the bier of the first vampire. She lay in her Un-Dead sleep, so full of life and beauty that it seemed they had come to do murder instead of rid the world of a devil. They delayed, as if hypnotized by the open eyes of the golden-haired sister.

Summoning up his memories of

her vile laughter, Jonathan raised his arm to plunge the stake into her heart. But Lord Holmwood, still under the vampire's spell, tried to stop the force of the blow. Jonathan pushed free and found his mark. One terrifying shriek and the grisly woman dissolved into dust, as had the Count.

Jonathan and Arthur resolved not to look into the eyes of the other sisters. Their powers of enchantment were too great.

They steeled themselves for the terrible task and located the other two graves. Twice more they hammered in the stakes made of wild rose wood. The horrid screeching and writhing of the vampires might have driven most men out of their minds. But each time, the moment before their bodies melted into dust, there passed over their faces a look of peace such as no one could ever imagine might have rested there.

It was over. No more terror — just pity for the tormented souls that at last were truly dead.

The friends stumbled into the light of the courtyard. The gypsies were waiting. Their leader stepped up and placed his hand on each of their shoulders in turn. His touch had the solemnity of a king saluting

brave warriors.

The first trace of spring was in the air when Jonathan and Arthur reached England. Professor Van Helsing met them at the station.

To their joy, they learned that on the evening of Dracula's destruction, the marks had disappeared 267 from Mina's neck and she had miraculously recovered her health.

Five years later, Mina and Jonathan Harker made a journey to Transylvania. They went over the path of adventure which was so full of vivid memories.

It was almost impossible to believe that the things which they had seen with their own eyes and heard with their own ears had ever happened. The countryside was fragrant with blossoms of fruit trees. The mountains were soft and green with new leaves and grass.

Castle Dracula was a hollow, ashen shell. Every trace of the tainted chapel was blotted out.

Peasants said it had been hit by lightning. None were sad to see it dissolve into flame.

Outside its wall was the grave of Quincey Morris. Happily, the fire had not touched his headstone and a profusion of wild roses bloomed all about.

Kneeling at the grave Mina said, "We have named our first son after you, Quincey. I have the secret hope that some of your brave spirit has passed into him. Goodbye, dear friend."